D0440174

Night Child

Ace Books by Jes Battis

NIGHT CHILD
A FLASH OF HEX
INHUMAN RESOURCES
INFERNAL AFFAIRS

Infernal Affairs

Jes Battis

ACE BOOKS, NEW YORK

THE BERKLEY PUBLISHING GROUP
Published by the Penguin Group
Penguin Group (USA) Inc.
375 Hudson Street, New York, New York 10014, USA
Penguin Group (Canada), 90 Eglinton Avenue East, Suite 700, Toronto, Ontario M4P 2Y3, Canada
(a division of Pearson Penguin Canada Inc.)
Penguin Books Ltd., 80 Strand, London WC2R 0RL, England
Penguin Group Ireland, 25 St. Stephen's Green, Dublin 2, Ireland (a division of Penguin Books Ltd.)
Penguin Group (Australia), 250 Camberwell Road, Camberwell, Victoria 3124, Australia
(a division of Pearson Australia Group Pty. Ltd.)
Penguin Books India Pvt. Ltd., 11 Community Centre, Panchsheel Park, New Delhi—110 017, India
Penguin Group (NZ), 67 Apollo Drive, Rosedale, Auckland 0632, New Zealand
(a division of Pearson New Zealand Ltd.)
Penguin Books (South Africa) (Pty.) Ltd., 24 Sturdee Avenue, Rosebank, Johannesburg 2196,
South Africa

Penguin Books Ltd., Registered Offices: 80 Strand, London WC2R 0RL, England

INFERNAL AFFAIRS

An Ace Book / published by arrangement with the author

PRINTING HISTORY
Ace mass-market edition / June 2011

Copyright © 2011 by Jes Battis.
Cover art by Timothy Lantz.
Cover design by Lesley Worrell.
Interior text design by Laura K. Corless.

ISBN: 978-0-441-02045-4

ACE
Ace Books are published by The Berkley Publishing Group,
a division of Penguin Group (USA) Inc.,
375 Hudson Street, New York, New York 10014.
ACE and the "A" design are trademarks of Penguin Group (USA) Inc.

PRINTED IN THE UNITED STATES OF AMERICA

10 9 8 7 6 5 4 3 2 1

EPISTLE DEDICATORY

For Papas

Acknowledgments

Thanks to people who have written to me in order to express any opinion at all about the series, from appreciation to ire. It's amazing and humbling to think that readers are actually interested in my characters and their stories. In particular, I need to thank Bea for being Bea, Medrie and Heather for being awesome, and the Cathedral Village in Regina for being such an inspiring neighborhood. Both Roca Jack's and the 13th Ave Coffee House conspired to keep me awake in order to finish edits. Buy the Book sold me four issues of *The Spectator* for twelve dollars, which is neither here nor there, but still, I'm thankful. The Filipino bakery supplied pork buns, and Mercury kept me in burgers and fries. A lovely dinner at the Fainting Goat helped give me the final push I needed to finish this book. Really, my laptop was the star, though. Thank you, *chiquito*. Where would I be without you?

1

I was in the middle of cleaning out my fridge
when I heard growling.

*Great. It's either a pit bull or a hellhound, and my
gun is in the bedroom.*

Currently, I was surrounded by pickle jars and other
condiments, along with an impressive pile of soy sauce
packets that I'd found hiding in the vegetable crisper.
Nothing close to a weapon.

I heard the noise again. It was definitely coming
from the living room. Could it be Mia? I wouldn't put
it past her to be moving furniture at three a.m. But it
didn't sound like furniture. It sounded like something
with teeth.

I slipped off the pair of latex gloves that I'd been
wearing and placed them gently on the counter. The

bulb in the fridge needed to be replaced, and it flickered as I closed the door. Now the kitchen was dark.

I walked slowly down the hallway. The hardwood was cold on my bare feet, but I preferred it to carpet because the wood was more conducive to drawing materia. With each step I tugged a little at the strands of earth energy below me, unsnarling them, convincing them to flow upward into the reservoir that I was building. If I drew too much too fast, I could crack the floorboards, and I didn't have the money to replace them.

The growling returned. I didn't sense anything particularly demonic, but higher-tier demons could cloak their essence. I couldn't imagine why something that powerful would be here, but if it was, I had about three seconds to act before it vivisected me.

It seemed unfair, though. I was wearing an old pair of Derrick's boxers and my UBC sweatshirt. So much for a dignified departure.

The living room was dark. Nothing but shadows and corners.

I inched forward. I'd drawn enough materia by now to raise a bit of hell, but I still wasn't sure what direction to go in. Earthquake? If we survived, the repair bill would bankrupt us. A kinetic wave might knock the creature for a loop, but it would also blow out the windows, and we'd just installed new storm glass. There was only so much I could do without my athame, which I'd left on the nightstand. I really had to stop using it as a bookmark.

I moved my hand slowly along the wall, searching for the light switch. The growling started again, and my stomach clenched. The earth materia was buzzing in my ears. It was now or never. Time to look death in the face.

I turned on the light.

The room was empty. I swallowed. Something invisible? I couldn't feel anything. Why the hell couldn't I feel anything?

I took a step forward. I heard the growling again, this time closer. It seemed to be right next to me, but there was nothing there.

Don't freak out. Don't lose the power that you've drawn.

I took another step, until I was standing next to the coffee table. Silence. Something caught my eye, though. A winking green light. I looked down, and this time the low growl made me jump backward, it was so close.

I swore.

My pager was inching across the table.

I'd left it on vibrate, and it was growling as it moved, inch by inch, about to fall off the edge. The message light blinked green.

"Christ."

I took a moment to let the adrenaline dissipate. Then I released the power that I'd been gathering, and it flowed back into the ground, warming my feet and the tips of my toes as it returned to its source.

I picked up the pager and looked at the screen, There was a 911 page from Selena Ward, my supervisor and the director of the forensics lab. I was in no mood to answer it, but I didn't have a choice. Working the night shift meant being perpetually on call, and we were short-staffed. It took so much effort to hide our investigations from the general public that we were always spread thin.

I walked back down the hallway and ran into Lucian, frozen in the act of putting on his shirt and stifling a yawn. The white lily tattoo on his neck seemed to glow slightly, as always. He handed me my athame, holding it gingerly by the handle, since the blade was hot.

"This woke me up," he said. "Then I felt the power that you were drawing. Was the fridge really so messy that you had to attack it with materia?"

I took the athame, which calmed down as soon as my fingers touched it. I didn't want to admit to Lucian that I'd nearly exploded my pager.

"I don't want to talk about it."

"Fair enough." He kissed me lightly on the cheek. "Time to go to work?"

"Looks like it."

"I'll make myself scarce, then."

"You don't have to leave. Just be quiet while I'm on the phone with her, and then you can go back to sleep."

"I was dreaming about you."

"Oh, yeah? What was I doing?"

"Building a model airplane. I think. Isn't that weird?"

"I never know what's weird anymore."

I passed him and ducked into the bedroom. My cell was on the dresser, and I dialed Selena's number while struggling into a pair of jeans. She answered before the phone could even ring.

"What took you so long? I paged you five minutes ago."

"My pager was in the other room." *And I thought it was a hellhound.* I decided to omit that. "Where do you need me?"

"Not just you. I need everyone."

I heard the door to Derrick's room open.

"Okay. Where are we going?"

"To the lab."

I blinked. "Someone died at work?"

"No. I need you all here for a debriefing. Get here as soon as possible. Do you know where Sedgwick is? I sent him a Teletype instant message."

"He's here."

There was a brief silence. Then I could practically sense her wry grin on the other end of the phone. "Fine. Just get everyone down to the lab." She paused. "That includes Lucian Agrado. If you can reach him at this hour."

Lucian was currently standing in the doorway, brushing his teeth. I put a finger to my lips. "Sure. I'll send him a text. He's probably still awake."

"I'll bet he is."

She hung up.

It was a matter of debate whether Selena knew about our relationship or not. If she did know, she seemed to have no interest in exposing us. Officially, he and I weren't supposed to be anything more than "colleagues," and even that was stretching it.

Unofficially, we'd been something else for nearly two years. Something largely unclassifiable. I wasn't sure that I could call it "dating," although we did see a lot of each other. Sometimes I felt like we were two ciphers trying to solve each other without any measurable success. Last year, he told me that he loved me, but he hadn't repeated the sentiment since then. We'd been arguing at the time, and I often thought that I'd misheard him. Maybe he'd really said *You're crazy* or *Get away from me*, and I'd merely heard whatever I wanted to hear.

That was the weird part, though. Of all the things that Lucian might have told me, *I love you* was never high on my list. I would have preferred to know anything about his past, where he'd been born, what his parents were like, or if Agrado was even his real last name. In retrospect, it was just about the least useful thing that he could have said.

Not that I wanted him to take it back.

"Can you hand me a hair elastic?"

Lucian walked over to where I was standing in front of the full-length mirror. He already had the elastic in his hand. "Here. It was under your athame."

"Yeah, that's where most things end up." I pulled my hair into something that resembled a lump, purely in order to get it out of my eyes.

Lucian put his hand on the back of my neck. His touch was cool. I shivered slightly, and paused, one hand raised, the other dangling at my side. I wanted to lean my head back, to settle myself into the crook of his neck. Instead, I turned around.

"You're coming with us."

"I know. That's why I was brushing my teeth."

"How did you know?"

He shrugged. "I just did."

"I can't imagine why she needs you there. It's not like you work for us."

"Please. I'm a highly sought-after consultant."

"You should be putting out fires in the hidden city."

"That's a job for those closer to Lord Nightingale. I'm only Seventh Solium. Let his favorites deal with whatever crisis is brewing."

"You won't get in trouble?"

"For what? Spending too much time here?" He put his hands on my shoulders. "Tess, I don't live in Trinovantum. I just work there. This is my home."

The city of Trinovantum was a diurnal melting pot for a number of demons, exiles, and other marginalized creatures who couldn't eke out a living (or undying) anywhere else. It was always night there.

I smiled slightly. "That's good to know."

"Besides. The food is better here."

"You don't miss the black watermelons from the night market?"

"No. They have a strange aftertaste."

Mia walked into my bedroom without knocking. "What's going on?"

"Work."

She looked at Lucian. "You're going, too?"

"So it seems."

"What about Derrick and Miles?"

"Affirmative," Derrick called from the hallway. "We'll bring you back something from Timmy's if you want."

"You'd better." She sighed. "I guess I can study while I'm up."

"Have you ever tried just relaxing?" Lucian asked. "I've heard it's amazing. You can just turn on the TV and forget all of your troubles."

"I don't have time for that."

"Mia, you're sixteen." He spread his hands. "You've got nothing but time. Why don't you try goofing off for once?"

"I don't even know what that means." She walked out of the bedroom. "I'm going to wake Patrick up."

"Careful," I called after her. "He's all fangs at this hour."

"So am I."

If someone had told me three years ago that I'd end up taking care of two teenaged vampires—one latent, the other very much active—I would have said they were crazy. But it was amazing what you could adjust to, especially when you didn't have a choice. I didn't exactly feel like an occult soccer mom, but I liked to think that I wasn't a complete failure as a guardian. Derrick provided the unconditional love, and I tried to keep both of them from getting into too much trouble.

Aside from exposure to several homicides and a few brushes with death, their lives were proceeding more or less normally. If normal still applied to us.

Sometimes I forgot that Mia was, technically, a vampire, since she'd never exhibited any symptoms of the vampiric retrovirus. She'd been infected at thirteen as part of a vampiric political coup, which had failed, but still left her with the virus burning in her blood.

The antiviral medication that she'd been taking for the last four years kept things in check.

She didn't talk about it much anymore, not since last year when she found out that drugs prescribed by the Central Occult Regulation Enterprise might also be dampening her latent mystical abilities. There didn't seem to be a practical way to prove this. *Hey, try to burn the house down and see if it works* wasn't the most motherly advice that I could give her.

Selena insisted that the medication, which resembled synthetic insulin, was designed purely to be an antiviral. But I saw the way that Mia looked at her EpiPen whenever I suggested she take her meds. She trusted it about as much as she trusted me. I was part of the CORE, and that made me suspect. I could hardly blame her. Most of the time I barely trusted myself.

I heard muttering coming from the hallway. Patrick had emerged, wrapped in a duvet and sporting some impressive bedhead. Mia now teased him ruthlessly about his chest hair, which had started to grow in as a perfect triangle. She called it Puppy, as in, *Hey, Puppy's looking pretty fierce this morning.*

It was mostly smoke and mirrors, though. Lately, I'd noticed a subtle difference in the way that she joked around with him. There was a prickly tension, along with furtive glances from both of them. The new dynamic made me nervous. When we'd first adopted Patrick, I was worried about anything romantic developing between them, but Mia had been barely fourteen then.

Now she was starting to notice things that she'd previously ignored. Like the fact that he was a cool glass of water with a killer smile. It was hard to tell where his vestigial human charm gave way to a captivating vampiric aura, and the last thing I wanted was for him to start hypnotizing her. Patrick was basically ethical, as much as a hormonal teen could be, so I trusted him up to a point. But I still wanted to install a dead bolt on Mia's door, even if it seemed a bit alarmist.

"Wow," I said. "She wasn't kidding about waking you up."

"She's evil."

"In all fairness, most vampires aren't asleep at this time of night."

"Most vampires didn't inherit a resistance to sunlight. I can thank Caitlin for that, at least. She didn't tell me much before she died and passed on her title to me, but at least she gave me the gift of walking by day." He scratched his head. "Is there coffee? If I'm going to be conscious, there should at least be coffee."

"I'm sure Derrick's making some."

"I'm not a domestic," he called from the kitchen.

"But you're making some, right?"

A pause. "Yeah."

"So what's the deal?" Patrick blinked. "Did everyone in the house get called to the crime scene, or is it just mass insomnia?"

"Everyone got paged. Chances are we'll be gone until morning."

He shrugged. "That's fine. I have a geography test that I should probably be studying for. Do you have any idea what a caldera is?"

"You're asking the wrong person."

Patrick had decided to enroll at Capilano College, and I was secretly quite proud that he'd been admitted, although he rolled his eyes whenever I mentioned it. Like most first-year undergrads, he was majoring in Everything. At first, it made me ache a little to return to school, but I thought better of it once I saw the bill for his textbooks. I had a problem with shelling out two hundred bucks for a hardcover sociology text called *Reflections*. Luckily, Derrick was a whiz at finding used copies online and didn't seem to mind visiting sketchy apartments in order to pick them up.

"I will never own a hot plate," he told me during the first week of classes, "and if you ever bring one into this house, I'll destroy it."

I suspected that Mia was helping Patrick with some of his homework, but I felt like I had to let it slide. He was already vampire magnate of Vancouver, and it was impressive that he managed to make it to school at all. I couldn't tell if he was opting for a normal life or just trying to distract himself from the grim politics that he encountered on a nightly basis.

Sometimes I felt like a voyeur watching my own life through a window (possibly a bullet-riddled window), and all I could do was stare in amazement. I was about to turn twenty-eight, and I lived in a house with two preternatural teens and a psychic. My boyfriend had already come back from the dead once, and my goblin therapist was almost certain that I had PTSD.

The door to Derrick's bedroom opened, and Miles

emerged, shirtless and wearing a pair of Canucks pajama bottoms.

"Nice jammies," I said.

His eyes widened. Then he blushed and practically ran for the bathroom.

I walked into the kitchen. Lucian was now fully dressed and sitting at the table, next to Mia. Both of them were staring at the coffeemaker expectantly. Derrick was rummaging around in the fridge.

"It's so clean. How much did you throw away?"

"About seventy percent of what was in there." I sat down. "I was going along at a nice clip, too, until my pager went off."

Lucian put his hand on my knee. "What's the plan for tonight? I can take a cab if you think we should arrive separately."

I shrugged. "We can just say we picked you up on the way. It shouldn't raise any eyebrows, and if it does, I'm too tired to care."

"Eventually you're going to have to tell her," Derrick said, closing the fridge. "I mean, she probably knows already."

"Selena's too busy to interpret subtext."

"That's fine." Lucian gave me a playful look. "I don't mind being your *amor clandestino*. It's hot."

"I hope you still think that when we're eighty, because it's never going to get any easier to come out to the CORE."

He grinned. "Do you think we'll still be together when we're eighty?"

"For all I know, you could be eighty already."

"Maybe I am."

"How does that work?" Mia asked. "I mean, do you have, like, eighty-year-old organs? Because that would be gross."

Lucian put his arm around me. "My father used to say that you're only as old as the woman you feel."

I made a face. "I'm not sure how to respond to that."

"Feminist ire?" Derrick poured the first cup of coffee. "Okay. I have no idea how to decide who gets this. Maybe you could all just make a case for who's the most deserving, and then we'll draw up some kind of chart."

Miles walked into the kitchen, now wearing jeans and a collared shirt. He adjusted his hearing aid, then smiled sweetly at Derrick.

"Is that coffee for me?"

Derrick looked uncertain for a moment. Then he handed Miles the cup, and everyone groaned.

"Unfair!" Mia pounded the table. "No special treatment for significant others."

This is a romance, Miles signed, *not a democracy.*

Derrick turned back to the coffee machine. "I think I can stretch the rest of this into two more cups. Maybe three."

"There's no time," I said. "Just fill up a travel mug, and we'll pass it around until we get to the Timmy's drive-through."

"Ugh. Haven't you heard of mononucleosis?"

"Have you heard of hysterical blindness caused by

caffeine deprivation? Because that's what I'm about to experience, and I doubt you want me driving the new SUV into the opposing lane of traffic."

"Fine. But I'm not sharing saliva with everyone here."

He was about to say something else when his pager started buzzing. I heard my pager buzzing in the next room as well.

"Selena's getting cranky." I turned to Mia. "Did Patrick remember to put gas in the car?"

"How should I know? It's not like you ever let me drive it."

"I lent you the car last week."

"Yeah, so that I could go to an SAT workshop. You lend it to him every other day so that he can drive his vampire buddies around."

"Fine." I stood up. "We'll make a schedule. Something official-looking with Excel. Derrick, make a note of it."

"When did I become your PA?"

"You and Miles are the only ones who know how to use the computer for anything other than playing FarmVille. And Miles is a guest, so any scheduling duties naturally fall to you."

"That doesn't seem natural at all," he muttered.

"Well, you know us. Always pushing the definition."

"What are you talking about?" Mia smiled. "We're practically a nuclear family. The only difference is that we have powers."

"And some of us can read minds," Derrick said.

"Quick. What am I thinking right now?" Mia leaned

forward. "It's not about you, and it's not something dirty. I promise."

His eyes narrowed for a moment. Then he shook his head.

"God. Why do I always fall for that?"

She laughed. "'Cause you're a sucker."

2

The first thing I noticed when I walked into the conference room was the snow globe sitting on the table. At least, it looked like a snow globe. Linus and Cindée were sitting next to each other, while Selena sat at the head of the table, surrounded by paperwork. She barely registered our presence.

"Sit. We don't have a lot of time."

I took a seat next to Cindée. "Is the world ending?"

"Neither of us know anything," she replied. "We're only here because we're getting paid time and a half."

Last year, Cindée had managed to live through the appearance of the manticore. She'd also been kidnapped, tied up, and subjected to the bad humor of a psychotic vampire (thankfully, Sabine Delacroix was now officially out of my life forever). I was kind of amazed at how quickly she'd returned to work. Maybe she needed the money.

I looked at Linus. "What's with the snow globe?"

"It's not a snow globe. It's a sophisticated piece of equipment."

"It looks like you bought it in Gastown."

"I didn't. It was designed in the lab."

"What does it do?"

He looked at Selena. "Do you want me to explain it now?"

"No. I have to debrief them first."

His expression was slightly disappointed. "Okay. I'll wait."

Derrick and Miles sat next to me. Lucian remained standing. Maybe he was feeling a bit of an outsider vibe, which made sense. Or maybe he wanted to keep his distance for the sake of appearances.

Selena finally looked up from the stack of papers. "We're all here. Now we can get down to business."

Derrick raised his hand. "I have one question."

"Okay."

"Can we order breakfast?"

"No."

"I have another question, then."

Selena closed her eyes. "Yes?"

"Is it true that the morning shift gets catered breakfast? Because that hardly seems fair, especially since they aren't on call."

"I'll make a note of your grievance. How's that?"

"I can live with it."

"Fine. Any more questions?"

Lucian raised his hand.

"Yes?"

"I'd like to know what I'm doing here."

"I'm about to explain that." She exhaled. "All right. Thirty minutes ago, we received a piece of intel from a reliable source. A body was recovered on Jericho Beach in the Kitsilano neighborhood. The VPD found the body, and after the coroner's examination it was transferred to the city morgue."

"If the VPD found the body," I asked, "what does it have to do with us? This sounds like a normate investigation."

"That's where things get complicated. The police department thinks that they've recovered a human body, but we have reason to believe that they're actually holding the body of a demon."

"What killed it?"

"We don't know. In fact, we don't even know for sure that it's dead." She looked at Lucian. "That's part of the reason that we've enlisted you. We're hoping that your expertise in necroid materia will be useful in determining whether the body is deceased or not. With some bodies, it's difficult to tell."

"I'll try," Lucian said. "Right now, though, I'd be more worried about someone else coming to recover the body."

"That's our concern at the moment," Selena replied. "We need to get the body somewhere secure, before it's intercepted. That's why I've assembled the four of you together tonight. We need you to break into the morgue."

"Wait a minute." I steepled my fingers. "You want us to infiltrate a government building and steal a body? What are we supposed to leave behind? A bag of sand?"

"No. It's safer and easier for us to delete all trace of the body. We've already isolated all of the officers and technicians involved in the body's recovery. It's a small group, and it shouldn't be too difficult to manage them."

"And by 'manage,' you mean erase their memories?"

Selena gave me a long look. "You've been spending too much time with vampires. The CORE isn't in the habit of inflicting brain damage on innocent people. We're simply going to modify their paperwork to make it appear as if the body was never there. The police officers have enough on their minds, and they won't be overly concerned with one more DB recovered on the beach. The coroner's office relies on computer records, and those can be altered. Instead of thinking that the body's vanished, everyone will just assume that it's been transferred to a government facility for advanced toxicology testing."

"I think we might be underestimating the competency of the VPD," Derrick said. "And it's not as if the coroner's office is being run by mindless drones. Sure, they're normates, but they aren't blind. If one file gets left behind by accident, we could have a paranormal incident on our hands."

"We can worry about that later. Right now, our priority is moving the body to a secure location. Once we have the decedent here, we'll be able to deal with the coroner's office remotely. It's the safest way. The less contact, the better."

"Do we know anything about the demon's ancestry?"

"No."

"Of course. Any idea where it's from?"

"Not yet."

Miles raised his hand.

"You can just speak up, Officer Sedgwick."

"Sorry. I wasn't sure if you were finished." Miles drummed his fingers on the table. Selena still made him nervous. "I was just thinking that if the deceased was a world-walker, that is, capable of interplanar travel, then there'll be an impression of sorts on its body. Your instruments couldn't detect it, but I might be able to."

"And that's exactly why you're here. That, and as an early-warning system."

His eyes widened. "You mean in case something comes after the body?"

"Right. You'll be the first to notice any spatial anomalies."

He managed to look uncomfortable. "That may be. But by the time I notice it, another demon could be ripping my throat out. I'm not sure I like this assignment."

"You'll have plenty of backup. We'll be monitoring you from every angle, and Agrado can also provide you with some defensive firepower."

"I wouldn't go that far," Lucian said. "I might be

able to distract a predator like that for a few minutes, tops. But necromancy can only do so much."

"You will have some technological assistance." Selena gestured to the globe. "Linus, do you want to explain further?"

"Do I ever." He smiled. "Okay, this is pretty cool. It's a temporal switch, but we call it a time bomb."

I could see what looked like strands of white light floating within the murkiness of the glass. The thing definitely had an aura, but there was a subtlety in its composition that my senses couldn't quite penetrate.

"Are we supposed to break it open?"

"Yes. But only at the right moment." Linus put his hand protectively over the globe. "There's a controlled singularity inside the glass, protected by a mesh of enlaced materia. If you break it, the singularity will expand to roughly a three-foot radius, which is just big enough to capture a single entity."

"Just throw it at whatever's coming toward you," Selena said. "It'll create a kind of temporal dead zone for about ten, maybe fifteen seconds. Anything caught within the blast radius will be slowed to a fraction of its normal speed. With a human, that would mean a dead stop. With a pureblood"—she shrugged—"you might slow it down to a crawl if you're lucky. It'll still be moving, but you should have enough time to grab the body and get away."

I exhaled. "This all sounds very sketchy."

Cindée opened up a small evidence bag, which I hadn't noticed before, and withdrew a metallic object. It looked like one of the miniature hand clappers with cymbals that belly dancers used. She handed me the clapper. It had bizarre symbols etched into its surface, and the rod connecting the two cymbals was slightly warm to the touch. I slid my thumb over it, and I could feel an invisible power source.

"We found this a few months ago on a Vailoid demon," she said, "and he probably stole it from someone. We call it a howler. Basically, if you click the two cymbals together, it emits a sonic pulse that only higher-tier demons—and some animals—can detect."

"Are we trying to give it a headache?"

"No. The pulse works as a kind of neural dampener. It should disrupt the demon's psychic defenses long enough for you to launch an attack."

"That's where Siegel comes in," Selena said.

Derrick stared at her. "Excuse me? You want me to get inside the mind of an unknown demon? Why don't I just get inside a giant food processor? It could be a brain-eater, or worse."

"The howler should distract it long enough for you to make a quick pass through its thoughts," Selena clarified. "We're hoping you can pick up something useful. The name of the decedent, or where it came from. Anything, really."

"Great. I'll try to write it all down while I'm being eviscerated from the inside. Do you have any idea how strong the thoughts of a demon like that are? It could make me gouge my own eyes out."

"We'll try not to let that happen, hon." I put a hand on his shoulder. "In the meantime, how are we getting into the morgue? Unless you've perfected a portable veil system, I don't see how we're supposed to move around undetected."

"Actually, it won't be as difficult as it sounds." Selena stood. "All we need are some uniforms and name tags. The rest will depend on your acting skills."

"Oh, God." I put my head on the table. "Please let me go back to bed."

"That's perfect," Selena said. "Now just channel that dramatic energy into your performance, and you'll be fine."

Vancouver had several morgues, all attached to urban hospitals, which were equipped with refrigeration units. When people died of natural causes within the hospital, they were transferred temporarily to the morgue before being moved either to a mortuary or a crematorium. There was also, however, a larger and more sophisticated autopsy facility attached to the Office of the Chief Coroner, which was in Burnaby, the city's most sprawling suburb. That was where we were heading. The coroner's office dealt with active criminal investigations and was frequented by the VPD, which meant that we had to get in quickly and quietly.

The office was on the bottom floor of a tall glass and steel building, and the entrance was flanked by security. Selena had furnished Miles and me with badges that identified us as autopsy technicians, while Derrick and Lucian were dressed as police officers. What amazed me was how easily Cindée had managed to replicate uniforms for us, all the way down to the shield and regulation Glock sidearm. They even had paperwork, which included detailed rotation schedules and personal history, compiled from both the RCMP and VPD databases.

We approached the entrance. One of the security guards walked over to us, and I couldn't help but notice that he was built like an ox.

Lucian showed the guard his badge. "I'm Officer Pérez, and this is Officer Sheldon. We're supposed to meet with the CC."

The guard looked us over. "I've never seen the two of you before."

"They were just transferred from the CCO in Toronto. They've got their recommendation letters from the chief coroner, if you want to see them."

He shrugged. "It's fine. You know where you're going?"

"Straight down this hallway to the service elevator on the right," Lucian said. "The autopsy suite is below the basement level, and we've got keys for the elevator."

The guard nodded. "Okay. Just remember to sign in at reception."

We made our way through the sliding glass doors. The reception desk was empty, which wasn't a surprise at this hour. Lucian leaned over as if to sign the book on the counter, knowing that the guard was watching him through the doors, but he didn't actually write anything.

"Let's hope they don't check for the next twenty minutes or so," he said.

"Wait." Miles tapped his hearing aid, which had

been equipped with a telecoil that could access the building's closed-loop transmissions. It also allowed Selena to transmit messages to him on the same frequency. "She says that the guards are about to switch rotation. The replacements shouldn't have any reason to check the sign-in book. So we're clear."

We continued down the hallway and turned right, which led us to a small vestibule with the service elevator that Lucian had mentioned. He'd studied the plans for the building beforehand, and I was impressed by how much he could retain. I guess his brain was more analytical than mine. I tended to rely on aesthetic landmarks, as in, *Turn at the coffee stand and walk down the hallway with the funny-smelling carpet.*

"This uniform itches like crazy," Derrick said, pulling at his collar. "I wish I could be one of the autopsy technicians."

"I don't know. I think it looks kind of hot." Miles laid a hand on his chest. "Maybe Selena wouldn't mind if we borrowed it for a while."

"Boys. Focus."

I pressed the call button, and the elevator doors opened. "There'll be time for role-playing after we get out of here."

Lucian swiped his stolen key card, and the panel on the wall lit up. He pressed the button marked LB, and the elevator began to descend, swiftly and silently.

"This belt is way heavier than it looks," Derrick said. "And I'm used to carrying my gun in a shoulder-holster. It's super uncomfortable."

"You could always create a distraction by undressing in the morgue. Other than that, you're just going to have to deal with it."

"Easy for you to say. You look like Lauren Ambrose in a lab coat."

"I'm going to take that as a veiled compliment."

The elevator stopped, and the doors opened. Everything smelled and sounded familiar: industrial-grade cleaning supplies, the chill of stainless steel, and the low hum of constant air-conditioning. Red and blue lines had been painted on the linoleum floor, directing the passage of carts and gurneys.

"Remember to say as little as possible." Lucian adjusted his belt, making the gun even more apparent. "They're used to seeing cops here, so Derrick and I lend you an aura of legitimacy. Do you remember the backstory?"

"We're replacing Timmons and O'Hara," I said. "They're on sick leave. Miles and I are both finishing a death-investigation internship at Carleton. I doubt they're going to ask us about our alma mater, though. They're more interested in whether we brought them coffee and doughnuts."

We continued down the passageway, which terminated at a heavy door with another card reader. Lucian swiped the key card again, and I was hit with a blast of subzero air. I could smell what lay beneath the layers of disinfectant, and it wasn't pretty. In fact, it was the opposite of all good things. If evil had a smell, decomposition was probably the only thing that came close.

Another door at the far end of the chamber opened, and an autopsy tech emerged. He was still wearing latex gloves and a face mask, and he stared at us in surprise.

"We're taking over for Timmons and O'Hara," I said.

He frowned for a second, then shrugged. "Fine. I'm taking my fifteen. Dr. Rashid just started working on the kid."

The kid?

Was that the body we were after? Selena hadn't said anything about it being a child's body. But demonic physiology could also be deceptive. It might look like a child and actually be several hundred years old.

The tech passed us and exited through the first door. I led the way, opening the door at the far end of the hall, which led to the autopsy suite. It was heavy and had a glass window, through which I could see the familiar tiled floor and steel tables with drains underneath them.

There were three autopsy tables in total, and the left side of the suite was taken up by a long steel counter. Sterile pads covered the counter, with freshly washed instruments laid atop them. Only one of the tables was occupied. A figure dressed in scrubs and a plastic apron, whom I assumed to be Dr. Rashid, had his back to us. He was leaning over the table, his body obscuring whoever or whatever lay on top of it.

The room was silent, save for the gentle shuffling of the doctor's feet as he positioned himself over the body. I noticed that he was wearing running shoes. For some reason, the small detail made me want to smile. But I didn't.

"Dr. Rashid?"

He turned, still holding a pair of shears in his right hand. "Who are you?"

"We're here to replace Timmons and O'Hara. They are on—"

"—sick leave. Yes, I know." All I could see behind the mask was his dark eyes, which fixed on me. "I didn't ask who you were replacing. I asked who you were."

Selena had given us the names of two grad students at Carleton University, who were enrolled in a death-investigation program but currently away doing field-work. It would be far too much trouble to track them down.

"My name's Christina Ross, and this is Bob Silver. I think our supervisor e-mailed you last week. Professor Ian Talbot."

Rashid frowned. "I don't know anyone by that name, and I received no e-mail. But as long as you're here, you can help me take notes." He glanced at Lucian and Derrick. "The two of you can leave. Thank you."

"We'll be right outside," Lucian murmured to me. Then he and Derrick left the autopsy suite. Now it was up to Miles and me to get rid of the doctor, and we didn't exactly have a lot of time.

I approached the autopsy table. Miles hung back a bit. He wasn't quite as accustomed yet to seeing dead bodies.

The body in question was surprisingly small. He couldn't have been more than eight or nine years old. His blond hair was matted in blood, and there was detritus on his face. He must have been lying facedown in the sand when the police found him. But if that were the case, there should have been blanching due to lividity on his face as well. It was untouched, aside from the streaks of dirt.

Dr. Rashid hadn't begun the autopsy yet, but he was about to. I had no idea what would happen if the kid woke up in the middle of being dissected.

"He's so little," Miles breathed.

I don't think he meant to say it. I looked at him and saw an expression of chagrin spread across his face.

Rashid looked up. "Yes. We can't know for sure, but I'd say that the subject is anywhere from eight to ten years old. If he's ten, then he'd be small for his age. There are no ligature marks, abrasions, or contusions of any kind on his body. No trauma that I can see. It might be a different story inside, though."

Miles frowned suddenly. I waited for Rashid to turn toward the counter, and then signed quickly to him:

What's up?

Not sure, he signed back. *Something's wrong.*

Great.

Fire alarm, I signed. *Tell Lucian.*

Dr. Rashid had just picked up a scalpel from the counter. "Start taking notes," he told me.

I walked over to the counter to grab his notebook. When I was a few inches away from him, I made a quick movement, nudging his leg. He stepped back, startled, and the scalpel dropped to the floor.

"I'm so sorry." I leaned over to pick it up. "This will need to be disinfected. I'll grab you another."

He didn't say anything. He just stared at me, as if I were the stupidest person alive. I doubted that Dr. Rashid was much of a pleasure to work for.

I washed my hands with pumice soap, then slipped on a pair of latex gloves. "I'm really sorry," I said again. "I'm never this clumsy. I swear."

I was just about to grab the second scalpel when the fire alarm sounded. Obviously, Selena had relayed my message to Lucian. Maybe we'd still manage to get out of here in one piece after all.

"We'd better go," I said. "They'll let us back in as soon as the fire department leaves. How annoying."

Dr. Rashid shrugged. "You can leave. I'm not going anywhere."

I stared at him. "You can't stay here."

"I'm not leaving. If there's any trace evidence on this body, it could dissolve in the next twenty minutes. The morgue is in no danger of burning down. I'm staying."

Really? Tonight of all nights we had to deal with the obstinate doctor who refused to abandon his post?

"I really think, for safety's sake—"

"Miss Ross." His voice had an edge to it. "My job is to conduct an autopsy on this child, and that's what I'm going to do. Now, you can either join everyone outside, or you can assist me."

I stared at Miles. He shrugged. He was out of ideas.

"Fine." I walked over to the counter and picked up the nearest scalpel. "Are you going to use the Rokitansky method, or—"

"Please stop stalling and give me the scalpel." He held out his gloved hand. "Every minute that we wait only makes it more difficult to determine a cause of death, and that's the least that we can do for this boy. Don't you think?"

I handed him the scalpel.

"Thank you." He positioned the blade against the child's sternum. "Now. Watch how I make this Y-incision. You might learn something."

He started to cut. I sucked in my breath.

Blood welled up in the wound.

"What the—" Rashid's eyes widened. "Quick, grab me gauze and sutures from the counter—"

Two things happened before I could move.

Miles started to sign something. I couldn't make out the exact words, but I could see that his hands were shaking. I realized that a patch of air directly behind us had suddenly taken on a dark cast. I could feel something in my gut. Something very bad. The hairs on the back of my neck were standing on end.

Something was about to join us in the autopsy suite. It was going to appear in a few seconds, and there was nothing we could do to stop it.

But no sooner had I realized that than something even more immediate caught my attention, along with Dr. Rashid's.

The boy's eyes were open.

He stared at us all in naked horror. For just a moment, his form seemed to shimmer, and I could see what lay underneath.

The demon was small, just like the false body that he'd formed for himself out of light, shadow, and will. He had skin the color of polished gray stone, and hard green eyes with slit pupils. He was hairless, with thin ears pressed close to his scalp. He also had a pair of small horns, made from some striated mineral substance, black and green.

His mouth hung open for a second. He saw the doctor. He saw me. Then he saw the scalpel, still in his flesh.

He screamed.

It was more than a scream, in fact. The force of it flung all three of us backward, and I felt its power hit me like a brick wall. I stumbled and tried to maintain my balance. Dr. Rashid fell to the ground, and Miles dropped to one knee.

The door to the autopsy suite opened, and Lucian burst in, followed by Derrick. He had his gun ready. But he stopped when he saw the figure of the small demon-boy, still lying on the autopsy table, his alien eyes darting in every direction.

The boy leapt off the table. His form shimmered again, and the blond-haired human returned. Had Rashid seen the demon's true form? I couldn't tell. He just kept staring at the boy. He still couldn't believe that he'd been about to cut into something that was very much alive.

The boy didn't seem to care that he was naked or bleeding. He was more terrified of us. He held out one hand, as if to keep us at a distance. I felt his power building again, and I took a step back instinctively.

"We're not going to hurt you," I said. "I promise. We're here to help you."

The boy stared at me. I felt his mind pushing against

mine. I let him in, let him sift through my thoughts and memories, despite how cold his touch was. I needed him to trust me. It was the only way he'd agree to leave with us.

"You're mage-born," he said, matter-of-factly.

His voice was slightly high-pitched and had a strange metallic quality to it. He also had an accent. I could only imagine what his native tongue was.

"Yes," I said. There was no use explaining any of this to Rashid. Selena would just have to deal with that particular mess later. "I don't know how you got here, but someone's coming after you. We have to leave now."

"He's not coming," the boy said, looking behind me. "He's already here."

I turned.

A four-legged creature was standing before us. Its bottom half was equine, with hooves sheathed in black metal that steamed as they touched the floor. Its top half was naked, bone white and covered in ink that writhed before my eyes. They were ritual tattoos, each one designating a mystical event in the demon's life. Judging from the amount of them, the creature had to be more than a thousand years old.

I couldn't decide what to reach for, my athame or the howler, which was in my pocket. Derrick had the time bomb, but there was no time to signal him. I had no idea where this demon came from, what its weaknesses were, or even if it had any. But I already knew that my gun was useless.

My hand closed around the hilt of the athame. I kept

my eyes on the centaur demon, trying not to shake beneath its gaze.

"I don't know exactly what you're after," I told it, "but maybe we can work something out here."

The demon made a sound deep in its throat. Possibly laughter.

Then it leapt at me.

3

A few things occurred to me.

Which bones would break first? My ribs, probably.

I imagined them pulverized, the way to my heart open and free of debris. The monster would reach in and plunder everything, my guts, my soul, my memories. All of it would be gone, all the connections, all the hardware, everything. Only a vegetal shell would be left behind.

But the impact never came.

I saw something flash forward out of the corner of my eye. A blurred gray form slammed into the demon, knocking it sideways. I stumbled and fell, hitting the ground hard, but the shock barely registered. I couldn't believe that I was still alive.

I looked up and saw both demons now facing each other. The massive equine demon towered over the small horned creature, which resembled something out of a Brian Froud picture book. But the demon-boy's eyes were bright, like green flames, and he stood his ground. The roughly five-foot height differential between them didn't seem to faze him at all.

"I'm here to collect you," the equine demon said. "Don't make this more difficult than it has to be."

"You're here to kill me, not collect me," the boy replied.

"You will come with me, one way or another."

"I'll die first."

The equine demon flexed its right hand. Blood sprayed out of its open palm, but instead of spattering the walls, it paused in midair, bubbling, turning to a mist like high-velocity spatter. It trembled for a second, a helix of dark fluid, dotted by particles of bone and mysterious limpid matter. Then it shimmered into the form of a long black whip.

It cracked the whip once, and curls of amber flame moved along its length. With all of the stainless steel in the autopsy suite, the reflections were dazzling.

"You'll die no matter what," it replied, holding the whip loosely. "But I can make it quick or make it last. That much is up to you."

"First you have to catch me."

The boy sprang backward. He leapt onto the counter, his movements so quick and precise that he didn't even disturb a single instrument. He perched there for a second, bare feet pressed against the steel. His toenails were long and black.

The equine demon cracked its whip again, and this

time the black rope stretched like a tendon, smashing into the counter. But the boy had already moved, and now he was balanced on the nearest autopsy table, where he'd been lying cold and inert only a few moments ago.

I noticed Dr. Rashid for the first time. He had taken his surgical mask and gloves off and was simply staring at the equine demon. I couldn't tell if he was about to scream, faint, or both. But he didn't move. He just stood there, absolutely fixed.

For a few seconds, nobody moved. Steam curled from the spot on the counter where the demon's whip had touched.

Now would have been a great time for Selena to arrive with backup. But the hallway remained silent. Nobody was bursting through the door.

Lucian took a step forward. "The boy is under our protection."

The equine demon turned slowly to regard him. "Return to Trinovantum, changeling. There's nothing for you here but the longest death, and you're too young to seek that."

"Well, I've already died once, and it wasn't so bad."

The demon chuckled. "You're funny. I enjoy funny things. They always amuse me when they expire."

"That's great. Were you planning to talk about that all night, or are you actually going to do something?"

I judged the distance between Lucian and the equine demon. About ten feet. I realized what he was doing. If he could get the creature to advance a bit, there'd be enough space for Derrick to throw the time bomb. It was dicey, though. If the demon moved too quickly, then the bomb would hit Lucian as well.

I looked at Derrick. He was reaching into his jacket slowly. He'd already anticipated Lucian's plan. But the equine demon stayed exactly where it was.

"How would you like it, then, necromancer?" It smiled. Its teeth were needle-sharp and made of metal. "I could do it from here. Or we could get closer. Dance a little before I split you down the middle and set fire to your entrails."

"Are you trying to frighten me or gross me out? Because you're doing both."

While Lucian was talking, the demon-boy had managed to inch forward slowly. The equine demon turned in his direction, about to say something. But before he could speak, the boy opened his mouth wide and spit out a jet of foaming green liquid.

The spray coated the larger demon's face, sizzling on contact. It screamed and clawed at its eyes. The liquid kept foaming, and I watched in amazement as its face began to melt like wax.

"He's like one of those little dinosaurs from *Jurassic Park*," Derrick said.

The equine demon recovered quickly. Although obviously in pain, it didn't seem overly concerned by the fact that its skin was bubbling. It reached for the boy, but the smaller demon moved too quickly, flitting out of the way.

Then the larger demon cracked its whip again. The black tendon snaked forward, catching the boy around the ankles. He cried out and fell to the ground. Fire began to move once more along the leathery surface of the whip, flowing from the handle downward. I could feel its heat, and so could the boy. He struggled to break free, but the whip held him tight. For the first time, I saw panic in his startling green eyes.

I looked around the autopsy room. Everything was completely sterile—the worst environment possible for conducting materia. Still, we were underground, and I could feel the currents of geothermic energy beneath my feet. They shied away from the fake tile and manufactured steel countertop, but they were still there, and I could hear them, subterranean lions growling absently in their sleep.

The amber light continued to flare along the length of the whip. I didn't want to know what it would do when it touched the boy's flesh, but I could imagine the result.

I reached beneath the tile, beneath the building's foundations, and into the cold matter of the rocks and earth below. They were outraged. Who did I think I was? They tried to ignore me. But I kept reaching, deeper and deeper, until I felt the plane of my consciousness sink into a dark pool.

I let the materia rise within me, until it enflamed every nerve ending. My athame was throwing off a corona of heat. I tightened my grip on the handle of the blade, focusing the power down to an incandescent line. Then I channeled it toward the end of the whip, still wrapped around the boy's legs.

Burst, I thought, with all of my might. *Burst.*

The tiles cracked.

A shaft of rock and molten material exploded upward from the ground, severing the coiled end of the whip. The flame stopped. The amputated piece of leather shriveled, then turned to dust.

The boy was free. Before the larger demon could crack the whip again, he leapt forward. I felt him gathering a surge of power, and then he hit the equine demon full in the chest, like a cannonball. A shock wave tore through the room. The demon stumbled, its four legs clawing at the ground. It fell onto its haunches.

Lucian pointed his hand at the fallen demon. A halo of red light coalesced around his fingertips. He shaped the light into a fizzing dart and then hurled it at the demon, like a Roman candle.

The equine demon raised its arm. I felt a vibration move through the floor, and then its power lashed out. The air in front of it went liquid, tracked with silver and filaments of icy blue.

For some reason, it made me think of being a small girl, sitting in the front seat with my mother while we went through the car wash. I'd always been captivated by the way that the soap moved down the windshield, coating everything in a soft, luminous pink, and making the glass seem to ripple like water.

Lucian's missile struck the liquid and dissipated, scattering into embers that seared and blackened the tile wherever they fell. He swore.

I heard a commotion in the hallway. Finally, Selena had arrived with reinforcements. I started to yell something, but the equine demon suddenly swiveled its head, golden eyes narrowing. Obviously, it had better hearing than I did.

The demon snarled something beneath its breath and gestured toward the door of the autopsy suite.

As I watched, the metal frame of the door began to blister and crack. Smoking and bubbling, it turned first red and then electric orange, shifting to an igneous curtain that spread across the walls and floor.

Great. They weren't getting through that anytime soon. Even if I could channel enough power to smother the flames, they'd still have to chip through all of the coagulated material left behind. The autopsy suite was an isolated, windowless room underground—no other points of entry besides that door.

We still had the power beneath us. Granted, if I channeled too much of it, I'd deep-fry myself. But as long as I was careful, I could keep borrowing from it.

Then something else occurred to me. Something I hadn't thought of before.

The equine demon had recovered its balance. It kept its eyes on the boy, who maintained his distance. I saw that the flesh around his ankles where the whip had touched them was seared black. He must have been in pain, but his expression was mechanically focused.

I moved slowly and quietly toward Lucian. Neither of the demons was paying attention to me.

"Hey," I whispered. "I have an idea."

He looked momentarily startled to see me, as if he'd forgotten I was there. I saw beads of sweat standing on his forehead. Whatever he'd thrown at the equine demon must have drained him considerably.

"I hope it's a good one," he said. "That thing's built like a Panzer tank, and it doesn't show any sign of slowing down."

"How many bodies are in the fridge?"

He stared at me. "What are you talking about?"

"The refrigeration unit at the far end of the room. It's used to hold corpses. Is it possible for you to tell how many bodies are in there?"

He frowned. Then his eyes narrowed for a second in concentration. I wondered how his particular senses worked. Death sonar? Or could he smell the sweet reek of decaying flesh from here?

"Five," he said. "It's full. They're all newly dead."

"That's amazing. You're like a bloodhound."

"What's your point?"

"Once, you told me that your power came from dead things—decomposing flesh, cadaverine, and compost. Theoretically, you should be able to use those dead bodies in there like batteries. Right?"

His eyes widened. "That is possible. But drawing energy from the bodies could also consume them."

"They're going to be cremated anyway. Does it really matter?"

"It seems disrespectful."

"Lucian, have you noticed that we're getting our asses kicked by something that just stepped out of another dimension? This thing has enough power to flatten all of us. The only way for us to get the upper hand is if we can stun it, even for just a few seconds. An epic blast of necroid materia might be enough to do that."

"I can try."

He stretched out his hand toward the closed door of the refrigeration unit. I felt him reaching out with his senses, like tendrils of plasma reached out from the earth during a storm, calling the lightning.

Translucent green vapors began to flow from the steel door. The air around them turned instantly cold. I watched as the vapors swirled between Lucian's fingertips, until his skin was rimed with frost. Cold sweat moved down his forehead as he continued to draw power, and the vapors flowed into his hand, up his arm, making his veins flare with sallow green light.

He gritted his teeth. "This is as much as I can hold. Step back."

I did so.

"Please don't miss," I said.

Lucian leveled his arm. The vapors flared for a moment, like an undead star about to go nova. Then a lance of green light exploded from his outstretched palm. It screamed as it cut through the air, and the sound was chilling.

The light tore through the equine demon's chest, blazing out the other side and striking the wall behind it.

The demon screamed. Blood sprayed from the glowing point of contact. It wasn't red, since most highertier demons lacked the hemoglobin and iron that gave blood its rust red color. Instead, it was black, like roof tar.

Then the light shimmered and winked out, leaving a clear hole in the demon's sternum. Foul smoke rose from the void in its flesh, and I could literally see through it. The demon staggered. But already the vessels, tendons, and bones were beginning to writhe and knit back together. We didn't have much time.

Lucian panted, leaning with one hand against the wall. He was out. No more necromantic battery power.

It seemed like the right time for the howler.

I drew the small metal clapper from my pocket. This close to the equine demon, it was already humming with energy. I had no idea where the artifact had come from, but I hoped it wasn't one of those things that went up in smoke once you used it. If we could replicate the technology, we'd have a dog whistle. Which was a lot better than our current strategy of *Throw everything at it, including the kitchen sink, and try not to catch on fire while you're doing it.*

I pressed the two cymbals together. They didn't make a sound, but their vibration grew more intense, until I could feel my fingers aching. Something like a low buzz started in the back of my head, never becoming entirely audible, but growing in density until I found myself wanting to squeeze my eyes shut.

The demon raised its head. It grunted. Then it began to twitch slightly, its eyes narrowing in silent pain.

My teeth were vibrating now. The demon made a sound like a snarl. It closed its eyes. Then it started to moan, clutching its head, as if it had a severe toothache. The howler was working.

"Derrick! Now's your chance!"

He and Miles had been keeping to the sidelines. Now he gave me a sharp look, as if to say, *I'll tell you where you can stick that chance.*

But he nodded, regardless. He was going to try, at least.

Derrick took a step forward. He kept eye contact with the equine demon, and I felt something flow between the two of them. The air around him stirred slightly as he channeled dendrite materia, which was what gave form to psychic energy. I'd seen his power in action many times before. He could pluck a thought lightly from someone's mind, or drill into it ruthlessly, drawing out information by force.

The demon looked at him strangely for a moment, still distracted by the pain of the howler. Then it began to laugh.

"Really? You think you can break into my mind?" It licked its lips. "Go ahead, you pathetic reader. Give it your best try. I invite you."

Derrick's eyes narrowed. I heard him suck in his breath. The flow of power between them intensified, and his hands closed into fists. Miles gave him a worried look, but he needn't have bothered. Derrick was beyond our reach now, searching the tracts of the demon's consciousness for a way in, the smallest gap, something that the blade edge of his power could wedge its way into.

"Your mind is like compost," the demon said. "I just have to squeeze, and all the sad, reeking bits of you will dribble out between my fingers. But I'm going to do it nice and slowly, so your friends can watch."

Despite its bravado, I could tell that Derrick was wearing it down. The howler's sonic energy was still throbbing in the air, and a few drops of black blood had begun to leak from the demon's nostrils. It was weakening.

Derrick pressed on with his attack. He was also bleeding—a slight trickle was running down his face and onto his chin. Miles saw it. His eyes widened.

Tess, he signed. *Stop him.*

Derrick kept pushing. The demon grunted. Then it coughed suddenly, and a clot of blood oozed from its mouth. It began to snarl. I heard Derrick groan.

"Get out!" the demon screamed. "Get out! I'll kill you! *Xxch'krr nsh nng!* Worm! Bag of pus and blood! I'll kill you!"

"*Nnnnnh.* Fuck—*you*—" Derrick hissed.

Blood was flowing freely from his nose now, reddening his jacket and the shirt beneath it. Flecks of spit had appeared at the edges of his mouth. He leaned forward, as if bracing himself against an arctic wind.

"*Enough!*" the demon shrieked. "Get *out!*"

It flung its arm out in a wide arc. I felt a vast pulse of energy move through the air. A killing current.

"Derrick!"

I channeled everything that I could, reaching deep into the earth node. Desperation lent me strength. The power scalded me. It roared its defiance as it moved through my body, electrifying every cell, until I felt like a negative with deadly light pouring through it. I cried out.

I flung the power in Derrick's direction, trying to deflect the energy that the demon had summoned.

It half worked. My attack sideswiped the demon's, knocking the majority of it off course, but a fragment of the power still slammed into Derrick's body. That was enough to send him flying backward. He sailed through the air, completely limp, the shock of the power having already knocked him out.

He bounced off the metal counter. I heard the crunch of bones breaking. Then he crumpled to the floor. His body lay still.

For a second, I couldn't move. I couldn't even breathe.

Miles, however, didn't suffer from the same paralysis.

He drew his gun—which he'd kept in an ankle holster—and fired at the demon's head. He kept firing, and each bullet ripped into the demon's face, tearing off chunks of its scalp, lacerating its ear, shattering its jaw. Blood the consistency of coffee grounds coated the walls and floor.

For all that, the demon barely moved. Its flesh had already begun to regenerate. The bone and muscle flowed back together, and the mushroomed .40-caliber rounds fell to the ground.

The howler had ceased vibrating as well. Our window had closed, and the demon was back to full form. No diversions left.

It advanced upon Miles. It gestured with its blood-spattered arm, and Miles cried out as an invisible force swept him into the air. He hung motionless, five feet off the ground, his eyes bulging slightly.

"That was really quite brave," it said. "Do you know what happens to brave boys? They get to die slowly."

It closed its hand into a fist. Miles choked. His hands trembled at his sides, but he couldn't move.

"For instance," the demon continued, "did you know that the human optic nerve can stretch up to a meter before it snaps? That means I can pull both of your eyes out, and you'll still be able to watch as I remove your heart. In fact, you'll get a stereoscopic view of it all. I think that makes you pretty lucky."

I saw a flash of green to the left of Miles. At first, I thought it was the demon-boy. Then I looked closer and realized that it was Dr. Rashid. I'd completely forgotten about him until now. He was slowly approaching the equine demon from behind. There was something in his hand.

A Stryker saw.

"Of course," the demon was saying, "we could make this even more interesting. I could start liquefying your organs from the inside. Or I can pull your legs off. How long do you think you'll survive as just a trunk with arms? I'm betting—"

His voice was cut off suddenly by the high-pitched buzz of the Stryker saw. Dr. Rashid plunged the spinning blade of the saw into the demon's naked scalp, using both of his hands to push it forward.

The demon screamed.

Blood hit Rashid's face, but he didn't even try to shield his eyes. He just kept cutting. The blade whined and groaned as it cut deeper, through flesh and muscle and into bone. It was designed to remove the calvarium of the skull to expose the brain, and it worked on demons as well as humans.

I didn't have much time. Keeping a firm grip on my athame, I ran toward the demon, channeling my last

reserve of power as I did so. I felt the pins and needles rushing up my arm. This was an old trick that my
teacher, Meredith Silver, had taught me long ago. She
called it "the Houdini."

I let the power flow along the hilt of the athame,
skimming along the surface of the earth node to boost
my own reserves. The blade grew hot. I concentrated,
and the double-edged knife began to tremble. Then it
grew, elongating into a saber that gleamed as I raised
it above my head.

The demon managed to turn around, and Rashid's
electric saw cut a deep gouge across its face. It opened
its mouth to scream something at me, but I kept moving. I used all of my momentum to drive the blade
straight down, through its chest.

It choked, lunging for me. But Rashid kept the
Stryker saw on its face, and the blade whined as it
continued to shear through the muscle tissue. I pushed
downward with all of my strength. I heard a sucking
noise, and then a crunch, as the blade passed through
the demon's rib cage.

Demonic anatomy could be idiosyncratic, so I was
relieved that I'd chosen the right angle. Blood welled
up within the wound, running down the surface of the
blade. I wrapped both of my hands around the hilt for
leverage. The demon howled something at me, possibly in its native language.

"Sorry," I grunted. "I don't speak asshole."

Then I pushed down on the hilt with all of my
might, using it as a fulcrum, which drove the blade
upward in an arc. I felt it meet resistance as it passed

through clusters of organs, some of which probably had no human equivalents. I gave the hilt one last push for good measure.

I was smart enough to shield my face, but hot blood still spattered my arms and chest, making my skin crawl. I was going to have to take six showers to get rid of the demonic funk. Maybe I'd bathe in tomato juice as well, just to be sure.

The demon kept screaming something, but its throat was ruined, so it all came out as a bubbling hiss. Blood seeped from its open mouth.

Miles had regained his footing now. He was rubbing his throat, but seemed fine. I grabbed his arm.

"Get the time bomb from Derrick's pocket. Now."

He nodded, then ran over to where Derrick was lying. I was impressed by his level of professional detachment. He didn't even look twice at the body of his lover, unconscious on the floor. He rifled through his pockets, found the globe, and returned to my side.

"Now what?"

Still gripping the athame with both hands, I gave it a sharp tug. The blade slid out of the demon's body. More blood came with it. I knew I should have worn a slicker.

I took the time bomb from him.

"Run. Grab Derrick and drag him out of the blast radius."

I kept a feverish grip on the globe as I turned and ran. I didn't allow myself to look back. I prayed that it would take the demon a few more seconds to regenerate, especially with the considerable damage that I'd done to its body.

My legs were shaking as I reached Lucian's side. He reached out to steady me. I must have had a truly insane look on my face, because he grabbed me lightly by the shoulders, looking into my eyes.

"What do you want me to do?" he asked.

"Just be ready to run," I told him. I looked up. The demon had taken a step forward, but it was still bleeding heavily. The front of its chest was slowly coming back together, the tendrils of flesh reknitting themselves with astonishing speed.

Dr. Rashid was kneeling beside Derrick's body, checking his vitals. The three of them had moved to a safe distance.

I looked at the time bomb one last time. It really did look just like a snow globe. But I trusted Linus.

I hurled it at the ground in front of the demon.

The glass shattered. White light enveloped the demon's form, and I felt a tremor pass through the air. Everything seemed to go a shade darker. The demon's writhing movements slowed, then ceased altogether.

It was frozen.

I stared at the cone of white light that was bathing the demon. Drops of blood hovered motionless within it, frozen in perfect meniscus. The demon's mouth remained open. Its eyes blazed.

Something exploded behind me.

I turned and saw the remnants of the door to the autopsy suite, now scattered in charred bits across the ground. Selena emerged through the ruined doorway, accompanied by two OSI agents dressed in protective gear.

"You're late," I told her. "You missed everything."

My bravado was already crumbling, though. I couldn't take my eyes off Derrick's still form. Selena saw the direction of my gaze.

"Don't worry. We'll get him patched up."

"What about the pureblood?"

"We have the technology to contain him. We'll be able to question him later, under controlled conditions."

The two agents had already surrounded the frozen demon and were weaving a complex field of infrared light with their athames.

I walked shakily over to Miles and Dr. Rashid. The coroner saw the expression on my face and cleared his throat.

"Your friend has a broken arm. Possibly a few broken ribs, and a concussion. But he's stable. I believe he'll recover completely."

"I thought you normally dealt with dead bodies, not live ones."

"I've dealt with a lot of things in my career." He blinked. "This is new, though. In fact, I'm not exactly sure what—" He blinked. "I mean, I don't know— What am I supposed to think about—"

He gestured wordlessly to the four-legged demon, still locked in midscream.

Suddenly, a small gray form appeared at his side. The demon-boy looked up at him. Rashid looked down at the boy. He had an expression of almost childlike wonder on his face.

"What exactly are you?" he asked softly.

The boy smiled. Then he reached up on tiptoes, as if to whisper something in the doctor's ear. Rashid leaned down, and the boy placed a hand on his cheek.

"Good night," he said simply.

Rashid stared at him, confused for a moment.

Then he dropped to the floor, unconscious.

The boy turned to me. "He won't remember any of this. I've damaged the specific neuronal clusters associated with this incident. He should wake up with a headache, but that's all."

"Nice trick," I said. "Want to come with us now?"

I held out my hand.

The boy looked solemnly at me for a moment. His eyes were the color of two peacock green marbles that I used to have as a child.

Then he took my hand. His skin was cool to the touch. His horns were gone, and he resembled a blond boy once again, face streaked with dirt, naked, shivering, and hopelessly small.

"I don't have anywhere else to go," he said.

I led him over to Selena. "Don't worry. That's kind of our specialty."

4

"Have you ever tried hot chocolate?"

The boy gave Selena a skeptical look as she held out the foam cup. He shook his head slowly.

"Try it. Our machine makes it pretty good. It's not fancy, but it'll warm you up."

"I'm ectothermic. I can regulate my own body temperature."

"Try it anyway."

He took the cup. "It smells strange."

"You'll like it. Trust me."

He took a sip of the hot liquid. He swallowed, then licked his lips. "You're right. I do like it." He drained the cup. "Do you have any more?"

"Sure. Follow me."

Selena led him to the coffee machine. He stared at it in fascination.

"It makes hot beverages," she said.

"How does it work?"

"See the buttons with the numbers? Press *B* and then four."

He did so. His eyes widened as the machine began to hiss and burble. Another foam cup dropped into the slot at the bottom, and he actually stepped back in surprise. "Where did it come from?"

"There's a stack of them inside the machine."

"Oh," he murmured.

The machine gave a final loud bubbling noise, and then a stream of hot chocolate poured into the cup. The boy's eyes never left it. When it was done, he just stood there, uncertain what to do next.

"Reach in and take it," Selena said. "It won't bite."

Slowly, as if reaching into the mouth of a tiger, he withdrew the foam cup. He sniffed it once again. Then he smiled and began to drink, this time more slowly.

"We don't have this where I come from," he said.

"Oh? And where's that?"

"I'm not sure what you would call it. In my language, it's called *Ptah'l*, which means Red Island. It's a small plane bordering several larger ones in a dimension adjacent to your own."

Selena had managed to find some clothes for him, but they were ill-fitting. As a consequence, he resembled a tween skater. She'd tried to convince him to wear shoes, but he preferred to go barefoot. His feet were small and white against the linoleum floor.

So far, we hadn't left the lobby of the forensics lab. He seemed most comfortable in the oversized leather chairs, and it wasn't the right moment to drag him into an interrogation chamber. Eventually, he'd have to submit to a full round of medical tests. But for now, Selena was working on him slowly. She had a surprisingly gentle touch with kids. Even if this "kid" only looked like one.

"You know," I said, sitting near him but not quite next to him, "you still haven't told me your name. You know my boss, Selena. And I'm Tess."

"My name is a combination of liquid and plosive sounds that you wouldn't be able to replicate with your larynx," he informed us, still sipping his hot chocolate. "But if you want, you can call me Ru. That's the closest approximation."

"Where did you learn our language, Ru?"

"Primary school."

Huh.

"Can you tell us how you got here?"

"I don't remember. I was running from them, and then I was just here." He grimaced. "There was pain, and dark, and sand in my mouth. Then just dark."

"Who's 'they'?"

He set down his cup, but made no reply.

"Do you mean the demon who came after you?" Selena pressed.

"No. He's one of the Kentauroi. A sentry. He was sent to recover me."

"Do the Kentauroi have any abilities that we haven't seen yet?" I asked. "Anything we should know about?"

Ru seemed to ponder this for a moment. "Well, there's the tissue regeneration. And the combustible fibrous appendages. Also, I believe that they're allergic to some microgametocytes."

Selena frowned. "You mean pollen?"

"Particularly *Asteraceae ambrosia*. I believe the vernacular term is . . . ragweed?"

I smiled. "There's a whole clump of it growing in the north parking lot. Maybe we should bring him back a nice bouquet."

"It's only an irritant," Ru said. "A distraction, at best. You'll have to keep a close watch on him, if you intend to hold him in this place. Are you using some manner of harmonic field that relies on weak nuclear energy?"

It was a little strange to answer these types of questions from someone who resembled a nine-year-old. But he seemed to value honesty.

"We're using something similar to what you describe, yes," Selena said.

"You may want to employ a green crystalline laser for diffraction purposes, then. If you don't disperse the valences as widely as possible, he'll sense any weak spots right away." Ru held up his empty cup. "May I use the chocolate machine again?"

"Of course."

He walked over to the corner of the room with his cup.

"What's our next move?"

"We need to get more information out of him. If we can figure out what's hunting him, we might be able to prepare an adequate defense."

"I'm a little confused, though, about our role in

this investigation. As far as I can tell, there's no crime apparent."

Selena stared at me. "Are you suggesting that we just let him go?"

"Of course not. But he says he doesn't remember anything. And I'm not even sure that we can hold him. Sure, he's discovered the wonders of the vending machine, and that's captivating him for now. But what happens when he gets bored, or restless? The kid can spit acid. It's going to be difficult to keep him here against his will."

"All we can do is convince him that this is the safest place to stay."

"Do you even believe that? I mean, okay, the lab's pretty secure. It's better than leaving him on the doorstep of the VPD. But what happens when 'they' send another bounty hunter to collect him? Maybe the next demon will be able to walk through walls or burn the whole place to the ground."

"You're not usually this alarmist," Selena said. "Have you been getting enough sleep lately?"

I sighed. "No. I never get enough sleep. But that's not the issue. I just keep thinking about three years ago, when we told Mia that we'd be able to keep her safe. We couldn't even protect her from one psychotic agent."

"Who's Mia?"

Ru was standing behind us, holding another steaming cup of hot chocolate.

"How much of that did you hear?" Selena asked.

"All of it. I can hear conversations on the floor

below us, as well. And the floor below that. Your species tends to yell a lot."

I nodded. "It's a habit."

"Who's Mia?" he repeated.

"She's a girl that lives with me. I adopted her a few years ago."

"Is she a demon?"

I frowned. "Technically."

"I don't understand."

I gave Selena a look.

She shrugged.

I turned back to Ru. "Mia was infected with a vampiric retrovirus. She takes medication to suppress the plasmids in her blood, but we can't eliminate them. She also has the genetic potential to manipulate materia, just like Selena and I."

"Why would you want to suppress the virus?"

"Well—because she doesn't want to be a vampire."

"Did she tell you that herself?"

I hesitated. "Not in so many words, no. But she was infected at an early age. If we'd let the virus run its course, there was a good chance that she'd be hurt, or killed, or that she'd hurt someone else."

"But vampirism would also make her stronger and give her more acute senses. It would eliminate any further genetic deficiencies in her body and lengthen her life span, perhaps indefinitely. Why wouldn't she want that?"

"Maybe she doesn't want to drink human blood," Selena said.

"She wouldn't have to. Synthetic blood is bottled

and sold in nearly every world, including my own. Some vampires also choose to subsist on animal blood." His green eyes surveyed me coolly. "It seems as though you took the decision away from her. That hardly seems fair."

"That's true. But—" I found myself groping. How could I explain to a pureblood demon that humans valued their own humanity? Maybe we overvalued it. But it seemed a lot better than the alternative. "Maybe she'd prefer to live a normal life."

"If she has demonic viral agents in her bloodstream, she isn't living a normal life. Just as neither of you two are living a normal life, by virtue of the genetic anomaly that allows you to manipulate your world's natural forces. What you call 'materia.'" He shrugged. "It just seems illogical to deny her the choice."

"But you never had the same choice," Selena said. "You were born pureblood. You've never known anything different."

"But I've thought about it," he said. "I may not be able to change what I am, but I still think about it. Perhaps that's worse."

I stared at him. Who exactly was this boy-shaped demon, sipping his third cup of hot chocolate in front of me?

"When the police found you," Selena said, "you appeared to have no vital signs."

"Like I said—there was dark, and then sand. That's all I remember."

"And you still don't want to talk about what was chasing you?"

"It was bad."

That was his only response.

"If you'll consent to it, we'd like to perform a physical exam on you."

"It's fine. Take your samples. I don't mind."

"Thank you."

He chuckled suddenly. "That's what the Ferid used to say. When they were first convincing us to leave our homes. *We just want to help*."

"The Ferid?" I asked. "Are those the demons who are after you?"

Ru didn't answer, but looked at me suddenly instead. "What happened to your friend? The one who was injured?"

"His name is Derrick. He's in the hospital right now."

"And his mate?"

I chuckled. "I'm not sure how Miles would feel about being called that. But yes, they're together. He's at the hospital as well."

"And your mate?" His eyes stayed on me.

"I—" I looked at Selena. Her expression was impossible to read. "I'm not sure who you mean."

He seemed to scan me for a moment. Then he shrugged. "It's not important. From what I understand, your species doesn't mate for life."

I thought about Lucian. How could you mate for life with someone whose power was entirely based on death? I still didn't even know how old he really was. He'd never told me anything about past partners. I felt strangely cheated by the lack of information. It's not as if I wanted him to talk about old lovers. But it would have been nice to have at least some basis for comparison.

Last year, we'd investigated the death of Luiz Ordeño, a very old, very powerful necromancer with entangled political connections. I remembered that there hadn't been a single picture of friends or family on his walls. No evidence of past loves, no tokens of affection, no mementos. Just a kind of relentless blank where human (or even nonhuman) connections should have been.

When I asked Lucian if he knew anything about Ordeño's romantic past, his reply didn't clear anything up. *Like most people who've lived for more than a few hundred years, I think that he was bisexual, or at the very least open-minded. But I never saw him with a partner of either gender.* Was that the only productive way to deal with the weight of all those years? Sexual variety? It seemed to make monogamy impossible. So where did that leave Lucian and me?

Ru was still staring at me. I cleared my throat.

"Sometimes we do mate for life," I said. "When the right partner comes along."

"But often you don't—correct?"

I nodded. "We try. We should at least get points for that."

"I'm too young to mate," he said.

The gravity of his tone made me want to laugh, but I managed to suppress it. "How old are you, exactly?"

"I am in my third ecdysis."

"What's that in years?"

He thought about it for a moment. "Two hundred thirty-one."

"Wow. That's a long childhood."

"We have a lot to learn."

"It's different here. We get tossed out of the nest at eighteen."

"How barbaric."

"This is quite educational," Selena said, "but it might be best, Ru, if you got some sleep. I mean—does your species require sleep?"

"Less than yours. But yes."

"We've prepared a room for you. It's not exactly the Hilton, but it should do for the time being. The pull-out bed is comfortable enough."

He looked around the lab, taking in the glass-partitioned rooms and walls lined with various equipment. "Do you all live here?"

"No. We have separate dwelling spaces. Apartments."

"I live in a house with a lot of crazy people," I clarified.

"My family and I live together in one place." His eyes surveyed a dark corner of the lobby. "We all sleep in the same chamber. At night, everything glows red from the hydrogen storms outside. I like to close my eyes and listen to the low hissing of the cloud layers. Then, in the morning, our windowpane is streaked with colors. From all the chromophores. Like the stained glass in your churches."

"Well," Selena said, "I can't promise you—um—chromophores. But we do have satellite TV installed in the room. And there's a minifridge."

"Will I be expected to remain here? In this room with the minifridge?"

"You aren't a prisoner. You can go if you like. But, frankly, it's not safe for you outside of this building. It's barely safe for you inside."

"Maybe you should just put me in the prison cell with the Kentauros. Then at least I can see my death coming."

"Death's not coming for anyone tonight," Selena said. "You've got around-the-clock protection. And the Kentauros won't be leaving its cell anytime soon."

Ru looked at me. "Will you be going back to your house tonight?"

I felt slightly uncomfortable beneath his gaze. "First I'll be going to the hospital, to check on Derrick. I may end up staying the night there. But I'll be back here in the morning. I can even bring you breakfast."

"What's breakfast?"

"The first meal of the day."

"You divide your food into cycles?"

"Basically, yes. What do you do?"

"We just eat all day long."

"That's called being a teenager. You and Patrick would get along well."

"Who's that?"

"Another person that I adopted. Less officially than Mia, granted. But he still lives with us."

"In the big crazy house?"

I smiled. "That's right."

"It sounds fun. Can I visit?"

I looked at Selena.

Absolutely not, she mouthed.

"Sure. Just not tonight."

"Okay."

"Sleep tight, Ru, and I'll see you in the morning."

"Thank you, Tess. I hope that you sleep tight as well."

"I'll try."

"Follow me," Selena said. "Your suite is down the hall. I think you'll be pleased by the snacks that we've assembled for you."

"What are snacks?"

"In my opinion, pretty much a reason for living."

He followed her down the hall. The sight of his bare feet receding into the dark made me suck in my breath.

Then I headed for the elevator.

The CORE clinic resembled a regular hospital, complete with vinyl chairs and offensive fluorescent lighting, only the inhabitants tended to have more creative injuries. Some patients could regenerate on their own, but still needed a little extra help. Others were suffering from materia burns, psychic shock, and other supernatural ailments that Demerol couldn't really help with. The nurses here had seen everything, from detached souls (a nasty condition called "exospiritus") to bodies rendered two-dimensional by a flatland curse. That was never pretty.

I wasn't entirely surprised to find Derrick's room

full of people. Miles had fallen asleep, his legs propped up on a chair. He was snoring gently. Lucian sat in a chair close by, doing a crossword puzzle with Mia.

"I don't understand this clue," he said. " 'May contain eggs.' Three letters."

Mia frowned. "Is it wrong that I want it to be 'egg'?"

"That seems too easy."

"I know. But it totally fits."

"Do you think it's just screwing with us?"

"Probably. We should have gotten the *Metro* puzzle. It's easier."

There was an empty chair near Derrick's bed. A small lump formed in my throat as I realized that it was for me.

Lucian looked up. "Hey. We sent Patrick out for coffee."

"God. I think I'm coffee'd out for one night."

"But it's almost morning."

"Well. You've got a point there." I collapsed into the chair. "Has he woken up at all? Said anything?"

Lucian shook his head. "He's pretty doped up. The nurse said he'll probably sleep for another few hours. Maybe more."

I looked at Derrick for the first time. His face was bruised from where he'd struck the ground, and he had a split lip. A cut on his forehead had been hastily stitched up. His right arm was in a sling. They'd shaved a patch of his head, which was now covered in gauze.

"He'd be horrified if he knew what that gown looked like."

Mia laughed. "I know, right?"

"When did Miles finally fall asleep?"

"Just a few minutes ago. He's out like a light, though."

"Did anyone check him for injuries?"

"Just some bruises," Lucian said. "Derrick definitely got the worst of it."

"Yeah." I reached out and held his hand. It was cold. "I tried to deflect the blast. It was just too powerful."

"We know." Lucian stood up and walked over to my side of the bed. "You did everything you could. And we all survived. He'll be fine."

"He went swimming inside the brain of a pure-blood demon. We don't know if he's going to be fine." I squeezed his hand. "There could be scars. Invisible ones. Has anyone examined him for psychic trauma?"

"I'm not sure."

"Did you call anyone? Did you even let them know?"

"Tess."

"I'm sorry. This has just been the longest night ever."

"Actually . . ." Mia pointed to the window. I could see a weak, grayish light seeping through the blinds. "I think it's morning."

"Great," I said. "Now it starts all over again."

"That's the good part, remember?" Lucian smiled at me.

"Sometimes I'm not so sure."

Patrick appeared in the doorway. He was holding two paper bags and a tray full of coffee cups. "Hey, Tess. I brought you a muffin."

"What kind?"

He peered into one of the bags. "Um. Carrot. I think."

"Butter?"

"Yup."

"Gimme."

"See?" Lucian patted my hand. "Starting over isn't so bad."

"No. Not as long as there's butter." I took the plastic knife and fork that Patrick offered me. "And chromophores."

Lucian raised an eyebrow. "What?"

I was already spreading the butter. "Nothing."

5

I woke up in a condo on the beach.

I was in a vast living room with high-beamed ceilings and polished hardwood floors. The room was an oval with wraparound bay windows, and sunlight streamed through them. I rose from the couch where I'd been sleeping, stretched to relieve the kink in my neck, and walked over to the nearest pane of glass. I could see a long, empty beach that gave way to turquoise water. There was no wind to stir the surface.

Two figures were sitting at the edge of the water. I squinted and realized that it was Derrick and Miles. They were both in shorts and appeared to be building a sand castle. Derrick had a bright red pail and shovel, and Miles was gently molding the edges of a tower with his hands. He said something that I couldn't hear, and Derrick laughed. Then he pointed to the castle's unfinished drawbridge, and Miles began working on it, kneading the sand as if it were soft dough.

I turned and walked to the middle of the room. There was a beautiful Persian rug laid across the floor, patterned in woven mandalas of red, green, and gold that danced before my eyes.

I noticed that a corner of the rug was turned up slightly, and there was a lump underneath it. I nudged the lump with my toe. It didn't move. Gently, I kicked the folded corner of the rug, and it fell away to reveal a pile of bones.

They were old and yellowed. Even the toughest tendons had rotted away, and they smelled of moss and earth. The skull was quite small. Possibly a child's. It looked Caucasoid in shape, but I lacked the expertise to tell with a glance. The eye sockets were deeply worn, like something that had slept for ages in a riverbed.

I looked out the window again. Derrick and Miles were gone, but their sand castle remained. Miniature sand knights on sand horses were gathered at the entrance to the keep, along with sand ladies, offering handkerchiefs and keepsakes. As I watched, the horses began to prance in their jeweled caparisons, and the knights lowered their visors, preparing for the tourney.

There was a long hallway next to me. I could hear something, a very faint something, coming from it.

The walls were clean and white. The floor was warm against my bare feet. I started walking down it, passing closed doors on either side. I walked and walked, but the hallway just kept going. I counted ten doors, then twenty, then thirty, all shut tight. Finally, I came to a door that was slightly ajar.

The sound was coming from beyond it. A gentle tapping.

I opened the door and stepped into a spacious bathroom, floored in marble. There was a pedestal sink in one corner, and a window dominating the entire south wall, which looked out over the water. I could see two shapes floating in the distance. Was it Derrick and Miles? They must have been swimming very far out. Derrick wasn't a particularly strong swimmer, which worried me. Perhaps Miles was.

A claw-foot bathtub sat in the opposite corner of the room. The brass faucet was dripping. I leaned over to tighten one of the knobs. As I stared into the empty tub, I noticed a smear of something red against the porcelain. A bloody handprint.

Something clattered in the hallway.

I could feel my pulse rising. I left the bathroom and saw that the door facing me had also been left ajar. I heard the clattering sound again.

"Hello?"

I pushed open the door. This seemed to be the master bedroom. The floor was carpeted, and a four-poster bed stood in the center. A window above the bed had been left open, and the casement moved slowly back and forth, banging against the wall. Wind stirred the sheets on the bed, and I realized that there was something underneath them. I took a step forward, and then stopped. My breath caught.

There was blood on the sheets. Blood on the pillows. Wind teased the edges of the top sheet, and I could see indistinct flashes of what lay underneath. I took another step forward, until I was standing at the foot of the bed. The bloodstains were still wet. I looked up at the walls. They were clean and bare. No parent stains and no spatter. All of it was passive blood flow. I stared at the carpet, but couldn't see so much as a stray drop. It didn't seem possible, unless someone had been killed in a vacuum. But it also wouldn't have been the strangest thing I'd ever seen.

Slowly, trying not to disturb any of the stains, I lifted up the sheet. A cold shock passed through me as I saw the body lying underneath.

It was mine.

I was wearing the same clothes. My jeans were soaked in blood, and my feet were bare. My hair lay across my face, obscuring one eye. The other eye was open, staring blindly. My lips were parted, my mouth flecked with blood. My throat was slit from ear to ear, completely transecting both carotid arteries. The cut was clean, and I could see where the fat and muscle tissue avulsed to reveal bone.

"Even dead," a voice said, "you're still beautiful."

I turned around, struggling to breathe.

A tall shape stood in the doorway. It seemed almost too angular, a piece of perverse trigonometry. It was made partly of smoke, but I recognized its eyes. They stood out against the darkness of its plastic face. Two burning pinholes. They were the color of dirty ice.

And they knew me.

The force of that knowledge slammed into me, devouring me, and I almost doubled over from the pain of being comprehended so perfectly. Its knowing seared me black from the inside. I wanted to scream, but I couldn't. I had no breath. There was nothing inside me, no blood, no torsion or fibrillation, just a dry puparial casing. It had sucked out everything I was with a single look.

I couldn't look at it anymore. I turned back to my body on the bed. I reached out with my fingers to brush my own flesh.

It was cold. I was cold.

"Not even necromancy will bring you back from that," it said. "Oh, it could bring back a few pieces of you, held together with willpower and a bit of duct tape. But never all of you. That's gone forever."

"Did you do this?" I asked.

"No. You did."

He was standing directly behind me now. The smoke of his limbs curled around me, his impossibly long fingers hesitating, just an inch away from my neck and shoulders. I turned. His eyes were level with my own. I looked deep into them, searching for something recognizable. All I could see was a crystalline structure, perfect, endlessly replicating itself. And beneath that, something dark and liquid, older than the first nanobacterium, but far from primitive. A radiant hunger.

"Why did you do it?" I asked.

"I told you. I didn't."

"Not the body. I mean *me*." I refused to look away. "Twenty-eight years ago, you attacked my mother. You left her broken and alone, bleeding in a parking lot. And you made me. I want to know why."

"You really want to know?"

"Yes."

"You're sure?"

"Tell me."

He smiled. "Because it was fun."

I screamed at him. I screamed every obscenity that I knew, in every language that I could think of. I screamed until my throat burned, until I was moaning, crying, choking, until I tasted blood welling up in my throat.

"I made you," he said, "so that I could own you."

I sank to my knees, bawling. He was shadow, and he was all around me. I couldn't breathe without taking him in. I couldn't smell anything except the putrescence of his satisfaction.

"Tess. I love you. I love you."

It was Lucian's voice.

"Get out!" I screamed. "Get out get out get *out*!"

"I love you. I love you."

I felt the bite of his love against my throat. I felt the blood.

Then nothing.

I woke up again, for real this time. I was in Der-rick's hospital room, folded into one of the uncomfortable chairs with my feet propped up. My neck was killing me. It felt as if I'd slept sideways, or maybe upside down. Light was coming through the open blinds, and I could hear the rain outside. I checked my watch. Six forty-five a.m.

Great. I had about twenty minutes to get to work if I wanted to avoid a reprimand. Selena was interrogating the Kentauros demon, and I had to be there.

The remaining chairs were empty. Miles must have finally taken my advice and gone home to get a few hours of sleep in an actual bed. I glanced down at my cell to see if Mia had texted me. There was a message: *at home and P bought groceries (strange i know!). see you after work.*

I shuddered to think what Patrick might have bought. Last time I sent him out for food, he came home with cereal and a jar of Nutella. But if Mia was there, at least she'd able to push for milk and bread. Derrick was the one who usually bought fresh pasta and produce. Ever since the day I brought home a slightly bruised avocado, he maintained that I wasn't discriminating enough.

Stifling a yawn, I looked up, expecting to see him asleep. Instead, he was wide-awake and sitting up, surrounded by pillows.

"Wow," he said, smiling. "Your hair looks like shit."

I stumbled out of the chair and ran over to the other side of the bed.

"You're awake! How long have you been awake?"

"Long enough to hear you snoring like a hockey player with a busted nose. It's actually quite impressive."

I kissed his forehead, then both of his cheeks. Then I grabbed his hand and kissed each knuckle for good measure. He laughed, pretending to swat me away. But he didn't let go of my hand.

"How are you feeling?"

"Like a centaur threw me against a steel counter."

"Well, that's pretty accurate."

"How long was I out for?"

"Close to eight hours."

He winced. "I hurt in a lot of different places. I think even my hair hurts."

"You've got a broken arm, two broken ribs, and you're recovering from a concussion. You've also got some serious floor-rash on your face. You hit the ground pretty hard back there."

"Yeah." He licked his lips. "I can feel the stitches. And my head is killing me. It's like an atomic hangover or something."

"I'm not surprised. You dove into the mind of an unfamiliar demon, and he was none too happy about it. You might as well have bashed your head against solid concrete. They're going to run some tests once you're feeling better, just to make sure there isn't any internal damage."

"You mean to make sure I'm not crazy."

"Essentially."

He gave me a long look. "What do you think?"

"About what?"

"Do you think I'm going to need time off?"

"Of course. Your body needs to recover."

"It's not my body I'm worried about."

"Derrick. I'm sure your brain is fine. Aside from the concussion."

"You don't know that."

"You're sitting here talking to me, aren't you? To-

tally lucid and normal. No ranting and raving, no apha-
sia, no psychosis."

"At least not yet."

"Are you worried? Do you feel different?"

"I don't know." He closed his eyes. "I can't tell. I
just feel thin. Like someone shaved away the top layer
of me, and everything's just a bit more intense—light,
sound, smells, everything. It's overwhelming."

"Do you want more Demerol?"

"No. I don't want to be high. I just want to feel
better."

"That's going to take time."

He sighed. "Yeah."

"Hey." I squeezed his hand. "You tangled with a
pureblood and survived. It could have been a lot worse.
And things are already starting to look up. We rescued
one demon, captured another, and nobody died. So
buck up."

"Really? 'Buck up'?"

"Stiff upper lip?"

He shook his head. "Sorry. Not doing it for me."

"What would you like to hear?"

"I'm not sure. Ask me again once they do the brain
scan."

I rubbed my thumb across his knuckles. "You're really worried about this, aren't you? Is it something that
you saw in the demon's head?"

"No. That was barely comprehensible. I don't even
know how I'm going to fill out the report about it.
Blood and ashes and a pile of bones."

"That's what you saw?"

"More or less."

"Well, nobody expects you to publish a paper on the imagery. Just tell Selena everything you can remember."

"Yeah. I know."

"So what is it that's actually freaking you out?"

"You mean besides the fact I'm wearing a dress that buttons up in the back? Because that's already stirring up all sorts of drag memories."

I smiled. "Yes. Fashion crimes aside, what is it?"

"Miles."

"Don't worry. The nurses checked him out, and he's fine. Just a couple of scratches and a bruised neck. He'll be back later today."

"It's not his health I'm worried about. It's us."

I blinked. "Call me crazy, but I'd think that surviving a demon attack would actually strengthen your relationship. I can't see that you have anything to worry about. He didn't leave your side all night."

"I know that he loves me. He's not the problem. I am."

"You cheated on him. God, where did you find the time?"

"No." He rolled his eyes. "And thanks so much for leaping to that conclusion first. It makes me feel like a real saint."

"Sorry. It's all I could think of."

"There's been no cheating, at least not to my knowledge. And I don't plan on changing that. I'm just worried about . . ." He sighed. "I don't know. I'm not even sure I can explain it. But I'm scared. Every day, whether I wake up in bed next to him, or I know I'm going to see him at work, or he sends me a sweet text—all I can feel is this unholy terror. Like it's all going to dissolve at any moment."

"Fear of the fuckup."

"Excuse me?"

"You've got fear of the fuckup. You think you're going to screw everything up, it'll be totally your fault, and you'll never forgive yourself."

"Well. Yes. Basically."

"Don't worry about it. I feel the same way. Every time Lucian says something nice to me, all I can hear is this voice in the back of my head screaming, *You are an asshole; you will totally destroy this.*"

"Really?"

"Absolutely. Sometimes I get so paranoid about it, I'll be afraid to say anything. So I'll just keep nodding like some kind of passive-aggressive bobblehead. Why do you think I agreed to get digital cable? Why do I continue to let him wear cargo shorts? I'm afraid to say no."

"But you guys are doing fine. He's crazy about you."

"And I could say the same thing about Miles."

He chuckled. "Maybe there really is something wrong with us."

"Yeah. It's called being damaged."

"But when did that happen?"

"If we knew that, things would be a lot simpler. We could fix it, or at least apply a patch. But it's all just a hazy memory. It's like someone anesthetized us when we were young, and when we woke up, there was suddenly this neurotic voice in our head. And the voice is a bastard."

"It is." He leaned back against the pillows. "It just feels like he's too good, you know? Too good to be true, too good for me—just too good in general. And my mind is a snake pit. I don't want him to see the worst parts."

"I think he already has. And he's still here. That must count for something."

"Maybe he just feels sorry for me."

"Man, this pity train has a lot of stops, doesn't it?"

He laughed. "Fine, fine. I get it. But you understand where I'm coming from, right? Our job is dark and messed up, and it has a high mortality rate. It's pretty much impossible for us to sustain a relationship with someone. And Miles isn't normate, but he isn't quite the same as us, either. He can't read minds. He can't dodge bullets."

"Would you rather he could? If you're only willing to date people with a yen for materia, you're seriously whittling down your choices."

"It's not that. I don't need him to be psychic, either. I'm just scared that something could go wrong. With me. Something inside. And he won't be able to understand, because it doesn't touch him the same way." He sighed. "I guess I feel like he could still be normal, you know? He could still date a normal guy. He could have a desk job and a nice condo and a real-estate agent for a boyfriend, and then he wouldn't have to deal with all of this."

"I'm pretty sure he wants to deal with all of it, hon.

Especially if you come with it. Because, as far as I can tell, he's a big fan of you and everything related to you. So he's willing to take on the drama."

"But maybe it would be more ethical to just give him an out, you know?"

I stared at him. "How hard did that demon hit you? Give him an 'out'? Derrick, guys like Miles don't come along very often. You don't want to give him an exit strategy. If anything, you want to strap him to a chair so he doesn't escape."

"Maybe."

I tried to smooth my hair for a moment. The effort was a failure. I looked back at Derrick and saw that he was avoiding my gaze by pretending to stare out the window.

"Just come out with it," I said. "This is more than a neurotic blip. Something's banging around in there, and I want to know what it is."

He rubbed his swollen eye. "Ouch."

"You want some ice?"

"No. I want a vacation."

"Me, too. But it's not coming. Unless you want to decorate the living room and pretend we're in a Mexican hostel."

"That could be fun."

"Stop stalling. Just tell me, or I'll never go away."

"You promise?"

"Yep."

He smiled slightly. Then the expression was gone. The fear returned to his eyes, and he held on tighter to my hand.

"I'm changing, Tess."

I tried to keep my tone neutral. "Changing how?"

"I'm not sure. I've felt it ever since we fought the Iblis. Before that, even. Do you remember when Miles was profiling the crime scene, back at the hotel, and the materia that the Iblis had left behind took control of him?"

"It's hard to forget. He called me a stupid fat bitch."

"Wow. Did you ever tell him that?"

"No. I decided to keep that little piece of sunshine under wraps."

"Do you remember what happened after that? To me?"

I nodded. "You channeled some fierce power. You traced a glowing sign in the air, and Miles obeyed you. It was kind of wild. I mean, I've felt your power before, but nothing like that."

"Did it feel strange to you?"

"Strange how?"

"I don't know. Just—off. Weird."

"You're going to have to give me a little more than that to go on."

"It felt like—" He closed his eyes for a moment. "Like someone opened a door inside of me. I didn't even know that it was there. But now it's open, and all of this *stuff* keeps pouring out. And I don't know how to close it."

"What kind of stuff?"

"I don't know how to describe it. Pictures. Sounds. Memories. I'm not even sure if they're my memories or not. I used to get déjà vu a lot, but now it's like a daily occurrence. Like, as soon as I get to a new place, I feel like I've already been there. And my powers are changing."

"Of course. The more you use them, the stronger they get. You're becoming a better psychic, and that's natural."

"No. I mean, yes, I'm better trained now. But they're changing in other ways. Sometimes I feel like I have even less control over them. Like I'm just a passenger in my own body."

"Materia can feel that way sometimes. If I channel too much power, too fast, it's like something's racing through my body. I can't control it, either."

"But you can. You always do." He stared at me strangely. "Tess, I'm afraid of losing control. There was one time—"

He bit the words off sharply. He couldn't meet my gaze again.

"Sweetheart. You can tell me anything."

Derrick exhaled. "It was a week ago. Miles and I got into a fight. Something really stupid about one of us forgetting to return a movie. I looked at him and said, *I don't give a shit. If you care so much about the fines, go return the movie yourself.* And he got the weirdest look on his face. Then he left, got into the car, and returned the movie. He came back twenty minutes later, got into bed, and didn't say a word about it the next day."

"I think that's called being a good boyfriend."

He shook his head. "No. I know his face. I know his expressions. I can tell when he's being sweet, or when he's trying to stop an argument, or when he's just humoring me. But this was different." I could feel his hand trembling slightly under mine. "Tess, when I said *Go return it yourself*, it was like I gave him a command. One minute he was mad at me, and the next, his expression was just blank. It was like I watched the personality drain out of his eyes, and all that was left was obedience. He did it because I ordered him to."

I frowned. "Were you using a control tone? I thought that only worked on normates and younger people. Miles would be less susceptible to it."

"That's the thing. I wasn't. I didn't channel any power. It was completely effortless. I told him to do something, and he did it. I feel like if I'd told him to smash his fist through the window, he would have done that, too."

"But you didn't. And I'm not sure you should get so worked up about convincing your boyfriend to return a movie. Even if you did slip in a bit of control tone, maybe it was by accident. Maybe he was already thinking of doing it, and you just kind of nudged him a little further. But I doubt it was coercion."

"I'm not so sure." He shook his head. "I don't want it to happen again. I don't ever want to control his mind, even for something so little and stupid."

"You just have to be careful."

"But I didn't even know it was happening. How can I keep myself from doing it again? And who's to say that the next time won't be worse?"

"You can't drive yourself crazy worrying about it. Just count to ten when you feel like you're about to freak out."

"It's not enough."

"There's nothing else you can do. And if you break up with him just to save him from a future of possible mind control, you aren't being ethical. You're just being an idiot. The only difference between your mind control and mine is that I have to work harder at it. And usually mine involves a bribe. But couples have been doing the same thing for centuries."

"You know it's not the same."

"Of course. But do you really want to beat yourself up every time the guy decides to do something nice for you? We can't always blame the occult world for our relationship disasters."

"I don't want to hurt him."

"What—like you're going to vaporize his brain while he's sleeping? I don't think your power works that way. You're not a zombie or a neural parasite. The worst you could do is accidentally give him a migraine."

"I don't know." He blinked. "I wish I could be so sure."

"Do you honestly feel dangerous? Because I live with you, and no offense, but I think even Mia outweighs you."

"I don't feel dangerous. I just feel—"

"Strange?"

"Yeah. All the time. And it's only getting worse."

"I'm sorry to say this, babe. But that's just who we are."

"You don't think we'll ever feel normal?"

"Not unless we move to an asylum."

"That might actually be nice."

"Are you kidding? It would be great. Three square meals a day, no rent, and all the Jell-O you could ever want." I laid my head on his shoulder. "Dream with me. No demons. No on-call shifts. No ectoplasm on our shoes."

"No more broken bones."

"No more bosses."

"No more training exercises."

"No more lying to the outside world."

"No more outside world."

"Yeah. We'd be totally sheltered."

"We wouldn't even have to read the paper or check our e-mail."

"We could do puzzles. Make collages."

"Mmm. With Elmer's Glue."

"Absolutely."

"And listen to books on tape. I could finally read Proust."

"I would only read *Vanity Fair*. But I'd cut out all the pictures of the skinny models, and then you could make papier-mâché effigies out of them."

"That sounds nice."

"And three times a week, Lucian and Miles would come visit us. They'd sneak in some alcohol, in a hidden flask maybe, and then read us the paper, but only the nice bits. Nothing about murders or lost animals."

"Actually . . ." Derrick chuckled. "Speaking of the normate news, we should probably watch it. I'd like to see exactly how Selena was able to spin what happened at the morgue. Can you switch on the TV for a second?"

"Sure. But only for a minute. Then we're watching cartoons."

"Don't you have to be at work soon?"

"Meh. I've got time for an episode of *Dora*, especially if it's fast-paced."

I grabbed the remote and flipped to the local news channel. A VPD officer was being interviewed by the media. He looked exhausted.

"This is an ongoing investigation," he was saying. *"All we can disclose at the moment is that, last night, at approximately four a.m., a group of individuals broke into the Chief Coroner's Office. Once inside, they did significant damage to the autopsy suite and stole a cadaver."*

My breath caught.

"Were there any witnesses?" a reporter asked.

"The forensic pathologist on duty last night is currently being held for questioning. We're not certain of his involvement in the commission of this crime, but we've not yet eliminated him as a suspect."

"Can you tell us the identity of the body that was stolen?"

"Not at this time, no."

"And is there any possible motive for stealing this particular body?"

"None that we know of yet. But we're investigating this closely."

I stared at Derrick, my mouth still open.

"Let's hide," he said.

6

Sometime during the night, the Kentauros demon had been moved to our special interrogation unit in the basement. I wasn't sure how Selena had done it, but something told me that I didn't want to know. There wasn't an opioid on the planet strong enough to knock out a pureblood. Pure heroin only made them more efficient.

I met Selena at the elevator doors. She looked drawn. Her expression barely changed when I produced a second coffee. She just took the cup numbly.

"You've been up all night."

"Can you tell? My head feels like a broken toaster."

"What broke the toaster? Was it Texas Toast? I always burn it."

She drank some of the coffee. "You saw the news?"

"Derrick and I watched it from the clinic."

"This is a first-rate shit show."

"I can only imagine. Where do you need me? Derrick's going to be on his back for at least the next few days, but I gave him permission to Skype in from time to time. As long as it's not during a knife fight."

"We need to get ahold of that doctor. Rashid."

I frowned. "They said they were holding him for questioning. I thought Ru wiped his memory, though."

"He may have left something behind. And if he did, we're in trouble."

"But there's only so much damage Rashid could possibly do, right? I mean, if he starts talking about a centaur demon, they'll just say that he's nuts."

"Maybe. But we don't want to take any chances. As soon as he's released from custody, we need to track him."

"You know, he actually held his own pretty well back at the morgue. He came at the demon with a Stryker saw. Nearly cut its scalp off."

She chuckled. "Probably just adrenaline. It wasn't easy keeping the Kentauros sedated. We all took turns. I even called in some of the trainees, just to lend power."

"What did you do? Sink its central nervous system?"

"We couldn't shut it down completely. But we used ultrasonic bombardment to give it constant reboots. Every time we hit the amygdala and lower brain, we managed to trigger the autonomic nervous system, which overrides the higher functions. But first we had to *find* the amygdala. That took a while."

"So it's under conscious sedation."

"It's about to wake up. Pissed."

We took the elevator to the subbasement level. The concrete walls were a mixture of dense particulate and extruded materia, created by power far beyond anything I knew. The woven strands of materia resembled filaments of quartz that provided constant resonance, like a murmuring hive. The air was thin, and very cold.

Selena swiped her key card, and we stepped into the interrogation chamber. The air inside was even colder, and crackling with static electricity. There was a broad steel table in the center of the room, with a chair on either side. The Kentauros demon was slumped in one of the chairs, seemingly still unconscious.

I noticed a length of gold chain looped around the demon's throat and anchored to a fixture on the floor. As I looked more closely at the chain, its links seemed to move of their own accord, shifting in and out of focus.

"There's no partition. And we're the only ones here." I stared at Selena. "Why are we alone with it?"

"Well, that's the rub. We can restrain its body, but it has to be conscious while we're questioning it. If it's conscious, we can dampen its psychic abilities, but we can't block them entirely. So filling the interrogation chamber with vulnerable minds didn't seem like the best idea."

"And you thought my mind would be a fortress?"

"No." She looked slightly guilty. "I mean, you're well trained. You're a senior agent, and you've dealt with psychic assaults before. But that's not why I chose you."

"Then—" I blinked. "Oh. I get it. My genetic material. Even if it's diluted, it still makes me resistant. And it gives us a certain sympathy."

"None of that has ever been completely proven, of course. But I'm willing to bet that it's going to do something for you. It can't possibly hurt."

"I feel kind of manipulated."

"That's only natural." She almost smiled.

"Are we sitting next to each other?"

"No. I'm sitting. You're standing. I want you near enough to see its face, but well out of striking range."

"Great."

Selena sat in the chair across from the demon. She extended her hand slowly forward. When it reached the middle of the table, the air around her fingers made a popping noise. She withdrew her hand quickly, and blue sparks danced in the space where it had been. I smelled ozone.

"Baryon field," she said. "We changed the flavor of its quarks to make it nasty. It's got a small radius, but it's highly effective on anything with soft tissue."

The demon was stirring. It coughed. The sound was so pedestrian. Then its equine half started to twitch. Its hooves scraped against the concrete floor. Its head snapped up, eyes open wide.

It snarled something that was all spittle and consonants.

"Good morning," Selena said.

The demon tried to lunge forward, but the chain held it in place. It touched the links around its neck, eyes widening in astonishment.

"What is this?"

Selena folded her hands on the table. "Supposedly, it's designed after the chain that held Fenris, the wolf who devoured the moon. I think our version is made of a mystical polymer, though."

"Am I supposed to be impressed?"

"Maybe a little."

"And you think this curtain of particles will stop me from killing you?"

"I think it's a safer bet than Plexiglas. And you don't actually want to kill me. If you kill me, you're trapped here forever. How many lifetimes do you want to spend in a maximum-security basement? It would get pretty boring after the first century."

It smiled suddenly. "You look exhausted. Have you been up all night?"

"Yes. I'm very dedicated."

"How long do you think all of this will hold me?"

"We're not sure yet."

"It's quite a risk you're taking. You must need information badly."

"Are you interested in working out a deal?"

"Sure. Until I discover a gap in your defenses. After that, I'll kill everyone in this building, starting with her."

Its golden eyes held me. I swallowed.

"You won't be the first who's tried. I can pencil you in, if you like."

"You smell familiar." Its eyes narrowed as it looked at me. "Sometimes you mixed-bloods reek of ambergris. But you're different."

"Is that supposed to be a compliment?"

"Yes. Considering the fact that the rest of you, the human half of you, smells of decaying matter and garbage. Your entire civilization smells, like spoiled meat. It's difficult just to be in the same room with you."

"We'll get you an air freshener," Selena said. "In the meantime, maybe you can breathe through your mouth and answer a few questions."

"Of course. I have absolutely nothing better to do."

"Excellent. Let's start with your name."

"Basuram."

"Age?"

"Irrelevant."

"Just ballpark it. A thousand? Are we talking pre–Dark Ages?"

"Yes."

"Late antiquity?"

"More or less. Although, as far as I'm concerned, your entire civilization has been one long, depressing dark age. You're very far behind most respectable life-forms."

Selena wrote something down. "You work for the Ferid, correct?"

Basuram stiffened slightly. "We don't work *for* them. We manage their forces."

"And you're satisfied with that relationship."

"For now. There are benefits. We're well compensated for our service."

"Why are the Ferid after Ru?"

It smirked. "*Ru?* Is that what he told you his name was? I suppose that is the closest approximation."

"Ru described a place called Ptah'l. Have the Ferid made contact there?"

"The Ferid are everywhere."

Selena flexed her shoulders. "I'm not interested in every place they've set down roots. I just want to know what they're doing in Ptah'l."

"What they're doing," Basuram said, "is none of your concern."

"Actually, it's a pretty big concern. If Ru is a refugee, we'll need to take steps in order to guarantee his safety."

"What you call Ru is a criminal. He's wanted in multiple worlds."

"What crime has he been convicted of?"

"Sedition. Grand theft. And attempted murder."

"Murder of whom?"

"The Ferid chancellor."

"Was this chancellor performing experiments on them?"

Basuram laughed. "Do you believe whatever a child with fangs tells you? He'd say anything to protect his coconspirators."

"Shouldn't they also have the chance to stand trial in a court of law?"

"We were collecting them for just that purpose. Every member of the terrorist cell received a summons to the Highest Court. But when we arrived to transport them, they attacked us. The boy escaped. The others died."

"I don't see why that had to happen," Selena said. "Judging from Ru's physiology, your species vastly outpowers his own. You should have been able to subdue them without killing them. Unless someone got whip-happy. Maybe it started out as a routine maneuver, but then everything fell apart."

The demon shrugged. "It's meaningless. Ru is in your space now, and he needs to be returned to ours, so that he can face the court."

Selena looked at her papers. "As far as we can tell, we've never encountered your species before. So we don't have a formal treaty with you. But other demonic communities have agreed to recognize our world as an asylum space. As long as Ru remains here, he should be safe and unharassed."

"What others? If they've managed to convince you of something so ludicrous, they must want something from you."

"So you're not interested in being our new neighbor."

"I'll sign nothing and promise nothing. My mission is to extract the boy, and as soon as I can do that, I will." It leaned forward. Selena didn't move, but I felt her body react slightly. A nervous twitch.

"You know as well as I do," Basuram said, "this motte-and-bailey shithouse you call a 'facility' won't hold me for long. I can hear the sinus rhythm of every human being on this floor. I can smell the odor of their fear and taste the disgusting buccal texture of their throats. The moment I break this chain, I will rush through each floor like a bloody wave, killing anything and everything I touch. And I'll accomplish it in less than five minutes."

" 'Bloody wave.' I've written that down." She met

the demon's gaze. "You don't have to convince me that you're a fine killing machine. I know that. I'm afraid of you, and you know that, too. Most living things must be afraid of you. But I'm not intimidated, and that's the difference. Threatening me won't help you."

This time she leaned forward. I couldn't believe it. Her eyelashes were practically touching the baryon field. I could hear it humming. Basuram looked at her with great interest.

"Because," she said, "even if you manage to get off this floor, our backup defenses will come sweeping down on you. And that is a world of hurt. You don't think we've stolen technology from your kind in the past? We've even improved some of it. We've got weapons that will liquefy your spinal column. There's one that turns your insides into a Crock-Pot and then kills you at a slow boil. If you don't believe me, read my mind. It's wide-open."

Basuram stared at her for a moment. Then it smiled. "I believe you. There's a considerable chance that I won't make it out of the building. But as soon as you kill me, two more will take my place. Eventually, we'll overrun you."

"I'm not sure about that. There's a lot of us."

"Then we'll kill all of you."

"It's not going to happen. We both know that."

It licked its lips. "All right. So you have a few contacts. It doesn't matter. You can't withstand what the Ferid will throw at you."

"Do you believe everything they tell you?"

"I've seen what they can do, and there's a reason they

don't mingle with your kind. It's because they don't even give one percent of a shit about your species."

It seemed to be staring at both Selena and me at the same time. I believed that it could be in two places at once. Its mind seemed to weigh upon me from all directions. I could feel it seeping through the cracks in me, tonguing the grooves of my defenses, just looking for a way in.

All I had to do was relax my guard for one second, and its will would slip into me like a curl of steam. It would even be sweet-smelling at first, relaxing, like settling into a warm bath. Then I'd go numb.

After that, it would have control of my body. Just a heavy pinch, like the dental needle passing into your gum, swiftly, a flash of silver and the feeling of sudden coldness. The tug of anesthetic. Then the undulating swell of you, everything that was you, spreading out slowly in a blank pool. And once the pool dispersed, you were gone.

Basuram was staring at me again. "Where do I know you from?"

I tried not to look at it. "Maybe we went to school together."

I didn't like the pressure of its eyes. But I couldn't look away. I kept breathing, kept covering my defenses. There couldn't be any weak spots. It sensed what I was working on, but didn't push too hard. It was still playing with me.

"Your odor makes me remember something." Its eyes widened. "I recognize it now. You're his daughter."

Selena looked at me sharply.

I swallowed. "Whose daughter?"

Basuram leaned back with a smile. "If you don't know his name, I'm not going to be the one to tell you. But I can see the resemblance now. It's undeniable."

"Tell me his name."

"I can't do that."

"Are you afraid of him?"

"Yes."

I approached the table. "Tell me."

"Tess." Selena gave me a warning look. "Let me handle this."

"I'd much prefer you let Tess handle it." Basuram was smiling. "I can't believe I'm looking at you in the flesh. His own daughter. And you weren't even hard to find."

"How do you know him? What is he? One of the Ferid?"

"What are you willing to give up for that information?"

"Do not answer that." Selena glared at me. "Tess, you need to leave."

"Not until he tells me—"

Basuram moved so fast that its arm was a blur. One second it was standing still. Then its hand plunged through the curtain of force that separated them. The baryon field devoured its hand, stripping the flesh and muscle tissue. It kept reaching, until its hand was almost entirely skeletonized.

I don't know how Selena anticipated it, but she managed to move out of the way. Its ruined fingers closed over empty air. Snarling, it withdrew its hand. The flesh was already regenerating.

Selena hit the intercom button on the far wall. "Re-activate it!" she yelled.

I felt a subtle vibration in the air. Nothing changed, but Basuram's eyes suddenly went blank. It stood absolutely still for a moment, hanging like an aimless puppet. Then its body slumped over the table. Its eyes remained open.

"I'm sorry," I said to Selena.

"It was goading you. Just smoke and mirrors."

"All of it?"

"Come on, Tess. I doubt it knows your father. Basuram was messing with you. It sensed that you're mixed-blood, and it wanted to manipulate you."

"Are you sure? We thought Ru was telling the truth, and now he may be hiding a weapon on us."

"I don't think either of them are telling the truth. And they'll keep lying until it profits them not to. For now, all we can do is explore every possibility."

We exited the interrogation room. Selena sealed it behind us. The elevator doors opened just as we were reaching the end of the hallway, and a group of agents poured out, all carrying athames.

"Don't wake it up," Selena said simply. "Call me once it's been transported."

They nodded and filed past us.

"What if something goes wrong?" I asked her.

She stepped into the elevator with me. "Something already has gone wrong. We've got one demon that we won't be able to hold for long, another who's probably lying to us, and a security leak on top of it all."

The doors closed. I leaned against the paneled wall. "You want me to check up on Rashid tonight? It may be tricky if he's still in custody."

"No. It can wait until tomorrow morning."

That was good. I had to meet with Mr. Corvid soon. I hadn't seen Corvid since the demon had given me Hex two years ago. It promised to be an interesting conversation.

"For now," Selena said, "I need you to come look at Ru's test results."

"Something weird?"

"That doesn't even begin to cover it."

"Can we get something to eat first? I'm starving."

Selena looked like she was about to say no. Then she blinked suddenly. "I wouldn't mind that, actually. I've barely eaten anything."

"I have an apple in my bag."

"I've got some instant oatmeal packets in my office. And soda crackers."

"That sounds amazing."

7 . . . .

When we got to the serology lab, we saw Linus
standing over a gas chromatograph, his back turned
to us. He placed something in the injector port and
switched on the heat. The chemicals grew volatile as
they were heated, separating from one another. Then a
rush of carrier gas swept them away in a stream. When
they reached the chromatography oven inside the heart
of the machine, they would enter their own steel capil-
lary column and begin to simmer.

Linus turned to face us. His blond hair was getting
longer, and I wondered if he was growing it out, or if
he'd just forgotten to cut it. Sometimes I liked shoulder-
length hair on guys. It was tricky, though. It had to be
well kept. And Linus obviously took care of his hair. It
was so shiny that I wanted to touch it.

"Liking the jeans," I said.

He didn't quite smile, but I saw the pleasure in his face. "Thank you."

"Did you process that last round of samples?" Selena asked.

"Nearly."

" 'Nearly,' as in, you'll be done in the next hour?"

"No. Each test has its own quirks. If you want a detailed restriction fragment length polymorphism analysis, you have to deal with the time-consuming process of electrifying a plate of gel and plotting out the numbers yourself. It's not fast food."

"The STRs must be almost done, though. Short tandem repeat testing is always a lot faster than—"

"I know that it's faster. It's faster because it's not as detailed. You can't have detailed and fast at the same time; you have to pick one."

"I need both."

"Then you need to buy me better equipment."

"The next budget meeting isn't for a week. You can put in a requisition form."

"The last time I did that, you claimed that my form was lost."

She blinked. "I promise that won't happen again. Let's just see what results you have so far from the serology panel."

Linus opened up a folder. "Results. That's all anyone ever talks about around here. I feel like I'm working at Walmart sometimes."

"Uh-huh."

He scanned the STR data. "These samples gave our machines a bit of trouble. They're calibrated to process demon epithelials, but we don't have many pureblood profiles in our archive."

"They don't tend to submit to needles," Selena said.

"Exactly. So we had to cobble together a few different profiles to use as an exemplar. But even that didn't make the job much easier. Most demons have double helices, like us, and a few purebloods have extra RNA helices that we can barely decipher. But these epithelials have a completely different shape. Take a look."

I leaned over the Fourier-transform microscope, adjusting the focus. It looked like I was staring at a cluster of pins, all squeezed very close together. As I looked closer, I realized that the "head" of each pin was actually a tiny chain composed of links. Each link was a collection of scales, and even the scales had a kind of chemical engraving on them.

"The human genome has about three billion base pairs of DNA, which are the chemical building blocks of life," Linus said. "Plants have a lot more, sometimes up to ten times more, but most of that space is empty. Their genomes are like abandoned rooms with a lot of cupboard space. But these strands are packed full. There must be close to one hundred million base pairs here. Imagine that as one hundred million drawers, and each one of them is full."

"The helices look more like chain mail." I stepped away from the microscope. "I'm not even sure what we're looking for inside of it."

"We need to figure out what has the Ferid so interested."

"We still have no evidence that the Ferid even

exist. Ru and Basuram could both be making up some shadow organization to cover their own tracks."

Selena gave me an odd look. "Are you sure about that? When I look at Ru, I see a kid suffering from post-traumatic stress. I don't think he has anything to gain by making things up."

"You don't *know* that you're seeing PTSD. Not for sure. He's a pureblood demon with DNA that looks like something out of *Beowulf*. We don't know what he's feeling, what his motivations are, just like we don't know anything about Basuram."

"Come on. Your mothering instincts didn't kick in when you saw him?"

"That seems like precisely the sort of thing you'd tell me to ignore."

Selena half smiled. "Professionalism is important. But when I look at him—I mean, he's not just a homeless demon. He's alone in this world. He may never make it back home, and now he's stuck here. I can't imagine what that feels like."

"It feels to me like you could both be having this conversation in another place," Linus said, returning to his computer. "Unless you have any more questions about base pairs. The more detailed restriction fragment length testing should be done within the next eight hours or so, but it may take longer."

"I won't ask how much longer," Selena replied sweetly. "Just page me when it's done. Whenever that might be."

"Of course." He didn't look up. "It'll be the highlight of my evening."

We both left the DNA lab. Selena chuckled. "Sometimes I think that Linus is the only professional working here."

"You're pretty professional."

"That's faint praise coming from you."

"Ouch!" I shook my head. "Still—it feels like our roles are reversed lately. You're lecturing me on empathy, and I'm talking about physical evidence."

Selena sighed. "It's just the direction my life is taking."

"What does that mean?"

"I'm not even sure. I barely understand it myself."

I suddenly remembered a moment last year. Selena was testing Derrick's intuitive abilities by using flash cards. At the end of the exercise, he was supposed to read her emotions, and he picked up something while she was staring at a drawing of a gun. Fear. Selena Ward, our director, afraid of a gun. It didn't make sense.

Who's Jessica?

Derrick had asked her that. It was a name that he'd heard by accident while reading her mind. As soon as he mentioned it, she shut down. Nobody had mentioned it since then, but I knew that it had something to do with Selena's change in behavior lately. I knew it in a way that wouldn't break down into numerical data or chemical peaks and valleys. It was like the footprint of a feeling.

"How much time have you been spending with Ru?" I asked.

"Not much. He'll only talk for a certain amount of

time. I get the impression that our language is very inefficient for him. He can't express himself as precisely as he'd like to, and he gets tired of it. Then he just goes quiet."

"Not precise enough? Have you heard him talk about quantum physics?"

"I don't mean grammatical precision. I think a component of his native language may be gestural, or even telepathic. It's not that he can't make himself understood perfectly in English. He'd probably pass the Graduate Record Exam with flying colors. But our language's innate shortcomings seem to bother him."

"They didn't seem to bother Basuram."

"He'd be a sadistic bastard in any language."

We came to a secure area. Selena gestured to the security guards standing on either side of the door. Both of them had an athame, sheathed but ready. I could sense that they were trained specifically in the use of thermal materia. Their auras smelled a bit like campfires.

They stepped aside. Selena swiped her key card, and we walked through the door into a short hallway. CT scanning panels had been positioned along the walls. As I walked, I saw my body being mapped on liquid crystal screens, from my bone structure all the way down to my cranial topography. I tried to ignore it. Data flickered past us. We were weighed, measured, and judged, like souls on an Egyptian scale.

A bell chimed as we reached the end of the hallway. The scans hadn't flagged anything, so we were free to pass into the secure chamber beyond. A second door opened, and I felt the temperature change. It was colder. I could sense faint lines of materia running from the hallway into the next room.

It actually resembled a hotel room instead of a storage chamber, which surprised me. I thought that Selena had set up something ad hoc, a converted closet of some kind, but this room had obviously been designed as a guest suite. There was a bed in one corner and a love seat against the opposite wall. There was even a flat-screen TV.

"Has this always been here?" I asked.

"It's new."

"But—just to be clear—we have a high-security hotel suite in the lab. With cable."

"You can't use it."

"But I hate sleeping on the couch in the break room."

"You don't have to. You can sleep at home, like other people."

"Is that bed a queen?"

"You're *never* using this room. Understand?"

I sighed. "It's not like we have paradimensional demons staying with us all of the time. What about when it's not in use? Am I just supposed to ignore it?"

"Yes. You need my key card to get in, so it doesn't matter."

"Where was this room when we needed somewhere for Mia to stay?"

"It hadn't been built yet."

"Is there a bathroom over—"

"Forget it."

"Fine."

Ru was sitting on the love seat with his feet folded underneath him. When he saw me, he got up and walked over, holding the remote control.

"I don't understand the transmission functions on this device."

"It's basically infrared," I said. "Just press the up and down buttons."

He gave me a sour look. "I know how to 'change channels,' as you call it. That was relatively simple. But some of the programs are demanding currency."

"That's pay-per-view."

"Yes. I'd like to watch it."

"No," Selena said. "We aren't budgeted for that."

"How disappointing." He returned to the couch.

He flipped through a series of channels until he found the Food Network. Then his expression became slightly glazed. It was as if we'd ceased to exist.

I sat down across from him on the sofa. "Ru? Would you mind talking to us for a minute? You can go back to your show as soon as we're done."

He turned to regard me. He was 99 percent human boy this time. To most observers, the biological photocopy would have been perfect. But as I looked into his eyes, I could see the barest hint of something nonhuman. Just a speck. The longer I stared at that speck, the bigger it seemed to grow, until I felt myself leaning over the edge of a vast alien consciousness.

I thought of the strange armored scales of his DNA. I could only imagine what Basuram's looked like. So far, his body had rejected all methods of DNA testing.

We couldn't even pierce the epidermis. We might have had better luck peeling back a dragon's skin.

Ru turned off the TV. "I can pay attention to both at the same time. But I've already seen this episode."

I turned to Selena. "Can we teach him how to download—"

"Absolutely not."

But I'd already piqued his interest. "Download?"

"We'll talk more about it later," I said. "First, we have a few questions."

He folded his hands on his lap. "All right."

I looked at Selena. She nodded.

"Okay. You've mentioned the Ferid," I began. "Basuram confirmed that they were looking for you, but wouldn't say more."

"I'm sure he said all sorts of things."

"Are the Ferid performing experiments on the Ptah'li?"

"I don't know. I don't remember."

"It would help if we had some physical evidence that this genetic testing was going on," Selena said. "But we don't know enough about your DNA. There's no way for us to tell if it's been manipulated without having an exemplar, and our only sample is from you. We need more."

"I've already given you blood and spinal fluid."

"Yes. You've been very cooperative, and we're grateful for that. But we need a different sample. Something for comparison."

"I have nothing more to give you."

"Then tell us more about the Ferid. What are they up to? Why would they be chasing someone like you?"

"Nobody knows why they do anything, except out of hunger."

"What kind of hunger?"

"It's difficult to explain."

I wanted to try a different tack. "Tell us about the chancellor," I said.

Ru looked at me. His eyes were opaque, like green glass. "Nobody sees the chancellor. We only hear his voice. Once or twice a day, he'll announce a new directive or enact a summons. If he says your name, you're bound by law to appear before him that very day."

"And what happens to those who appear before him?"

"They vanish."

I turned to Selena. "This sounds like an interplanar civil rights case. We have no real reason to hold Basuram, and we don't even know how either of them got here. I'm not sure what our next step is here."

"Ru"—Selena held his eyes—"Basuram said that you tried to kill the Ferid chancellor. He said that you were part of an anarchist group."

"He's lying. I'm not part of any group."

"You mentioned your family. Could any of them have been involved?"

"I don't know. I don't remember." He closed his eyes. "I can almost see their faces, but it all goes dark so quickly."

"It's fine," I said. "Don't push yourself too hard. Basuram's not going anywhere, and you're safe for the moment."

"We need to return to the scene where Ru was found." Selena stood. "There could be some trace evidence that hasn't yet been obliterated by the elements."

"The beach felt haunted," Ru said.

"What do you mean by that?" I asked him.

"I don't know how else to say it." He hugged his knees. "I could hear voices. There was something alive in the sand and the shells, something groaning underwater. I heard it before everything went dark."

"Well, we're not the Ghostbusters," Selena replied. "But we do have a topographical mapping device. Let's see what we can do."

8

Jericho Beach was cold and empty when the CORE forensics team arrived. Although we did have the technology to keep onlookers from wandering onto a common scene, that worked only under controlled conditions. There wasn't enough materia in the world to keep people away from the beach in Vancouver's Kitsilano neighborhood during the day. Our only alternative was to analyze the scene at night. Instead of crafting a veil, we posted agents at key spots where early-morning joggers and drunk kids might accidentally wander in too close. I'd heard they were working on some kind of personal veil, something to do with our athames. But I so rarely asked questions anymore unless they pertained to my salary.

We marked out a search zone in four bands, using small sensors that looked like garden lights. Needle-thin wafers of xenon, a heavy metal, were stacked inside, acting as attractors for the unpredictable family of particles that we called "materia" for lack of a better descriptor. Our technology was similar to dark-matter detectors in Italy and Switzerland, only designed to work on a much smaller scale. The physicist Elena Aprile was trying to discover dark matter itself with her XENON100 detector in Gran Sasso. We already knew it existed and just needed to entice it.

We'd already been over the site with a flux magnetometer, testing for wave echoes that might indicate something buried. The lines of energy would bend around certain objects, especially metallic ones, whose presence created a ripple in the ground-mapping data. The magnetometer itself was small, but the battery pack was awkward and heavy. Selena complained that it was giving her tendonitis.

"Are the photomultipliers set up?" I asked. "I don't help with those anymore. I accidentally broke one, back when Marcus Tremblay was still unit chief."

"I know," she replied. "I was the one who cosigned the expense report."

"In my defense, the calculations were only a millimeter off."

"And that millimeter ended up being the difference between finding nothing and discovering the buried skeleton of a *tortuga* demon."

"He was so small, though. Poor little guy."

"He ate souls."

"Yeah. He did. But, to be fair, that was his natural sustenance. He couldn't help himself. But, really, can you imagine this cute little turtle with bony spurs on his marbled blue shell, just sort of waddling up to you in the middle of the night? You don't think he's going to suck out your soul."

Selena frowned at me. "You work for an occult organization. A mean-looking turtle appears in your house, at night, and starts crawling up your stairs. You wouldn't even take a moment to think that it might not have your best interest at heart?"

"He wasn't mean-looking. He reminded me of the Dr. Seuss turtle."

"Hate to break up this conversation," Linus said, pushing the ground-penetrating radar device in front of him. "But we've got less than two hours."

The GPR locator resembled a fusion between a push lawn mower on wheels and a battery-powered generator. The radar was mounted on an orange steel chassis, and a white plate stuck out in front to comb the ground. The data would be sent to a laptop in peaks and valleys of yellow and mauve light, which Linus would then get to sift through for the next forty-eight hours.

He'd worn a lot of hats in the department since last year, when our budget was slashed. With Becka on sick leave, our herd had definitely been thinned, and we were all feeling the crunch. But we'd really lucked out when Linus agreed to come work for the CORE. Marcus had found him through the alma mater registry at his university. My former boss may have been a psychotic killer, but he was also a phenomenal headhunter. Office gossip suggested that Linus had experienced some sort of mystical "accident" while he was a grad student. It was low-level, but Marcus still used it to his advantage in convincing Linus to come on board with the CORE. Nobody was sure if Linus had been pressured to join, or if he'd entered willingly into employment with us.

"Where's Ru?" I asked.

"At the lab. There's a marathon of *Chef at Home* on."

"And Basuram?"

"Sedated. Under twenty-four-hour watch."

"Do you think what we're doing to the Kentauros demon is humane?"

"I think you just contradicted yourself in that sentence."

"You know what I mean. The Kentauros has rights, just the same as Ru does. But we're not too bothered at the idea of pumping him full of soporific drugs and forcing him into a zombie existence."

Selena sighed. "I get your point. And no, it doesn't feel good. But it's a danger to the entire building. We don't have a lot of other options."

"It just bothers me that I think of Basuram as an 'it,' and Ru as a 'he.' I'm the one who looks like an 'it' to them."

"Right. And we all just have to see past our otherness. In the meantime, this scene is waiting, and eventually, we're going to run out of drugs."

"Also—" Linus interjected, as he pushed the GPR mower slowly past us. "I get paid time and a half for doing fieldwork. I was hired as a lab director."

"You're right," Selena said. "And we appreciate your extra efforts."

"He's the only one, right?" I asked Selena once he'd passed.

"Yes. Absolutely the only person in the lab who knows how to work the GPR. Between this and the weapons locker, his salary must be close to mine."

"Or higher."

"I was trying not to think about that."

"How did he end up getting the weapons gig again?"

"He used to be in the army."

I blinked. "Seriously? I mean, in a research capacity?"

"I don't know the details. He's got military training, though."

I watched the tall, skinny blond man gently pushing an oversized metal detector across an empty beach. He didn't look particularly like an expert on weapons.

"Ru was found on this spot," Selena said, "so we're interested in any thermal signature changes in the area. We need to figure out how he got here. Basuram isn't about to tell us, and both of them must have some kind of transit device. Especially if the Ptah'li home world is as far away as it seems."

"It might not be made of metal. It could be partially organic."

"We're scanning for just about everything."

"I'm about to turn on the photomultipliers," Linus said. "Is everyone's cell off?"

Selena and I both nodded.

Linus pressed a button on a remote control. The xenon towers clicked open, and dozens of highly sensitive one-pixel cameras emerged from them. The air seemed to thicken slightly. It tasted metallic, heavier. The currents of materia being harvested by the xenon cells were laying invisible lines of tension across the square of beach. The power was almost syrupy and reminded me of a car heater gone bad.

For a while, all we did was watch Linus pushing the GPR over squares of sand demarcated by colored tape. We drank coffee silently. It was too early in the morning to make small talk. Selena's phone vibrated once, but she ignored it.

"Here's something," Linus said, after an hour. "Come and look."

We walked over and examined the laptop screen. There was a long bar of green with an x-axis at the bottom. The top layer of soil was a yellow plane, and beneath that, there was a green layer that seemed to roil, more liquid than turf, as the radar illumined it. A line of purple, slightly deeper, bisected the green layer, and beneath that was only a cloud of dark, like spilled ink.

Linus pointed to a dark shape, adjacent to the purple. "This could be a lot of things," he said. "But it's not a shell or a rock. It's giving off weak radiation."

Selena was already dialing a number on her cell. "How far away do I need to be to make this call?"

"Thirty meters. We won't know where to dig until we've processed the radargrams, though. Don't get too excited."

"Right." She was already walking away from us.

I stood in silence for a moment, staring at the black mark on the screen.

"It could be anything," I said. "And we've got less than an hour of darkness left. Maybe it's just someone's piggy bank."

"They don't generally give off weak radiation."

"You think it's made of uranium?"

"It's made of something that's buzzing with energy like a hornet's nest."

Selena came walking back.

"Who did you call?" I asked.

"Cindée. If we can use carbon markers to get a radioactive signature from the debris, she may be able to match it to mystical trace that we have on file. Or at least to something we've heard of."

"The sun's rising soon."

"We'll keep crowds away for as long as we can. Then we'll just have to pack up and come back tomorrow. We can make it look like a construction site."

"On a beach."

"You'd be amazed what people will believe if you just throw up some caution tape and orange signs. It's one of the few things that makes our job easier."

I rolled up my sleeves. "Where do you want me?"

"Nowhere." She gave me a look of moderate exasperation. "Go home. Get some sleep. You'll be back in the lab soon enough, and there are plenty of competent shovelers on their way already. I don't need you here every second."

"You're an amazing boss. You do know that, right?"

She shrugged. "I get things done. I cut people too much slack most of the time, but I'd like to think I'm buying my way into heaven."

"That seems sensible." I signed the exit log and handed it to her. "I appreciate this. I haven't been spending a lot of time at home lately."

"Won't everyone be in bed?"

"Not in my house. Right now it's practically cock-tail hour."

The lights were off when I got home, but I could see the glow of the television coming from the den. I could barely hear the sound of canned laughter. It seemed like a classic case of Derrick falling asleep on the couch. But I was surprised that Mia wasn't still awake. Often at this hour, I'd find her at the kitchen table, drinking strong tea and filling out index cards with facts that I couldn't possibly imagine.

I threw my purse on the table by the door. It was covered in a layer of spare change and expired bus tick-ets. It really seemed like we'd cleaned just yesterday. Perhaps we had. I remembered holding a mop at some point, although I wasn't quite sure what I'd actually done with it.

I hung up my coat and walked into the den, which was really a living room, but I could only think of it as a den because it was usually full of guys. The room was empty, but not without signs of previous habitation. My fuzzy brown Costco blanket had been neatly folded, and there was a glass of water sitting on a coaster. These signs pointed to Derrick or Miles, but the TV was playing an old music video, and Derrick never watched any of those channels. And usually when he was up this late, I'd smell microwave popcorn or cof-fee, sometimes in combination. Now I wasn't sure what I smelled. It was almost sour, but not totally unfamiliar. I could think of a few demons who smelled, for lack of a better word, tangy, but not like this.

Really? Am I going to try to explode my pager twice in one week?

This time I wasn't going to draw my athame. I couldn't, anyways, since it was still in my purse. I'd been using it to conceal stolen creamer from the break room. Maybe we couldn't save money on tuition, books, or clothes, but I'd be damned if I was going to pay for creamer every week.

In fact, this time, I wasn't even going to draw any power. If there really was a maniac in my kitchen, I felt like handling it in a more medieval style. I had a lot of tense energy, and currently, none of my bones were broken. It was as good a time as any to get into a fight, and I was on home territory.

I stepped through the kitchen doorway.

The glow was coming from a small lamp on the table. Miles was sitting in a chair, concentrating on something that he was holding beneath the lamplight. When he saw me, his eyes widened. He touched his right hand flat to his forehead and moved it in small salute. It was the ASL version of a startled *Hey*.

"Sorry if I scared you."

He quickly reached for his hearing aids, which were next to the lamp. After he'd adjusted them, he looked up again. "It's okay. I just wasn't expecting you to be home for another few hours."

"It's fine. You're always welcome here, and we do tend to be at our highest efficiency around this time of night. Speaking of which, did you want some coffee?"

"I'm good, thanks. Don't you have to wake up early?"

"Too much coffee can make me sleepy. It's like a warm, slightly neurotic hug before the end of the day."

"I prefer tea most of the time."

"My mom drinks tea."

"My mom drinks gin."

I laughed. "Nothing wrong with that. I do have one question, though."

"Yes?"

"Is that a joint you're holding, Miles?"

"Oh. This?" He looked at the tightly rolled cigarette. "It is."

I sat down next to him. "Officer Sedgwick. It's like I hardly know you."

"This is awful, I know." He closed his eyes. "I'm sorry. Derrick was snoring, the dog's hogging the rest of the bed, and I couldn't sleep anyway. Mia went to bed early, and Patrick's been in his room for the last four hours. I figured there was no harm in it." He started to rise. "But this is your kitchen, and I'm being negligible, or something along those lines, so I'm just going to clean this up."

"Are you kidding?" I gestured toward the patio. "Fire it up and we'll go outside. There's virtually no wind tonight, for some reason."

He raised an eyebrow. "Should we—"

"No. We should wake up no one and do nothing. I'm tired, and you're pretty much my favorite person right now. Let's just keep it between us."

"Okay. We don't have to kill it."

"Why not? We kill everything else, don't we?"

Miles and I stepped onto the patio, sliding the door shut behind us. I left the barest inch open, as anyone who's ever been accidentally locked out of their house before tends to do. Miles fished a lighter out of his jeans pocket and lit the end.

I made a face. "That stinks."

"I know. Sorry."

"It's not necessarily a bad smell. Just a strong one."

"It's okay. I've got this little thing."

He pulled a battery-powered fan out of his other pocket. The blades were so small that they barely made any sound when he turned it on, and the breeze, although not exactly refreshing, was more than adequate.

"I can't believe you carry that thing around in your pocket."

"Kind of unsexy, right?"

"No way. Adorable."

"Thanks."

He took a drag, coughed a little, then handed it to me. I inhaled. It tasted kind of dark-roasted, with just the right amount of skunky attitude. I held the smoke in my lungs for a beat, then exhaled. Miles pointed the fan in my direction, and the cloud dispersed before it could start to smell.

"That's a pretty good system," I said, handing the cigarette back to him.

"I know."

"Almost makes me think this isn't your first time doing this."

He winced visibly. He was too nice to keep secrets.

"You're right. I'm sorry; I'm a monster."

"Are you kidding? You can do whatever you want on this patio. Don't ever feel bad about coming out here to relax."

"It's pretty stupid, though. I mean, we're practically police."

"Practically. But not totally."

"Were you one of those bad girls when you were at school? One of the ones who used to hang out on the other side of the tennis courts?"

"I was a big fat nothing in high school. And every one of those words is true."

"I don't believe that."

"It's true. I'm not sad about it. I don't think you're meant to have fun during that time. I think it's hell for everybody."

It must have really been hell for you, I almost blurted out. But then the rational side of my brain kicked in, and I realized that, aside from the statement being totally unverifiable, I had no idea when Miles had even lost the bulk of his hearing.

"I went to a school for the deaf," he said. "We learned sign first and lip-reading only as a kind of last resort. So it took me a long time to become fluent." He took another drag and handed it back to me. "It made for some awkward moments. Especially at the doctor's office."

"I'll bet." I took my last drag and handed it back to him. "I'm done. Thanks. This is better than the ginger ale I was excited about having earlier."

Miles stubbed out the cigarette and put it away.

"Lucian has a deaf brother, right? I remember him telling me that."

"His name's Lorenzo. He died, though."

"When?"

"I have no idea. I don't know how old Lucian is. He could be some kind of creepy litch-lord, and I'd have no idea."

"I'm sure he's not a"—he blinked—"whatever that thing is you just said. It sounded gross. I don't like necromancers, but Lucian doesn't seem like the others I've met. I don't stay awake at night worrying about what he's doing."

"Why don't you like them?" I asked. "I mean, aside from the obvious reasons: They're scary, they run on corpse power, and they live in a weird city filled with oblong black fruit and singing trees."

Miles looked slightly uncomfortable. "I'm not a necrophobe. There's nothing wrong, per se, with necroid materia. Death is a part of life. I understand that. But my mother was a necromancer. And when I was born with eighty percent hearing loss, the doctors told her it was rubella."

He was staring at the patio furniture as he spoke. He couldn't quite look me in the eye, but his voice was calm. "It wasn't rubella. I saw it in her face every time she looked at me. She was so guilty. She'd been warned by people in the community, people that knew she was trying to conceive. They told her about the risks, but in the end, she chose the power. She couldn't separate herself from it. She chose it over her son."

"Miles. That's awful." I looked squarely at him. "But look at you now. You're amazing. You wouldn't be working with us otherwise."

He shrugged. "She was smart, and my dad was smart, so I'm smart. It's a basic equation. Would I have had an easier life being able to hear? Yeah. But I don't blame her for choosing herself over me. In the end, she made the choice that kept us both alive, so I guess I should be thankful."

"My mom just lies to me constantly," I said. "That's all I've got."

He rolled his eyes. "Mothers. Why are they so puzzling?"

"I know. It's like, my mother doesn't flat-out lie; she just casts these little deceptions wherever she goes, like she's dropping handkerchiefs or something. She does it in such a pleasant way that when you find out the truth later, you miss the lie. Because at least the lie felt good, and the lie made you waffles."

"My dad's the liar in the family," Miles said. "Mostly, though, he just lies to himself about how tremendously unhappy he is."

"Are they still married?"

"No, they divorced a long time ago. They both live alone now. My mom's happy as long as she's got work to do, but my dad never really had that. Now it's like he's just unraveling, like he's this crooked thread with nowhere to go."

"My stepdad runs an electronics store. My real dad's a demon."

"I know. I mean, Derrick told me a little about that." His eyes widened. "It sounds really intense."

"It is, Miles. It's really intense."

We were both silent for a while.

"With Derrick, things are simpler," Miles said. "I spend most of my day concentrating on people's faces, trying to understand what they're asking me to do. And they're always asking me to do something." He sighed. "But when we're together, Derrick talks with his hands. And then I get to watch his hands. Which is nice."

"I wish my ASL were better."

"It's fine. You pick up on most things."

"Right. I'm like the stupid cousin."

"You're not the stupid cousin."

"If you put me in a room full of people speaking in sign, I'd be reduced to the language of a baby. It'd be exhausting."

"But you know how to listen, and you remember the hand signs that you've learned. It's a start. And if you want to learn more, I can help you."

"Derrick's too mean."

"That doesn't surprise me."

"He always gets that look on his face, like, *Why aren't you getting this immediately?* And then I just want to kick him."

"You should. He kicks me sometimes while we're sleeping, and in the morning, when I show him the bruise, he's so barely concerned. As if this happens to every guy that's ever slept in his bed."

"There haven't been a lot."

Miles snapped to attention. "Oh—no?"

I stood up. "Sorry. I shouldn't have said that. Obviously, I need to go to bed and stop thinking that I can enter into grown-up conversations."

Miles followed me back into the kitchen. "How many is not a lot?"

"This avenue of questioning is closed for the evening. I've already said too much." I kissed him on the cheek. "Good night."

"Good night. Thanks for the company."

"Thanks for listening to me blather on."

"The blathering was consensual. Night, Tess."

I closed my bedroom door behind me. The bed was empty and unmade.

Lucian might have been older than the foundations of this house. He might have been older than the city itself. So why was I the one who suddenly felt so old? Sure, there was a beauty to being alone in one's room, in the dark, about to shed all of your clothing and slip into bed. But the silence and the humidity of the chamber didn't make me feel liberated. Standing there, I felt more like an overturned bucket. I felt *achicado*, which in Spanish means shrunken, but also, bailed out, like a leaking vessel.

I opened the window, just to let in a bit of street noise. Then I got into bed and fell asleep twenty minutes later, completely overtaken.

9

I began the morning by staring at a pile of radar-grams. They were all variations on a blue plane with faint ripples in its surface. In some of the scans, the ripples were slightly distorted. It looked as if someone had dropped a small stone into a pool of liquid cement. The interference was subtle, but still visible.

"I still have a lot of data to go over," Linus said. He looked exhausted. "There's the dewowing. And something called a Butterworth pass. I have to strip away multiple layers of distortion."

"Dewowing?" I asked.

Linus shrugged. "Don't ask me; ask the GPR-SLICE interface."

"Selena wants to start digging tonight."

"That's nice for her. If I'm done by nightfall, I'll text you."

"Thanks, Linus. You're a peach."

"I slept for an hour last night. I feel more like a rotten plum."

"Rakish looks good on you, though."

"Stop sucking up. It'll be done when it's done."

I told Selena exactly that, but was careful to leave it on a Post-it rather than actually breaching her office. I had another appointment to keep, and I was already on the verge of being late.

Dr. Hinzelmann looked up from his yellow notepad as I walked in. "Tess. Good to see you. Have a seat."

I sat down in the plush chair. The air-conditioning in his office was turned up to high, and I could feel the goose bumps rising on my flesh. I kept rubbing my arms unconsciously, as if trying to start a small fire.

"Do you need a refill on your sleep medication?"

"No. I think I'm okay for now."

"So you've been getting enough sleep, then."

"I'm not sure I'd go that far. I'm sleeping better than I was a few months ago. I still feel like I could pass out on the photocopier most of the time, though."

"Have you considered decreasing your hours? Maybe spending a bit of time away from the lab would help you resume a normal sleeping pattern."

"I don't think I've ever had a normal sleeping pattern. And I'd love to take time off, but the case I'm working on now is kind of exploding in all directions. Selena needs me pretty much at all times."

"She's said as much?"

I bit my lip. I wasn't going to fall into one of his snares. "Let's just say she strongly intimated it."

"Or, you inferred that her need was urgent, when, in fact, she doesn't need your presence any more or less than she needs the presence of any other employee. Are you certain that she needs *you*, and not that you simply need to be here?"

"I don't need to be here. I need to be with my family. But I also have a job, which, currently, is an enormous pain in my ass."

"And how is family life?"

I blinked. "Fine. I mean, I'm absolutely the worst parent in the world. But if you ignore that, things are fine."

"What makes you think you're the worst parent in the world?"

I shifted in the chair. "I feel like I have no real influence over them. Realistically, they're both powerful enough to do whatever they want."

"But they must listen to you sometimes. That's almost the best you can hope for with adolescents."

"It's not that they don't listen to me. It's that I can't help them."

"With what? Clothes, school, sustenance—you seem to be providing for all of their needs as well as you can."

"No. I can do that. Tampons and textbooks and minutes for their cell phones, that much I can do. But I can't protect them from *this*." I gestured around me. "This life. This eternal cosmic shit-fest. That, I can't save them from."

"I'm not even sure how you'd try," Dr. Hinzelmann said. "They're in the paranormal life. Patrick's a vampire who can walk by day, the only one of his kind in the city. And Mia doesn't yet know what she wants to be, or who she is. Which is pretty common ground for a girl about to turn sixteen."

"I understand your implication. We're facing the same adversity as any family. But every time I leave my house, I'm scared to death that something's going to happen to them. Not that they'll get drunk, or make bad sex choices, or have their hearts broken." I folded my arms. "I'm scared that a demon will set fire to our house. I'm scared of seeing Mia or Patrick on an autopsy table."

"Every mother has that fear, to some extent."

"But I'm not their mother. Mia's an orphan. And we don't know much about Patrick's life before he was turned by Caitlin. We've never found his parents."

"Sounds like they both need you, then."

I massaged my temples. "They need Derrick to make them a palatable supper. Mia needs a haircut, although she's fighting me every step of the way. I'm just tired of having to unclog the drain every week."

"Is Derrick still recuperating?"

"He's getting better. And by better, I mean bitchier, which signals to me that his health is improving."

"It must be a relief to share the parenting duties with him."

"Patrick and Mia help, too. I mean, they're part-demon, but they're still pretty well-behaved teens, all things considered."

"Plus, you're part-demon as well."

I chuckled. "Yeah. My genetic legacy has prepared me to deal with the greatest amount of insanity possible."

"Your mother still worked for the CORE when you were conceived, correct? That must have been quite trying for her."

I felt myself grow cold. "I imagine it was."

"You must wonder about your father all the time. Have you ever thought of using this lab's facilities in order to locate him?"

Dr. Hinzelmann lowered his chair, then hopped gently to the ground. Standing, he came up to my waist. The natural light coming through the office window made his brown skin look especially like bark.

"My DNA has no match," I said carefully. "There's no way I'd be able to use the CORE's genome database for that kind of searching, because there's nothing to search for. I don't even know what dimension he came from. I probably never will."

But all I could think of was what Basuram had said. *His daughter. And you weren't even hard to find.*

Maybe he was one of the Ferid. Maybe he was something like the Iblis, one of the shadow-creatures that guarded the doors between worlds. Or maybe he was like the manticore, immeasurably old and removed from the rest of the world, trapped in a spell laid by a Renaissance alchemist who thirsted for immortality. The last two I'd already dealt with, and in the span of two years, no less. I was starting to think that every year, the Monster Committee got together and decided what nasty, primordial mofo I was going to have to deal with. Like an early Christmas present.

"There's more than one database," Hinzelmann said.

I'd checked out of the conversation for a moment. But his statement brought me back with a small start.

"What do you mean?"

"Just what I said." He smiled. "You've worked here long enough to know that there's always two versions of everything. There's the program that you see, and the program they keep underground."

"Underground where?"

"I just mean it generally, as in buried."

"Huh." I sat back in the chair. "This whole building is practically storage for things that were never supposed to see the light of day."

"Including us." His yellow eyes met my own.

"Right," I said.

Linus texted me about the radargrams.

Still processing. No digging until tomorrow night.

This news I gave to Selena in person.

Her look darkened. "Processing. I'll give him processing."

I didn't stick around to hear the rest of what she proposed. They could duke it out themselves. I was in no hurry to pick up a shovel and start digging for what could very well be radioactive remains.

I don't know what brought me to Lucian's apartment. I drove around Yaletown in a fog, parking my car on the edge of Pacific Street. His loft was part of a brick warehouse, one of the original buildings that had survived this neighborhood's inexorable march toward trendiness. In place of factories, there were now dance clubs, *chocolateries*, and furniture stores where you could drop four hundred bucks on a white leather ottoman.

I crossed over to Drake Street. My phone buzzed. It was a text from Mia, asking where I put the coffee, because it's not in the cupboard above the fridge, and a certain person doesn't want to go to the store to buy more, even though he could just walk over to Norman's Fruit Salad. *And I can't go because my hair's wet, plus it's after nine, and I could get accosted. By a man.*

I set the phone to silent. If Mia really needed my help, she could bypass her BlackBerry and throw a psych-blast my way.

That's for emergencies only, Derrick had told her. *Needing a ride home is not a good enough reason for giving Tess or myself a debilitating migraine.*

I knocked on Lucian's door. My hands were sweating, and I felt trills of energy racing through my body. Was I getting sick? Maybe it was just the caffeine.

Or maybe it was something else. I kind of doubted it, though. Every time I looked at a bed lately, I didn't think *sex* so much as *sleep*. I fell asleep in the break room today and woke up with the waffle pattern of the chesterfield pressed into one side of my face. My hair was sweaty and tangled. I was starving, but the thought of food also nauseated me. Unless it was porridge, which I thought I might be able to handle.

Lord Nightingale opened the door.

For a second, all I could do was stare at him. The

last time I'd seen him had been during my first and only visit to Trinovantum, the hidden city of the necromancers. Then, he'd been wearing a breastplate that looked like an insect's carapace. Now he was wearing a herringbone jacket, slacks, and knee-high leather boots.

He smiled when he saw me. "Agent Corday. How have you been?"

"Good. I've been—good." I frowned. "Sorry. Do I curtsy? I've forgotten the etiquette."

"You may do whatever comes naturally."

I extended my hand. "Shake?"

He looked at me strangely. "Very well."

We shook hands. I knew we weren't supposed to touch, but nothing had happened last time, despite Lucian's warning. His hands were cool, soft. He'd grown his hair a bit longer, and it settled in black curls around his face. He leaned in close.

"I was just discoursing with Lucian. I don't mean to monopolize him. I'm sure you two must have a lot to talk about."

"I planned on watching TV," I replied, taking a small step back.

"There's only one channel in Trinovantum," he said. "It does get tedious."

"What do they play?"

"Epic poetry, mostly."

"Yikes."

He smiled. "Good night, Tess. If I don't get back soon, I'll turn into a pumpkin. A very dangerous pumpkin."

Lord Nightingale vanished into the rainy street. The first step he took may have been ordinary, but I blinked once, and he was just a faint impression against the dark. Then he was gone completely. I felt a humming in my head. The ozone bite of necroid materia hung on the air.

Lucian was washing dishes. He looked up. "Hey. Sorry about that."

"No worries." I kissed him on the cheek. "What sorts of dealings were you two having? God forbid it was anything homosocial."

He raised an eyebrow. "Would that bother you?"

"No. But I'd much rather be there. It's no fun if I just hear about it later."

"Well, there was nothing serious. A little flirtation, but that's natural."

"Oh, is it?"

"He's my lord. I'm one of his men."

I sat down on the couch. "How much flirting, exactly?"

"It's not quantifiable."

"Just give me an idea."

Lucian dried his hands, then sat down next to me. "I'm only Seventh Solium. There are a lot of people closer to the top than I, and I leave the ass-kissing to them. But Theresa does have favorites."

"Theresa. That's a girl's name."

"Yes. In Portuguese, it's Tareja."

I blinked. "Lord Nightingale has a girl's name?"

"Well, yes. He was born a woman."

"In Portugal?"

"He was the bastard daughter of Alfonso the Sixth."

"So . . . at what point did Theresa become a man?"

"I have no idea. Frankly, it seems like too personal a question."

"But you know for certain that he was born a woman."

"In ten eighty. We can Google him, if it would make you feel better."

"No. I believe you. It's just—" I squinted. "Okay, he's born a woman, a princess, and now he's—"

"Nine hundred and thirty years old."

"And at some point, he pulled an *Orlando*."

"You've read Virginia Woolf?"

"Yes, Lucian. I am aware of Modernist women writers."

"Sexy." He slid closer. "What's your favorite Virginia Woolf novel?"

"*The Waves*."

"I found that one sad. A bit ephemeral, too."

"I know. That's why I like it."

He put his hand on top of mine. Everything felt a bit fuzzy. The logical part of my brain had quietly begun its shutdown process. His hand was soft from the warm water and felt good. A bit too good.

"Wait. What exactly does it mean to be one of Theresa's men?"

"I don't really want to talk about Lord Nightingale anymore."

"Oh, is it just that convenient?"

"It is." He kissed me lightly. "I want to try a new subject."

I pulled away. "Is it like a sire thing? Like with vampires?"

"For fuck's sake." He took my hand in both of his. "I'm not sleeping with Lord Nightingale. Please believe me."

"I do."

"Good." He started to lean forward again.

"And you've never?"

He closed his eyes. "No. I mean, yes. Once."

"Oh?" I felt my voice rising an octave. "When was that? Recently?"

"God, no. Years ago."

"How many?"

"It was a long time ago. We were in Lisbon. It just sort of happened."

"Well. I mean—" I sighed. "Obviously, it's your body; you can do whatever you want with it. I didn't know you then. I really have no reason to be jealous."

"That's right."

"And you've said that you prefer girls."

"I prefer you, at the moment."

"But you might prefer Theresa next time?"

He laughed. "No. I have no plans to revisit that night."

"Does he, like—" I made a weird motion with my hand. "Can he change back to a woman? Or will he always be a man?"

"I don't know. You'd have to ask him."

"But when the two of you were together, he was a man?"

Lucian smiled wryly. "He sure was."

"Jesus."

"I doubt he had very much to do with it."

I crawled into his lap. "Were you drunk, at least?"

"Quite."

"Did it cause a political coup?"

"Not that I know of."

"Should I shut up now?"

"I'd never say something so crass. Not to you."

He kissed me.

Lord Nightingale hadn't tasted like anything, just emptiness. Lucian's mouth was a very different story.

I bit his ear, which was a favorite pastime. He sucked in his breath. I moved my tongue down the length of his neck. He smelled like clean sheets and vanilla.

I unbuttoned my shirt. He rubbed small circles on my back with his hands. I curled into him. I could feel my whole body starting to move to its own rhythm. He kissed me again. His fingers were in my hair. I could feel what my body was doing to him. I could hear it in his breathing. His legs were shivering.

He reached under my skirt. Everything got very warm.

We took off the rest of our clothes. Lucian folded his boxers, placing them off to the side. For a moment, he just sat there, bacchanalian, legs spread, grinning at me.

Then I climbed on top of him. I wrapped my arms around his neck. He took one of my breasts in his mouth, and I closed my eyes. It was the first time all day I'd managed to squeeze out the rest of the world. Now there was only the heat of his mouth, the drag of his tongue, the barest press of his teeth. My consciousness was slowly becoming a merry-go-round, or a golden comet, flying faster and faster until I could no longer make out its trajectory. It spun and threw off sparks.

He slid away from me, getting down on his knees on the carpet. His tongue found me, and I grabbed onto his shoulders for support. He pulled me closer to his face, while his hands stroked me from behind. I must have been vibrating at a high frequency. The whole living room had a pale, crystalline cast to it, as if I'd already become a waveform. I grabbed a fistful of his hair, pulling him closer, deeper. For the first time, I realized that his black hair was touched with silver.

His breath stirred me. I felt like he might tear something out, and I wanted it to happen. I wanted to feel riven clean, every part of me exposed to the air, the sting of palpation, the threat of contracting something, anything. Like a body on a slab, open for viewing. *Take it all. We're going out of business. Even the organs are for sale.*

I pulled him back onto the couch, settling on top of him. I guided him in, and we froze for a moment, both trembling slightly. He drew me close, kissing me. I bit his lip. He groaned. I knew that if I pressed deeper, I could draw blood. And for a moment, I wanted to. Instead, I traced his mouth with my tongue.

It was my rhythm. I began it, moving my hips, and he responded from beneath me. His hands were all over my body. I reached behind me, stroking his legs, then his feet. I grabbed onto his ankles, using them for leverage. He arched his back, pressing against me, and I thought we might shatter because we ground so hard into each other, rendering our bodies to sweat, salt, and oil.

He moved as I moved. His pace quickened.

"Wait," I said. "I want you against the wall."

We rose. The concrete floor was cold on my bare feet, but I was also sweating, which evened things out. I lifted my leg, mounting him. My hair was in his face. He wrapped his arms around me, and I climbed, and climbed, wondering at how good he felt, and at how precise my need had become. I climbed until there was nowhere left to go, and then I felt everything contract, like laces suddenly pulled tight.

I moaned. Lucian buried his face in my neck. He shuddered. I kept moving, still on fire, every curtain lifted and exposed to the darkness that lay beyond.

"Tess—"

I felt him let go. His breath hissed in my ear. I wrapped my fingers around his neck, holding him still. He sighed.

My thumb brushed the lily tattoo, just above his clavicle. I felt a shock. It was slight, but still very real.

I put my mark on you, the Iblis had said. But what had it really meant? I'd seen the creature melt into a pool of bloody wax, so I knew that it wasn't about to answer any of my questions. Still, I wanted to know. I wanted to know more about the man who belonged to this body, his body, still locked inside mine.

We stood for a while, breathing hard, unable to speak. Finally, when he'd recovered his composure enough, he took my hand and led me upstairs. It was already like a dream. I slipped into my side of the bed and was barely conscious of him throwing the comforter on top of me. I closed my eyes. He laid his feet atop mine. His hand was on my back, still.

I can't remember anything else.

10

It was Derrick's first day back in the lab.

He walked with a slight limp, and there was still some bruising visible on his face. Other than that, he seemed his regular self. I kicked myself mentally for not pressing the matter with Miles when we'd last talked. Something had seemed wrong about the moment. And really, how do you bring up a question like, *Hey, do you feel like your boyfriend may have assaulted your mind lately?*

Still, it might have been nothing but a hiccup.

He looked around as we stepped into the guest suite. "Hey, this place is swank. You should charge by the night."

"It's kind of a holding cell," I said in a low voice.

Ru was sitting on the couch with his headphones on.

When he saw us, he took out the earbuds. He looked Derrick up and down.

"You were at the morgue," he said.

"I was. I like your pants. They're a bit big, though."

"Yes. They are voluminous." He extended his hand. "I'm Ru. Am I doing this right? With my hand?"

Derrick took it. "Absolutely. Good shake."

"Good shake to you, too. I assume you've come to read my thoughts."

Derrick sat on the opposite end of the couch. "It doesn't quite work that way. I might be able to get a blurry picture from your mind, but it's not like reading an e-mail. If you don't want me to see something, I won't be able to."

"I'm not sure that I believe you."

"Ru—" I chose my next words carefully. "Derrick also has memories from that night, but he needs help recovering them. It's not his intention to comb your mind for data. He just wants to try to reconstruct the events as faithfully as possible."

Ru's expression bordered on resignation, which seemed odd coming from someone who looked like a child. Then he shrugged. "You're already digging into the earth. You might as well dig into my brain."

"You must want to remember something about what happened to you."

I felt like a terrible person as the words left my mouth. I was coaxing a young demon into reliving what was probably the worst night of his life.

"Remembering is hard," he said. "But I guess it's necessary. What must I do in order to assist you?"

"Just be still." Derrick put his hands in his lap. "I don't have to touch you. But you may feel something almost like a touch."

Ru looked at me. "What's your job? Do you guard the door?"

I sat in the wingback chair next to the couch. "I provide neutral energy. It lessens the chance that you and Derrick might cross wires."

"And what does it mean to cross wires?"

"It's nothing bad," Derrick assured him. "Just think of her as a dehumidifier."

Ru frowned. "That doesn't make me feel better."

"Relax. I'm going to start now. If you feel uncomfortable, even a little bit, she'll be right there. All you have to do is say her name."

He nodded. "All right. Proceed."

Derrick looked at the ground. As he began to draw slowly into himself, I heard his voice clearly. *If things get weird, grab him and close the door behind you. Don't let me out of the room.*

A chill went through me. *Is that really necessary?* I started to ask. But the conscious part of him was already gone.

All three of us were silent for about twenty seconds.

"What?" Ru asked suddenly. "I can't hear you."

Derrick said nothing.

Ru frowned. Then he swallowed thickly and made a face, like someone with a sore throat. "What is that? What are you doing?"

I wanted to ask the same question. Usually, Derrick was employed to read the minds of demons who were already dead. The last time I'd seen him read a human's mind was when he was doing telepathy exercises with Selena. That was when he'd pulled a mysterious name from her mind. *Jessica.*

"That's a weird question," Ru said, although now he wasn't looking at either of us. "What kind of neighborhood do *you* live in?"

Derrick's expression didn't change. His pupils were pinned, and he stared at the carpet. His hands remained folded neatly in his lap.

Ru gave a small shudder.

His eyes lost their focus. He sank into the couch, seeming to wilt slightly. For what seemed like a minute, all I could hear was the sound of my own breathing. Then Ru spoke. His voice was the same, but his expression was almost vegetative.

"My dam's name is Tyr. My sire's name is Osh. We live in Four, under the cloud cover." He was silent for a bit. Then: "I had a vapor-worm. He was my pet. One night he broke into the pantry and ate his way through my mother's preserves. I wasn't allowed to play with worms after that."

I could see the dendrite materia gathering around Derrick's body in white pops and flashes. I felt the hairs on the back of my neck rising.

"I see him in the mirror," Ru said. "I see his room. The walls are dark and made of wood. The floor is plastic, melted in places. The light makes it hard to see. My head's spinning. But then it passes. I pass."

Derrick's hand moved slightly. I felt something cold and heavy brush past me.

Ru stood up, his expression changing.

"I don't want to."

I tensed. "Ru," I said. "If you can hear me, squeeze my hand."

But Ru wasn't looking at me. He was looking at something invisible, something that brought tears to his eyes.

"There was blood," he said, his lip trembling. "On my shoes. And his eyes were closed, but he knew that I was there. He said my name. I put my head in his lap, and he touched my hair. I could feel it."

"Derrick." I rose. "Stop. He needs a breather."

He didn't react. His eyes were glued to the carpet. His hands moved slowly up and down his jeans, as if ironing out creases. His mouth remained slightly parted, and I almost thought he was going to break into a smile. But there was nothing behind his eyes. They were wide, unlit rooms.

"He keeps telling me to go," Ru whispered. "He keeps saying the same thing, over and over. There's blood on my shirt, too. I don't want to leave. What if I can't ever come back? I don't want him to be alone. I don't want to be alone."

I snapped my fingers in front of Derrick's face. "Quit it."

He grabbed my wrist.

His grip was surprisingly strong. I tried to yank my hand away, but he held on. His eyes narrowed slightly.

I felt an echo stir in my mind.

Derrick's fingers were like ice. Colors danced at the edges of my vision. I raised a psychic defense. He leaned against my wall, gently at first, then with re-newed vigor. The foundation started to crack.

"El!" Ru screamed. "Don't! Please! I want to stay with you!"

I drew my athame, reversing it so that the hilt was extended. Derrick's mind was scrabbling for purchase within my own. He was tugging on the substrate of my consciousness, shining light into the dark corners. His grip intensified, and I felt him pulling up threads of memory and desire, their root systems exposed.

I touched the hilt of the blade to his neck.

"Derrick."

Light flared between us. I smelled smoke and pulled the blade away immediately. The pressure in my head dissolved.

"Did you just *burn* me?"

I winced as I saw the red mark already forming on his neck. "Sorry, hon. You were kind of trampling through Ru's brain. And mine."

"Oh, God. I'm so sorry." He looked at Ru. "Are you all right? I didn't hurt you or anything, did I?"

Ru didn't answer. When Derrick stretched out his hand, the demon flinched.

"I think we should leave Ru alone for a bit," I said.

Derrick nodded slowly, rising.

"I'm really sorry," he said again. His voice was bro-ken. "I don't know what happened. I didn't mean to—"

Ru stared at the ground. He couldn't look Derrick in the eyes.

"You can page Selena if you need anything," I told

the demon. "You know the number. We'll be right out-side."

He was frozen for a moment. Then, like someone waking up from a dream, he slowly retrieved the re-mote from the arm of the couch. He turned on the TV and began watching a food documentary. He didn't look at either of us.

I followed Derrick into the hallway. Once the door was closed, I started to say something. But his look of utter devastation stopped me.

"I don't know what's happening to me," he whis-pered.

He was shaking. I hugged him close.

"We're going to figure it out," I said.

The Sawbones was packed when we arrived. I hadn't been to the paranormal bar in quite some time, but tonight, it seemed like the perfect place for Der-rick. He didn't have to worry about violating any minds here. Nobody was going to open their dark, dirty thoughts to him, and some of them didn't even have what could properly be called "brains," at least neurologically speaking.

More important, alcohol deadened his powers. Until I could figure out what we might be dealing with, I wanted to keep his ESP as dull as possible. It less-ened the chance that we'd have a repeat of his session with Ru.

We sat down at the only remaining table. There was

no point in looking at the menu, since I already knew I was going to order the zucchini sticks, in spite of their dubious reputation. I also wanted an ale.

"So, this is how we're figuring things out?" he asked.

"Absolutely."

"And what are we figuring out, exactly?"

"How to get you drunk."

"I'm not really sure how that helps."

"Beer helps everything. Haven't you learned that?"

He sighed. "I broke into the mind of a child. I made him cry. What kind of a twisted freak *does* that?"

"He's older than Angelus. He's not a child. And that wasn't you back there. It was something else entirely."

"You think I'm possessed? Oh, God." He put his head on the table.

"Not possessed, sweetheart." I rubbed his hair. "It's your gears. Something's out of alignment, that's all."

"My soul," he mumbled. "It's gone. Replaced by a void."

"Okay. We're going to need a pitcher right now. And I don't mean Miles." I giggled. "Sorry; that came out before I could stop it. I may already be a little drunk from the air in this place."

He groaned something incomprehensible in response.

A waitress came over. She had blond hair, and I recognized her, although we hadn't seen each other in nearly two years. "Hi, Joanie."

Joanie did a double take. Then she smiled shyly. "Wow, it's been forever. How's it going with all your"— she glanced at Derrick, facedown—"stuff?"

"Stuff is stuff. Messy and constant."

"Kitchen's closed," she said. "On account of an incident I'm not supposed to be talking about."

"Bar pixies?"

She shook her head. "I *really* can't talk about it."

"Gotcha. We'll have two pitchers of Alexander Keith's."

"How many glasses?"

"Three."

"'Kay. Back in a bit." Joanie left.

"Why three glasses?"

"What's that?"

Derrick was staring at me. "Tess. Who else is coming?"

I stared at my BlackBerry. I'd insisted we buy them so the family could keep in contact, but they also worked well as distracting fetish-objects. Really, Miles had been the one to ruin us all, with his device's seductive messaging features.

"Tess—"

The door to the Sawbones opened. I can't exactly say that a hush fell over the bar, but those with acute senses definitely felt something. A slight distortion in everyone's immediate perception, like the ripple I'd seen on the radargrams. It was the feeling of power bending around a heavy element.

Duessa and Wolfie stepped into the bar. Derrick kicked me.

"Ow. Shit." I glared at him.

"You suck," he whispered. "And I'll kick you again before the night's over. What are you trying to do, give me a heart attack?"

"They're actually nice people, you know."

"I'm not disputing their niceness. I'm just a bit nervous about the fact that Duessa is a scary immortal. And when Wolfie's mad, he sets fire to people."

"*Things*. Not people."

"The Iblis?"

"That wasn't strictly a person."

They reached the table. Derrick, who was always good for his word, kicked me again underneath the table.

"Duessa." I smiled. My shin was throbbing. Derrick had worn his chocolate brown Steve Maddens, which had vicious points. "Thanks for coming. It's good to see both of you again, under more relaxing circumstances."

Wolfie pulled the chair out for Duessa. "Wouldn't you all prefer a classier venue? This place is full of wasted thugs and lost souls."

Duessa took a seat. "Every soul's got to have someplace to settle for a night. Even if it's just to get fed."

"Or laid." Wolfie sat down. "The necromancers in the back booth are up to no good. I can smell whatever they're channeling."

"They're always here. I barely notice them anymore." I turned to Duessa. "I'm afraid I've been a bit rude, asking you to come without giving you very much info."

"That's fine. I live in this neighborhood." She looked around with a slightly flat expression. "Although I don't usually come here."

Joanie came by, setting down two pitchers. She noticed Duessa, and her eyes widened. "Oh—hello." She curtsied.

"Damn," Wolfie said. "That was an honest curtsy."

Duessa smiled at Joanie. "Well, she's a lady."

"I can get another glass—"

"It's fine, honey. I brought my own." She reached into her handbag and withdrew a stein with a gilded handle.

"That's gorgeous," Derrick said.

"I know." Duessa pulled out a handkerchief and placed it on the table. Then she set the glass on top of it. "A pirate from Kinsale gave it to me. Anne." She smiled, shaking her head. "Mad, that one."

"Kitchen's closed," Joanie reiterated. "Sorry."

"It's fine. We ate already."

Joanie left, heading for the kitchen. I started to say something, but Duessa beat me to it. She looked squarely at Derrick.

"Let's see your eyes," she said.

He flinched. "What exactly did she tell you?"

"Just look at me."

They stared at each other for a moment. It was the opposite of the "conversation" with Ru, when neither had been able to meet the other's gaze. I felt nothing in the way of power. Duessa seemed to just be looking closely at him.

Then it was over. Duessa grabbed the pitcher and began pouring glasses. "I think we could all use some of this."

"It's bad. I knew it was bad." Derrick sighed. "Maybe there's a little demon inside my brain. Like that guy from the *Teenage Mutant Ninja Turtles* who lived inside the robot's stomach. Krang."

I frowned. "But didn't he build the robot—"

Duessa cleared her throat, cutting me off. "It's not a case of inside versus outside. That's too binary. What you've got is an impact."

Derrick frowned. "Like—a car hit my brain?"

"Close. A demon gave you a concussion. Your mind's wounded, and it's got to heal before things will get back to normal."

"Am I dangerous?"

She took a sip of her beer. "It's not as simple as that."

I could feel Derrick clamping down on his natural sarcasm. He kept his tone even and polite. "I imagine it isn't. But is there anything else you can tell me? I don't want to go brain-snatching at random, you know?"

"It's not brain-snatching. Not yet." Duessa patted his hand. "Look. Here's what happened. You got cross-checked by something old and powerful. Your mind's a little beat-up. It may do some odd things. Hiccups."

"I've broken into people's brains," Derrick said. "First my boyfriend, and now someone who really shouldn't have any connection to me at all. That's a bit more than a hiccup. I don't want to hurt people. At least be honest with me—if you think I need to be locked away, then tell me."

"Isolation isn't the answer. If you're really going to heal, you need good people around you, people who are willing to give you their energy."

"That sounds like mooching."

"It is. But it's the good kind."

"And you don't see anything else?"

Duessa sighed. "All right. Think of your mind as a house. Some rooms are open, and some aren't. When a demon shakes you around, it's like a storm going right through your house. It can stir things up. It can open doors."

"I don't like whatever door it's opened."

"That's tough. If it really is open, then it's open for good. You've got to deal with whatever comes out."

"We can all help," I said. "You're not alone."

Derrick stared at his glass. "You were right. Beer is the only answer that really makes sense to me right now."

Wolfie's phone rang. He looked down at it, then groaned. "It's the supplier. I'm going to take this outside."

"It's awfully late for them to be calling," Duessa said.

"But we like them because of the flexible hours they keep, remember?" He answered the phone, heading for the door.

"Is he running the House?" I asked her.

"Nearly. I do very little administrative work anymore. I have to tell you, it's been an enormous relief."

"You must need a vacation."

"That only comes when you die. And I'm not quite ready to give up the ghost yet. But it's nice to have some time off, at least."

"I already miss my time off," Derrick said. "I should have pretended that the pain was a lot worse. I was really getting used to sleeping in."

"Yeah, sorry, buddy." I patted his shoulder. "Those halcyon days are over now. You're back in the trenches. Drink up."

Duessa turned to me. "What were *you* going to tell me?"

"I can't recall anything specific."

"That's strange. I was almost certain I heard it in your voice."

It was nearly impossible to lie to her. I exhaled.

"We were interrogating a demon—the same one who attacked Derrick. The demon claimed to know my father."

Derrick stared at me. "Holy shit. Why didn't you tell me that?"

"You've got enough on your plate."

"Yeah, but we're supposed to share plates."

"I'd rather take my crazy to go. At least for right now."

"What sort of demon?"

"I'm not allowed to say. I'm sorry. Maybe it was lying. Maybe it just wanted to get a rise out of me. But it didn't seem like a lie."

"Your dad was a pureblood, no?"

"I think so. I mean, that's what my mother told me, although lately she's become an unreliable source of information."

"Well, it's possible. They could run in the same circles."

"The Iblis knew my father, too. He seems to be quite the popular guy with murderers and assassins."

"And the manticore," Derrick said softly. "It seemed

to recognize you. It said, *She's something.* Maybe it knew your dad as well."

"Well, I wish we could have a psychotic family reunion, but two of those creatures are already dead. The third's in a holding cell."

"That may not last for long," Duessa said. "I hope it's under close watch. And very far underground."

I started to say something. Then I blushed slightly, shaking my head. "Sorry. Never mind. I was about to ask something inappropriate."

"Go ahead."

"Well—" I gave Derrick a guilty look. "Is it true that Lord Nightingale used to be the Condessa of Portugal?"

"That gossip is nine centuries old. I imagine Lucito blabbed it to you?"

"He said they hooked up."

"And you're jealous."

"Well. Yes."

"I'm confused," Derrick said. "Lucian hooked up with Lord Nightingale, when he used to be a woman?"

"No. He was a guy at the time."

"Oh." His eyes widened. "*Oh.* This must be killing you."

"Shut up." I turned back to Duessa. "I've got nothing to worry about, right? I mean, they hooked up while they were on vacation. Big deal."

She chuckled. "Theresa's a rover. Lucian's always been just the opposite. When he's with someone, he's with them. He'd tell you if something was up."

"So, wait." Derrick was still a beat behind us. "He's Portuguese?"

I sighed, returning my attention to Duessa. "I know I'm just being paranoid. And I mean, realistically, if he likes boys, too—there's nothing wrong with that."

"Hear, hear." Derrick took a drink. "Even though they're all bastards."

"Yes. In spite of that."

"He seems to like only you, at the moment," Duessa said. "I guess you'll just have to be content with that."

"I suppose you're right."

"Besides." She drained her glass. "We're not all the things we used to be. People change. Nothing can stand in the way of that."

"We'll need more beer soon," Derrick observed.

Duessa looked at me. "You're paying?"

"Yes."

"Then I'd be delighted to have another pitcher."

I stood up, taking out a twenty. "Derrick? Any special shots? I can get you the one with whipped cream again."

"No. I'm done with blow jobs."

"That's a lie, and you know it."

He sighed. "Get me something that tastes like candy."

11

I arrived at the lab hungover, but focused. Derrick had agreed to meet me for coffee in the break room. I stifled a yawn as I was swiping my card to get in the building. That would definitely end up being the security snapshot of the day: me with my eyes closed, looking like I'm eating my own fist.

Cindée was examining a tray filled with fragments. They resembled grayish black shards of porcelain. They'd been charred, and bits of soil matrix still clung to them in places. They reminded me of a broken mug, or at least its aftermath. It's a reality in forensics that we often have to work with small, broken, dirty things.

"There's glass mixed in there," Cindée said, "as well as what could be pottery shards. But they also have a faint porosity."

"Like bone?"

"Possibly. We don't know yet if they're mineral or artificial."

"How far down were they?"

"Less than two meters."

I looked at the fragments. "They aren't metal. The GPR only bounced off them because they're radioactive."

"They have a fraction of the energy released by a dental X-ray. But because it's gamma radiation, it registers a lot stronger."

The lab itself had materia-fed screens, which reconstituted nonexotic forms of radiation into low-band ultraviolet energy. The most I was going to get from these fragments was a mild suntan.

"What sort of trace are we looking for?"

"I doubt we'll find a fingerprint. The pieces are too small. But we might find a few lazy amino acids still hanging around. We'll bake the materia at a steady temperature. The charring may reveal something."

I spaced out for a second. When I came back, Cindée was saying something about using a wet powder suspension on the fragments.

"Where'dja go, sweetheart?" she asked.

"I have no idea. I need a coffee."

"Don't taunt me."

"Do you want one?"

"Nah. I just had my break, and I'm jittery as it is. Thanks, though."

"Should I tell Selena something about the . . . wet powder suspension?"

Cindée grinned. "That's not necessary. It's kind of a

Byzantine process, if you want to know the truth. Just tell her the fragments are being thoroughly analyzed. Oh—and Linus had a message for her. It's on a Post-it he left."

"Damn. I thought I was the only one using Post-its."

"No, he pretty much invented it." She pulled the Post-it off the keyboard and handed it to me. It read:

Boss, if you want me to run a Refractive Index test on any glass from the debris, we need to update our GRIM software. This will cost 1200.00.

"Really? I get to be the one who gives her this?"

"Just slip it under a file. She'll notice it after you've left."

"We're awful employees."

Cindée shrugged. "She has better things to worry about than a software update. And we don't really need it tonight. But Linus will feel better if he knows that his request was delivered in due course."

"You're good, woman."

"Yeah. Well, I've survived this long." She rapped her knuckles against the counter. "Knock on Pyrex."

I headed for the break room. As I walked down the hallway, I noticed that the door to Selena's office was closed. I made sure that nobody was looking, then stuck the Post-it note to her office door. I needed Linus on my side as well.

Derrick was already sitting on the couch, unpacking something that smelled amazing. Patrick and Mia were both with him. When Mia saw me, she instantly rose and grabbed my arm. "Oh, my God, we need to talk right now."

I followed her back into the hallway.

"Okay. Sorry; this is important."

"I really just want to sit down and relax. The four of us are hardly ever in the same room anymore."

"I know—we're a broken family, et cetera. I don't care. I'm talking about something far more important." She lowered her voice. "Patrick got a tattoo."

I walked past her. "Show it to me," I said.

Patrick sighed. Then he lifted up his shirt slightly. There was a vampiric rune, red and blue, inked just below his navel.

"It's my original mark, from the Magnate," he said. "I just had it filled in, so that it's more visible."

"I don't think you need to be outing yourself as a paranormal right now."

"That's kind of self-hating, don't you think?"

I sat down. "Fine. I have no sensible advice for you. Just do whatever you feel like from now on."

Derrick handed me a plate of chow mein.

"Is this from Sky Dragon?"

"It is."

"How did you get them to deliver downtown?"

"I paid them a lot of money. Now, eat your noodles."

"Mmm. They're so fat. And there's so many of them."

"He got the tattoo at Sacred Heart," Derrick said.

I stared at Patrick. "You went to a normate tattoo parlor and asked them to touch up your vampire rune?"

"I heard the girl there had really steady hands."

"You had a crush. Shocking."

"I chose her based on her reputation."

"Uh-huh. I absolutely believe that."

"I'm over eighteen."

"You are. Which means"—I pointed a fork speared with noodles at him—"you get to make your own dumbass decisions."

Patrick sat down, grabbing a plate. "Thanks. I think."

"I think it's kind of cool," Mia said. "He's proud of his heritage. I mean, there's nothing wrong with that, right?"

"I just don't want him to attract too much attention. He can wear his pride on the inside, but it's quite another thing to brand himself."

"Isn't it like getting a rainbow tattoo?"

"Those aren't especially attractive, either," Derrick said.

The last thing I wanted to talk about right now was vampire pride. Mia was already curious as hell about Patrick's "heritage," as she called it. The problem was that her power and her vampire DNA were inseparable. If we tried to access one, we risked increasing the strength of the vampiric viral plasmids, which meant potentially losing a part of what made Mia who she was.

You must want to remember what happened.

I could have asked the same thing of Mia that I'd asked of Ru. So much about her life before the last five years was still buried, including the identity of her real parents. That was a secret that both Marcus Tremblay and Sabine Delacroix had taken with them to the grave (and, in Sabine's case, to whatever alien shore awaited her after undeath).

"Tess?"

I looked at Mia. The expression on her face made my skin go cold.

This is it, I thought. *She's really going to say it. "I'm becoming a vampire, and there's nothing you can do to stop me."*

I swallowed. "What is it?"

"Don't forget about your Dr Pepper."

I smiled. "Thanks for remembering."

"It was Patrick who remembered, actually. But I was the one who remembered that you *didn't* like the vanilla flavor. Which averted a potential disaster."

"You're my hero," I said. And it was true. "Why are you and Patrick both here, by the way? Did you really want Chinese food that bad?"

Derrick gave me a look. "Okay. Don't freak. Selena asked Patrick if he'd be willing to examine the Kentauros demon."

"Examine it how?"

"She wants me to smell it," Patrick said. "She called it 'olfactory trace detection.' Maybe it'll have some kind of bacteria that I'll be able to distinguish or something."

"Maybe it has a specific body odor," Mia said. "And *you* get to identify that. How lucky does that make you?"

"Shut up."

Selena popped her head into the break room. "Oh,

Patrick, you're here already. That's good. Come with me."

"Nobody's going anywhere yet." I turned to Selena. "Are you seriously going to put him in the same room as Basuram?"

"No. We're putting him in the room next to the demon's cell. The two of them can communicate by microphone."

"I should be able to smell it through the walls," Patrick said. "Modred's been teaching me how to maximize my sense potential. He's really nasal at the moment. So we've been smelling a lot of things together."

I glared at Selena. "Were you even going to tell me about this?"

"I sent you two texts about it."

"When?"

"Forty minutes ago, when I first had the idea."

I looked down at my phone. It was pretty much a warzone of unanswered text messages, e-mails, and BBMs. I felt like I'd put it down for only a moment, but suddenly, I couldn't remember when I'd last looked at it. I felt real panic. I'd become so conditioned by its regular updates that I feared missing anything, even a relevant Facebook announcement.

I got up. "Okay. I dropped the ball on that one. I'm still concerned, though. I don't even like the fact that these two are in the same building, and you want to put them practically in the same cell."

"In adjoining cells," she repeated. "Both heavily reinforced. Neither of them are even going to get a look at each other."

"Are you kidding? You have no idea if the Kentauros demon can see through walls. Can we at least disguise Patrick's voice?"

"Yes. He'll have a filter."

"Like a real informant," Patrick said. "It's kind of cool."

"No. This is not cool. It's dangerous and unnecessary. And with all due respect, Selena, it pisses me off that you want to use him like this."

"She's not using me," Patrick snapped. "I wanted to help. It also helps me focus my powers, and I need to learn more. It's good experience."

"He is right," Selena said. "Although, touché about me being nasty and going over your head. I understand that Patrick's old enough to be making his own decisions, but you and Derrick are also an important part of his life. I assure you, I don't plan to put him in any significant danger. And there's the real possibility that Basuram might let something slip."

"I can also take care of myself," Patrick said.

"Aww." Mia sighed. "I remember when I used to think that. Then I woke up with my hands tied behind my back, and watched a guy get blown away, right in front of me. Now I just kind of assume that things are going to go south right away."

"You probably get that from me," I said.

"For the record," Selena added, "Derrick already chewed me out about this very issue, twenty minutes ago."

I looked at him. "Had you had coffee first? What kind of mood were you in?"

"I was curt," Derrick said. "But respectful. In the end, though, I agreed with all of her points. I don't think Patrick's going to be in any immediate danger, and really, there's no one else with his sensory abilities—at least, no one who'd be willing to work for us. It's a bit of a win-win."

"I'd just like to point out," Mia said, eyes glued to her phone, "that nobody invited me here for anything. I came because I was very bored, and Derrick promised that we'd go to Spartacus Books, after the smelling's over."

"You're picking up a Marxist tract?"

"They have good 'zines. And I know the 'moment' of 'zines has already come and gone, or whatever, but I still like them."

"Are 'zines over? I hadn't realized."

"They were pretty much over once you heard about them, Tess."

"Ouch. You're in a fine vapor today."

"Sorry. I guess that was low even for me."

"We're going now," Selena said. "Derrick, you're not coming near Basuram again, for obvious reasons."

"Understood," he said. "I'll chill with Mia."

"Oh, can we chill? Like actual thugs?"

"Good luck with that," I said.

The three of us left and took the elevator down to the level where Basuram had been relocated. It got distinctly colder as we hit the basement level. The lights were dim, and our shoes echoed on the hard floors.

"How many demons are kept down here?" Patrick asked.

"Depends if you're counting the employees or not," Selena replied. "Basuram is the only demon currently incarcerated. This facility was only designed for short-term holding purposes."

"Should I be nervous about this?" Patrick asked me.

"There's nothing wrong with being a little nervous. But Selena's right. The two of you will be segregated. You'll be able to sense each other without seeing each other, and Basuram won't ever hear your real voice."

Linus met us at the cell door. He ushered us in, then retreated. "The audio's set up. All Patrick has to do is speak into the microphone."

"Thanks, Linus," Selena said. "You can lock us in."

Linus shut the door to the cell. "I'll be out here recording."

"You know what to do if something goes awry."

"Yeah. I'll get my ass out of here."

Selena exhaled. "Do at least try to sound the alarm as you're running in the opposite direction."

"I will. Don't worry."

I sat down next to Patrick. Selena remained standing.

"Should I say something?" Patrick asked.

"Not yet," Selena said. "Just reach out with your senses. Tell us whatever you manage to pick up."

Patrick's expression went distant. I felt nothing.

"It's old," Patrick said, his eyes still closed. "Really old. The smell is like"—he frowned—"plaster? It's strong. It's making me a little dizzy."

"Don't push too hard," I said.

"It's fine, Tess. I can do this."

"Who is that?"

Basuram's voice echoed through the microphone. We all went silent. Patrick shifted in his seat.

"I'm a vampire," he said, into the mic. "My sire was the Magnate of this area."

"Magnate." Basuram laughed. "Is that vampire middle management? Why would they send you to question me? I have no idea what they think you might glean by sniffing around me like a dog."

"You'd be surprised what I can pick up on," Patrick said. "You've got bacteria on you that's not from around here. And I sense that you eat a lot of red meat, which is something I can respect."

"You're no closer to me than the rest of them," Basuram said. "I've spent my whole life at war. But I can taste how young you are. You don't know the first thing about being an immortal."

"I'm a pretty quick study, though. I've been learning how to sniff out memories."

"You can try. But if you open your senses to me, there's the chance I'll move in and make myself right at home in your brain. Is that something you're willing to risk, vampire? Because once I get control of your central nervous system, I'm going to start breaking necks."

"My brain's dead," Patrick said. "I mean, technically. I'm animated, but my organs are toast. You can't invade something that has no electrical impulses."

Basuram seemed to digest this in silence.

"I smell ashes," Patrick said. "Something made of bones."

Ash and bones. That was what Derrick had seen in Basuram's mind.

"That memory is close to the surface," the demon replied.

"What does it mean?"

"I'm not about to tell you."

"Why do the bones feel so smooth? They're almost like glass." He made a face. "They taste bitter. I need something to drink."

Basuram was silent.

"Are you ignoring me now?" Patrick asked. "Is this a sore spot?"

It was quiet for a little while longer. Then a different voice came through the microphone. It was slightly higher in octave. It still sounded like it was coming from Basuram's throat, but the intonation was entirely different.

"Who am I speaking to?"

Patrick frowned. "We've already been introduced."

"The slave that you spoke with is under my collar. Now we are in direct communication. What is your name?"

He looked at Selena. She nodded slowly.

"Patrick," he said.

"Are you a vampire, Patrick?"

"Yes."

"When were you turned?"

"That's kind of a personal question."

"How old are you, Patrick?"

"Eighteen."

"Eighteen." The voice sounded almost nostalgic. "Patrick, I am a very old thing. I am probably the oldest thing you've ever met."

"I met a manticore," he said. "They're really old, right?"

"They are long-lived. But I'm older than the manticore that you met. So you should understand me very carefully. Stop questioning the slave."

"Why? Was the demon about to tell us something?"

"It knows only a few flashes of a much larger design. You won't learn anything from it that will help your investigation."

"Why are you talking through it now?" Patrick asked. "It kind of suggests that Basuram was going to tell us something."

"It was not, I assure you. In order to fulfill its orders, the Kentauros must apprehend the Ptah'li fugitive. That is all it cares about."

"I doubt it would appreciate you using it as a puppet."

"It does not appreciate anything, nor feel anything. It works for the Ferid. It manages palatinate affairs."

Patrick looked at me blankly.

"Like a border guard," I whispered.

"Is that what you are?" he asked. "One of the Ferid?"

"Good-bye, Patrick."

"Wait—" I grabbed the microphone. "Who are you?"

There was silence.

"Tess—" Selena put a hand on my arm. "This isn't the time."

"Tessa." The voice changed. It was slightly harder. "I had no desire to uncover you, but it seems our paths have crossed."

"Do you know my father?"

"Yes."

"Can you tell me his name?"

"No."

"Can you tell me your name?"

Silence. Then: "Arcadia."

"How do you know my father, Arcadia?"

There was no reply.

We waited for a bit, afraid almost to breathe. Then Linus opened the cell door. "The demon's asleep," he said. "Passed out on the floor. I'd go nearer to check, but I'm not crazy."

"I may be," I said, sinking into the chair.

"You think your dad might be one of them?" Patrick asked me. "One of those Ferid creatures?"

"I don't know. That psychic presence could have belonged to anyone."

"It felt very far away," he said. "If that makes you feel any better."

"It doesn't. But thanks."

"Arcadia." Patrick looked at me as we walked out of the cell. "Is it a girl's name? How do you think she knows your father?"

I sighed. "With my luck, she's an ex."

12

My mother was cooking dinner when I got home from work. This might have been normal, except for the fact that I hadn't talked to her in two weeks. I'd left messages on her answering machine, but she hadn't returned any of my calls.

"She went on a cruise," Kevin said. "Something she won at work."

"Didn't she invite you?"

"She only got one ticket."

"That hardly seems fair."

"Tell me about it. I've got inventory to deal with at the store, and she's off in the Mayan Riviera somewhere."

My mother was not the type of person to go on cruises on the spur of the moment without telling me. She also wasn't the type of person to ignore my phone calls after she'd been back for days. Now she was standing in my kitchen, stirring a pot of something that smelled absolutely delicious, and smiling.

Smiling as if nothing had happened, as if nothing was happening, anywhere, ever. It was what I'd come to think of as her smile of denial.

She leaned in and kissed me on the cheek. "I wanted to surprise you. I hope you're hungry."

In truth, I felt nauseous, and the thought of food made me want to start breathing into a paper bag. But the smells from the oven were working their magic, and I knew what a good cook my mother was. So I just nodded.

"Sure. I'm starving."

"Excellent. I'm making the turnips just how you like them, with butter and lots of sugar. And I brought a jar of pickled beets. You remember how your auntie Kay and I made all those pickles? Well, they're finally ready, and let me tell you, they're to die for. We made pickled beets as well, and they're just as good."

I sat down numbly at the table. "Thank you. Derrick and Miles are eating out tonight. Patrick and Mia are most likely avoiding me after today."

"It's okay, dear. I know how hard you work. I took some of the vacation time that I've been banking for a while. So I don't mind at all. I'm free as a bird."

"Yeah. Kevin said you went on a cruise."

She kept stirring the turnips. "I'd hardly call it that. I just stayed with some old friends in Tulum. It was very relaxing."

"Since when do you have friends in Tulum?"

"I have friends in a lot of places."

I stared at the clock. "Mia won't be home for another hour. She's got some kind of around-the-clock study group. And Patrick's staying over at a friend's tonight. Or maybe he's out disturbing the peace. I don't know."

"They can warm it up when they get home. And don't worry. You're doing fine with both of them."

"I didn't say I was worried."

"But you are. I can tell."

She walked over to the table and handed me a steaming mug. I was about to say for the millionth time, *Mom, I don't drink tea; only you do*— But then I smelled the coffee. I stared at her.

"Did you make this for me?"

"Yes. Aren't you proud of me? Derrick showed me how to use the coffeemaker over text message. He was very informative. If it doesn't explode in the next fifteen minutes, I'll be confident that I actually did it right."

My eyes narrowed. "What's going on?"

"What do you mean?"

"Come on. You vanish for two weeks. Then you show up in my kitchen, cook me dinner, and make me coffee. It's weird."

"I don't see anything weird about it."

"It's weird, Mom. You're being weird."

"How?"

"I can't explain it."

"You're just tired. You need a home-cooked meal."

"We're not refugees. We do cook for ourselves.

Derrick is a great cook, and I can throw something together. Under pressure."

"Nobody's denying that." She grabbed a plate from the counter. "But everyone needs a little help now and then."

She put the food in front of me. Suddenly, I felt as if I'd never been so hungry in my entire life. I wolfed it down, pausing only to drink coffee in between bites. She sat across from me, eating slowly, like a regular person. She sipped her tea. I watched her rings, which sparkled slightly as she moved her hands.

My mother and I had always been telepathic in a way that had nothing to do with Derrick's power. We talked, certainly. But often we could just sit in perfect silence and be open with each other. We didn't need to say anything. Sometimes I thought of her as a particularly strong wireless signal, tuned only to me. All I had to do was match her frequency, and we could just stay like that, in perfect discourse, without saying a word to each other. Barely even looking at each other.

Kevin, my stepfather, had never really understood our connection. My mother loved him, and he knew that. She wasn't a miser with her feelings. She let him know that he was cared for in all sorts of ways. But I was her daughter. I'd grown inside of her; we shared mitochondrial DNA. Her love was imprinted on every one of my cells.

And yet, sometimes I felt that I knew very little about her. Sometimes she seemed like the most mysterious person in the world to me. Tonight was definitely one of those times. She was sitting across the table from me, smiling, dabbing at the corner of her mouth with a cloth napkin, and I suddenly felt as if I were looking at a stranger.

Who was this woman? When had she found the time to cultivate friendships in the Mayan Riviera? And how had she managed to lie to me for so many years, pretending not to know that I was mage-born when *she* was the one who'd initiated my training with the CORE? What else had she lied about? Lately, that question kept chasing itself through my brain whenever I talked to her. The mistrust was driving us further apart, and I didn't know what to do about it.

"Honey?"

I blinked. "Sorry. Did I space out?"

"A little. Would you like some dessert?"

"I'm pretty full."

"Are you sure? It's pumpkin pie with homemade whipped cream."

I stared at her. "You made a pie?"

"Yes. I do that sometimes, remember? Twice a year."

"But when—I mean—" I felt like I was losing my mind. "We don't have pie crust. Not even the frozen Tenderflake kind. Did you buy groceries?"

"Some. I asked Derrick what you needed."

"Oh, God. He didn't tell you to buy pumpernickel bread, did he? He just wants the whole loaf to himself."

"No. I just got a few essentials. Now. Pie? Yes."

Having answered her own question, she stood up and walked to the fridge. "The cream hasn't been in here for long. It should be fine. Your blender is hopeless, so I had to use that strange Moulinex that you keep in the cupboard. You really should get yourself a KitchenAid. They're starting to come down in price."

She had her back turned to me and was scooping out the whipped cream while she talked. "You know, I bought mine through the catalogue. I cashed in all of the points I'd been saving for years, and Kevin showed me how to order it online. It's amazing." She set down a perfect slice of pie in front of me.

"Sometimes it's nice to cash in. I've never liked saving. No matter what they tell you, spending is more fun. And I was even able to choose my color. It was easy. I just clicked on the beautiful green one, and two weeks later, it was in my kitchen."

I took a small bite of the pie. It tasted better than anything I'd ever made in my life. The cinnamon and the pumpkin spice and the buttery crust were Aristotelian, they were so perfect.

"Is it okay?" she asked. "I had to use the canned stuff. I didn't feel like gutting a pumpkin, especially in this kitchen."

"It's great." I kept swallowing. As long as there was constantly food in my mouth, I didn't have to worry about anything. Just the taste, and the repetition, and the comforting fullness. I could see why people ate themselves to death.

"Do you want some more?"

I pushed the empty plate away. "No, thank you."

"But it was good?"

"Yes. It was very good."

She smiled. "I always knew how to cook for you. I know what you like. Even when you were a baby, you were so picky. Nothing but carrots and squash. I was always afraid you were going to turn orange."

She took my plate before I could say anything. Actually, I didn't know what to say. Or maybe I just didn't know where to start.

"Let's go for a drive," she said.

I stared at her. "I just got home."

"Trust me. I have something to show you."

"This is getting weird again."

"Come on. It won't take all night."

I rose. "Where are we going?"

"It's close by. You'll see."

"So . . . you're not going to answer any of my questions?"

"Sometimes you just have to be patient."

"But I'm not. I never have been."

"No." She sighed. "Me, neither. But it's an acquired skill."

I looked at the clock again. "I guess we've got some time until Mia gets home. It won't hurt to take a quick drive."

"That's the spirit." She smiled.

Something was definitely up.

We took her car. She drove, and at first it felt strange to be a passenger when I was so used to driving other people around. But within a few minutes I had already slipped into that trancelike state that sometimes sneaks up on you, especially at night, when you find yourself being driven somewhere. There's something about the passivity of it, the stillness and the surrender to someone else's will. I watched my mother's hands on the steering wheel. I watched her take slow, careful turns, obeying every traffic light, even when there was nobody else on the road. I let myself drift.

As we passed Commercial Drive and Victoria, the neighborhood became more industrial. After a certain point, the quaint shops and restaurants disappeared, replaced by warehouses and factories. We didn't speak. The heater in the car was making me slightly groggy. I closed my eyes.

When I opened them again, we were parking. I looked out the window. I could barely make out anything in the dark.

"Where are we?"

"Someplace where no one will bother us."

"Mom, this is creepy."

"Don't worry. Just follow me."

"You're going to leave the car here?"

"It'll be fine."

We got out and locked the doors. I shivered.

"This looks like a construction site."

"It is."

I blinked. "Why are we here?"

"I told you. I have something to show you."

With that, she started walking. I had no choice but to follow her. The street was dark and dead-ended at a chain-link fence. As I watched in amazement, my mother reached into her purse and withdrew her athame. I recognized its pearl hilt. She touched the tip of the blade to the lock.

"Careful," she said. "There are pointy bits on the fence. You don't want to tear your jacket."

"This is breaking and entering."

"Nobody cares, dear."

She stepped through the narrow opening in the fence. I followed her, drawing my own athame from its boot-sheath. We must have looked like a crazy couple, mother and daughter, both with matching knives.

There were steel girders, rebar, and chunks of concrete everywhere, along with the partial foundations of an unfinished building. It resembled a kind of skeleton divided into dirt-filled chambers, dark, damp, and still. My mother didn't seem concerned by any of the chaos around her. She just kept walking, right into the middle of the site, which was taken up by a mound of gravel. She stopped at the base of the mound, turned, and then inclined her head slightly.

"This is as good a place as any for a duel," she said.

"A duel? What are you talking about?"

Her athame suddenly flared blue, illuminating the sharp angles of the industrial park. I hadn't even felt her draw any power.

"Can you hold this for a minute? I need both hands."

Gingerly, I took her athame, which was still glowing. The last time I'd held it, I was fighting with the Iblis. That had been two years ago, but it still felt natural in my hand.

She drew a slim wooden case out of her purse. There was some brass etching on the top, but I couldn't read it, not even with the light from the dagger. She flipped open the case and removed its contents, something slender and dark.

"This is for you," my mother said. "It was hidden

for nearly fifteen years. But you're ready for it now. It's time."

I stepped closer. I realized that she was holding another athame. Its hilt was braided in silver, and the guard was an elegant U shape, carved into the likeness of enwrapped vines. I stared at it. She was right. I hadn't seen the blade in fifteen years. But I remembered it.

"This was Meredith's," I breathed.

"It's yours now." She took back her own athame from me, handing me Meredith's as she did so. It felt heavy in my left hand.

"This was why you went to Tulum?"

"Yes. When she died, I inherited most of her possessions. I left them with some friends. Two weeks ago, I had a dream about her. I booked a flight that morning."

"Kevin thinks you went on a cruise."

"I brought him back a T-shirt and a necklace. He's happy."

"Why are you giving this to me now?"

"Because you need it to complete your training. There was a lot that Meredith wanted to teach you. Now it's up to me."

I shook my head. "She's been dead for fifteen years. What am I supposed to do with this?"

"It's easier to feel than it is to understand. Watch me."

She held out her athame. I felt a slow, dark current of power, rising like mist between us. The dagger in her hand began to shimmer. It became liquid. She held it with both hands. Then, carefully, she moved her hands in opposite directions. The liquid divided, still rippling, as if driven by an unseen current. Now she was holding two daggers. I felt her concentrate again, and the blades solidified. They were both exact copies of each other. I couldn't tell which was the original.

"I think I saw her do that once," I breathed. "Meredith, I mean."

"Yes. She's the one who taught me." She held the blades comfortably. "It's not the same as having two real ones, of course. But it works in a pinch."

"How long will they stay like that?"

"Until I lose my concentration. I haven't done this in a while, so you'll have to forgive me. "

"I don't understand what you're trying to teach me."

"The most valuable lesson that my mother taught me." She leveled both of the blades, assuming a combative stance. "To stay alive."

I stared at her. "You know something about this case, don't you? The Ptah'li, the Ferid, the Kentauroi—you know something that you're not telling me."

"That's part of being a mother. Now. Are you ready?"

"For what—"

Suddenly she was in front of me. Her hands moved so fast that they were nearly a blur. One of the knives rushed toward my face, while the other slashed downward at my midsection. I stumbled backward, bringing up both athames in a clumsy defense.

"The CORE only teaches you to fight with a single weapon," she said, advancing upon me again. "Unless you count guns, which are basically useless. But there's an art to fighting with two athames in tandem. If you can master it, you'll always have an advantage in combat."

"Mom, you're freaking me out."

"Get over it, dear. You have to defend yourself."

She slashed at me again with both blades. I caught the guard of her right blade with my own athame. I used Meredith's athame to deflect her second blade, and the two weapons hissed as they met each other.

"Good." She took a step back. "You're learning. The trick is to move both blades at the same time, as if you were using a single weapon. You'll get faster as you practice, but for now, we need to work on your balance."

"What's wrong with my balance?"

She lunged. I parried both of her strikes with some difficulty.

Then she kicked me in the stomach.

It wasn't a hard blow, but it was enough to send me scrambling backward. I nearly fell, but managed to recover myself.

"That was dirty."

"Yes. It's also possible to do what I just did without moving any part of your body. You can channel force directly through the blades."

"Like kinetic energy?"

"Exactly. Why don't you try it?"

"I don't want to hurt you."

"I gave birth to you. I doubt you can hurt me any more than you did when you came out breach."

"All right, then."

I lunged at her. She brought up both of her blades in defense, and when our weapons touched, I channeled a spike of materia from the ground. It made my teeth chatter, but I let it flow through me, out of my fingertips, into the tempered steel of the twin blades. The air between us sang. Then the power struck out.

She was expecting it, so she didn't stumble. But it still pushed her backward. She bent her knees, making a small sound.

"Are you okay?"

"Of course. I'm just not as young as I used to be."

"Should we stop?"

She glanced at her watch. "We've got at least another half hour until Mia gets home. That should give me enough time to show you some crossover lunges. Perhaps even a *coulé*."

I smiled. "I'm game."

"Good." She raised both of her blades. "Ready?"

"I think so."

"All right. Come at me again."

We continued to fight, our weapons ringing out against the silence of the empty lot, smiling as we struck at each other.

13

"Hey. I was hoping to run into you." I handed Cindée a coffee. "Here. I got an extra mocha for Derrick, but then he wimped out and decided he wanted to have tea. So I mocked him as I was getting out of the car, but now—free mocha for you."

I'd just been passing the break room when I saw her, closing up a Tupperware container of something she'd heated in the microwave.

"That's sweet! Thanks. And I'll take it."

I sat down on the couch, struggling out of my jacket. "Is your break over? I'm not quite ready to look at any data, at least not for another minute or so."

"I've still got another five." She sipped her coffee. "Mmm. Thanks again. This is really going to push me through the next four hours."

"How's the fragment analysis going?"

"It's easier to show you than tell you, at this point."

"Yeah, that's usually the case."

"Let's not run over to Trace just yet, though." She shifted position. "I've eaten too much weird food today. I feel bloated."

"I know that feeling. My stomach's already angry at me. And who can blame it? Last night, I had chips and salsa before going to bed."

"That actually sounds pretty good."

"I had to floss after. But I got this new flossing thing."

"Oh, the plastic one, with the handle?"

"Yes! It's incredible. It's like I can feel myself actually becoming a slightly more responsible person each time I use it."

"I know exactly what you mean."

We were silent for a beat. My phone buzzed. I looked down.

"It's Mia," I said. "She and Patrick want to borrow the car."

"Let 'em. From what you tell me, Mia's like an anchorite or something, always studying and saving herself for Berkeley. Let her have some fun."

I texted back my assent. "Done. See? I can make decisions."

"You seem to be doing fine. I saw both of them yesterday, and it's clear that they idolize you and Derrick."

I chuckled. "Maybe you mean it in the sense of Roman house idols—the kind of statues you could break or throw in the closet. If anything, Patrick and Mia are hypersensitive to all of our tiniest flaws. They're like these two little bitchy microscopes."

"I grew up with three sisters. No need to explain it." Cindée looked at her watch. "Okay, break's over. Follow me, and I'll show you something that's pretty much going to blow your mind."

"It's too early to get fully blown. And I mean that with all due respect."

Cindée led me to the trace lab. The fragments had been pieced together and were displayed on a metal tray. About half of the shape was missing, but the piece that remained looked almost like a small cabinet, or even a reliquary of some kind. The inside was hollow and obviously meant to contain something.

"This is amazing." I peered closer. "What are these little grooves?"

"I think they might be hinges. For a small door to swing open. If there was a latch, it's been lost. But the design seems to suggest a kind of semi-organic vessel."

"Any idea what might have been kept inside?"

"None at all. But we've found a residue on the inside. Have a look."

I looked through the eyepiece of the scanning electron microscope. Blue granules of powder appeared like frozen limestone cliffs under the lens. I could also see irregular clumps of a lighter material, clinging to the substrate in places. Those patches were probably the result of whatever acid had been applied during the wet powder suspension.

"What's in it?" I asked, rising from the microscope.

"High levels of nitrocellulose."

"As in gunpowder?"

"Yes. But also like nitrate film."

"Huh. That makes very little sense. A fine blue powder left over that's full of nitrates, and it's sticking to the inside of—what, exactly?"

"We're cautiously describing it as a vessel."

"Great." I looked at the vessel. "What are we doing with the powder?"

"Various atomic absorption tests. But I also had a bit of a maverick idea."

"I'm listening."

"Well, the nitrates could be acting as a cellular medium for all sorts of different energies. I thought we could apply some alternating materia currents to it, like we might do if we were electrifying a gel strip for an STR test."

"Are you trying to create Frankenstein's monster out of blue dust?"

"Possibly."

"I can ask Ru about it. I doubt he'll be forthcoming, though. And I'm not even sure how I'd begin the conversation. *Hey, we found what might be a broken birdcage, with some dust in it. Anything like that ring a bell?*"

"Maybe phrase it a bit differently."

My phone started ringing.

"Sorry. It's Mia. But good work on the powder, Cindée."

"Thanks. Be sure to mention it to Selena when she's

signing my overtime authorization. Which needs to be in by *six* today."

"Gotcha! I'll tell her!" I left the trace lab. "Mia? What's up?"

"Can I spend twenty dollars?"

"Well, you do have your own bank account. Would there be anything *in* said bank account at the moment?"

"Yes. But if I spend twenty tonight, I won't have enough money for coffee tomorrow, and I need coffee to stay awake. So, it's a bit of a crisis."

"Basically, you're asking me for money."

"If you want to put it that way. Yes."

"Where are you?"

"At the *daegred*."

I blinked. "At the *daegred*. You're hanging out with vampires."

"It's a safe house. Besides, Patrick's with me. And Modred."

"Oh really. How's Modred?"

"He's teaching me how to smell stuff. I know I made fun of Patrick for doing it, but it's actually kind of cool."

I swore inwardly. "Don't move. I'm coming to get you."

"No, don't worry; I'm having a nice time."

"I'm picking you up, and we're going to Stanley Park."

"Are you serious?"

"I'm putting on my coat as we speak."

"God. You suck."

She hung up.

I sighed, heading for the door. It wasn't that I didn't trust Modred. And Patrick wasn't exactly a bad influence. He did seem to watch out for her, most of the time. But the last thing I needed was a room full of emo vampires convincing Mia that she needed to get further in touch with her dark legacy.

Other than Derrick, who now appeared to be damaged, Mia was the last un-screwed-up thing in my life. She wasn't about to transition to vampirism. She'd stay mortal if I had to chain her up.

Mia stared fixedly out the window as we crossed the Lion's Gate Bridge on our way to Stanley Park. She'd been silent the whole drive here. I knew that she was fuming on the inside, but I didn't have time to chat about it now. I guess I could have handled her visit to Patrick's court in a sweeter, less hostile way. After all, the *daegred*, an Anglo-Saxon word for "safe house," was really no more than a vampire community center. If Mia was in danger of anything there, it was the possibility of getting bored to death by teenaged boys talking about computers.

I'm not saying it was rational, but I needed to know where she was, if only for the next twenty minutes. I needed to feel like a parent, even if I had to force the issue and make us both feel bad about it. Selfishness, it seemed, didn't magically vaporize upon inheriting a guardianship. I parked at the foot of the bridge, in the lot I knew was free. This happened to be where I'd parked when I got attacked by a necromancer wearing a Vorpal gauntlet. Even if I was thumbing my nose at fortune, it seemed worth it for free parking, especially in this neighborhood, where every acre of land was saturated with old money.

I switched off the ignition.

My eyes hurt from driving at dusk. A hazy porosity lay over the whole landscape. I thought it would probably rain, and was already cursing the fact that I'd driven here in my Birkenstocks. They always smelled funky after they got wet. Unless it was just my feet. The thought was mildly depressing.

"Nobody was raping me," Mia said.

"Well, that's good to know."

"I wasn't in any danger." She kept staring out the window. "*Both* Patrick and Modred were there. Patrick's my brother, and Mo has no interest in me. I have no idea what kind of person he likes to feed from, actually."

"I don't know what should be more distressing—the thought of someone feeding on you, or the fact that you've started calling a vampire Mo."

"Patrick started it. We'd never call him that to his face."

"I would like to see his expression if it happened, though."

She laughed. "He'd be like, *Your modern slang confuses me*, and then I'd have to watch him play with his lip piercing for, like, the next thirty seconds."

We both got out of the car. I set the alarm. "I know you can handle yourself," I said. "I'm not daft. It just makes me nervous."

"Why? Because they're vampires? Or because I'm one?"

"You're not a vampire."

"I was infected with the virus."

"Yes, but it's always been dormant. And you're on medication that regulates your viral load, keeps you asymptomatic."

"What if I don't want to be asymptomatic anymore?"

I stopped walking. I could feel a sigh building within me, but I pushed it down. I turned and looked at her.

"You're old enough to decide how you want to live your life. If you want to become a vampire, I can't do anything to stop you. But if you have one scrap of respect for me as a mother figure, even a half-assed one, then you'll listen to me when I say—*don't*. It'll solve nothing and destroy everything."

"How can you be so sure?"

"I don't know—maybe because your parents were killed by a vampire? Maybe because I watched a vampire break my mentor's neck with a chain when I was your age? Or maybe because the *same* vampire who killed your parents just tried to kill you, less than a year ago? Personally, I think those are enough reasons."

"Tess. Come on." She glared at me. "You're a hypocrite. You're dating a guy who draws his power from corpses."

"Vampires and necromancers are not the same thing."

"Why? Necromancers are hotter?"

"This conversation is going nowhere."

"My brother's a vampire. It wasn't his choice to get

turned, either, but it was done to him. It's made him who he is, and that's nothing to be ashamed of, because there's no shame inside of him. He's happy, Tess. And he's a vampire. You can't do his laundry for him, pick up after him, treat him like your kid, and then say that all of his friends are bloodsucking half-lifes."

"Your path isn't going to be the same as his." I put my hands on her shoulders. She tensed, but didn't throw them off. "Patrick has the ability to live in sunlight. He can't spend too long outdoors, but he can manage it for long enough to live a human life. If you were turned, you'd start smoldering the minute you walked outside."

She shook her head. "That's not totally true. Modred says there are, like, these artifacts that can protect a vampire from sun poisoning."

"That's a vampire urban legend. There are no artifacts that will protect a vampire from dying by sunlight. And it's not like in *Buffy*. They burn for a long time before they actually die. It's revolting. And, I imagine, excruciating, as it happens to you."

"This is your scared-straight speech?"

"Yeah. How am I doing?"

"Pretty good, actually." She laughed. "You do make some valid points."

"So we can agree to disagree about this for a while?"

"I guess it would be more efficient to drop it," she said. "At least for now." Some of the tension had left her body. "But can we have a bit less vampire hating?"

"Agreed. We can even get a nice bumper sticker for the car."

We kept walking, following the line of trees, until

we came to the darkest thicket, where the Seneschal lived. I mean, he didn't live in a thicket, per se. He lived in a small underground condo whose entrance was disguised by brambles.

"Why are we talking to the bird-guy again?"

"Because he may know something about what we found buried at the scene."

"Patrick told me he's like a Skeksi."

"Do not say that to him." I knocked on the door, whose outline I could barely distinguish from thorns. "Be polite."

The door opened, but the entryway was vacant. I shrugged and walked in. The passage broadened, until we were standing in a well-lit den. The walls of the chamber were largely organic, but full of alcoves that, in their turn, were full of random things. Some of the things I recognized instantly as dangerous, while others were literally pieces of junk. The ones that worried me were the only half-broken pieces that were still quite powerful. I hoped that he kept a good inventory.

The Seneschal sat at a desk, which was new. He turned around in his Kirk-style chair. His eyes still resembled the blue of an acetylene torch.

"Door's automatic now," he said. "Easier."

"What's with the desk?"

"Writing memoir."

I tried to keep my expression neutral. "That sounds fascinating. What language are you writing it in?"

"Several."

"Good times. Well, we just came with a quick question for you. Something involving what you might call a broken treasure."

The Seneschal gestured for me to come closer. "Let me see. Not everything is treasure, you know. Some things only look."

"Why am I here, exactly?" Mia asked. "Not that here isn't interesting. I just feel like a third wheel."

"You're here so I can keep an eye on you."

"Really? After that whole *You're a capable woman* speech?"

"I suck. You did say it yourself."

"Deeply." She began to walk around the Seneschal's den. "This stuff is weird and interesting, though."

"Is sold if she breaks," he whispered to me.

I nodded. "Right. Here's a reproduction of something that we found buried not far from here. It seems to be for holding something. Have you ever come across anything like this before?"

I showed him a digital photo of the broken container. He stared at it for a few seconds, then handed me back the picture.

"Don't need."

"I'm not asking if you need it. I'm asking if you've ever seen one before."

He nodded. "Once. Was useless, though. Broken, like yours."

"What was it meant to hold?"

"Memories."

I blinked. "Can you be more specific?"

"For memories," he repeated. "Don't usually see them."

"Why not?"

The Seneschal looked at me as if I were profoundly stupid. "Because they are on the inside of the body. That is where they reside." He shrugged. "In general. But an accident might produce one like yours."

"You mean—" I frowned. "We're looking at some-one's organ?"

"Is more container," he said. "But yes."

"Do you know what species it might be found in?"

The Seneschal looked distant. Then he frowned. "I forget."

I sighed. "Okay. Well, if you remember, you know how to reach us."

He nodded. "Sure. You want something to take?"

"What—you mean, like a present?"

"Yeah, yeah." He gestured at the walls filled with alcoves. "Take something. But don't let the girl take the box that she's holding right now."

I ran over to Mia, who was fiddling with a small metal cube.

"Hey, there. Let's just put that back on the shelf."

"I'm not simple, Tess. I won't make anything ex-plode."

"Those are everyone's famous last words in my business. You can browse with me, though. The Sen-eschal said we could take something with us."

"Cool. Like at the dentist."

"This might be a bigger payoff than mint floss, though."

We scanned the nooks and crannies filled with bizarre things, most of them in states of disrepair or shaky metamorphosis. We avoided the reptile shelf altogether. Finally, Mia spied what looked like a small brass teapot.

"What's that?"

"I have no idea."

"I kind of like it."

"All right. That's good enough for me."

"Wait, though. You must know what some of this stuff does. Isn't there something much cooler than this teapot?"

"Probably. But this is what you want. So it's what I want."

She looked at me. "God, you're so lame sometimes." But she was smiling. She handed me the teapot, which I put in my purse.

"What should we have for supper?"

"I was thinking tacos."

She made a face. "Don't let Derrick toast the shells. Make sure Miles does it. He toasts them so perfectly."

"I'm sorry; are you seriously asking me to cause a full-scale tempest in the kitchen? I'll do no such thing."

"Aww. But they're still good when Derrick toasts them."

"He'll be happy to hear that."

We walked back across the parking lot. The car was exactly where I'd left it, which, although small reassurance, was still better than nothing. We got in, and I started the engine. I yawned.

"I'll drive, if you're too tired," Mia said.

"You do a terrible job of hiding your eagerness."

"Well?"

I hesitated. Then I handed her the keys. "I guess if I can trust you with vampires, I have to trust you behind the wheel."

"You totally can. I swear."

"Uh-huh." I relinquished the driver's seat. "But if we have to call roadside assistance, you're definitely not getting that twenty bucks."

14

It was Selena's idea to take Ru for lunch. The thought of him being in such close proximity to Basuram made her nervous. Plus, we'd let slip that there were actually more varieties of hot chocolate than could be found in the vending machine, and he was eager to try something new.

"I want the creamed whip," he'd told me.

"Whipped cream."

"Yes. That. Selena says it makes the drink better."

"It actually makes life better."

We settled on Caffè Artigiano, on Smithe Street, which stood in the shadow of the art gallery. Street kids gathered on the steps of the art gallery, smoking pot, laughing, and letting their dogs drink water from plastic thermos cups. At this time of day, Artigiano, and the sort of blissed-out yet caffeinated brusqueness of the environment, increased the turnover of customers. If anyone was going to try something in daylight, they'd have to think twice about engaging so many random bystanders, since foot traffic from Robson always choked up side streets like this one. The lab was still close enough to be reassuring.

Really, we all just wanted to stretch our legs. Ru spent most of his time watching TV in a nice but empty room. Selena was cramped in her office, and I kept finding myself squashed behind the wheel of a car, shuttling someone somewhere. I dreamt about each of the routes, remapping them, as I found myself endlessly drawn back to the lab and everything it meant. Everything that CORE meant, or would mean. Because, not for the first time in my life, I was wondering if I belonged there.

"How many languages are there in your world?" Ru asked.

"Over six thousand," Selena replied. "Lots of dead or dying ones, too. Plus, there's machine languages, and other sign systems."

"What you do with your powers—is that like a language?"

"It's more of a chemical reaction, as far as we've ever been able to tell."

"But you've developed ways of communicating with the power. You can make it work for you. That seems like a language." He looked around the café. "Most people here are speaking the same dialect."

"The city's predominantly English-speaking," I said, "with a significant infusion of Mandarin and Cantonese. Also French, Italian, and Spanish."

"English—is that what the language we're speaking is actually called?" Ru laughed. "On Ptah'l, we learned it as High and Low Great British."

"That's bizarre."

"It makes a lot of sense when it's divided that way. Your sarcasm is difficult, as well as your words with humorous adjacent meanings."

"Puns?"

"Yes. They are hard sometimes. We call everything like that Low Great British, so it's easier to memorize the irregular words."

I'd been waiting for the right moment to ask Ru about the vessel. I wasn't sure how to bring it up. I was pretty much relying on Selena to mention it, but part of me didn't want her to. I just wanted us all to have hot chocolate in peace.

Ru gestured to the people sitting around us. "It's so easy to fool them. I don't even have to maintain the shift in waveform that modifies my appearance. Nobody here notices anyone but themselves."

"It's part of our charm," I said.

"But why haven't they figured out that you exist? Your lab and your machines that analyze blood from demons. It seems so obvious."

"Because," Selena said, "some of us are them, and some of them are us. A lot of it has to do with money, unfortunately."

"I like my chocolate, though. I think this is the best one I've had yet."

"It certainly cost the most. But the barista did make

a maple leaf out of foam, and you don't see that just anywhere."

"Ru," I said, hating myself. "We discovered something buried. It was close to where we found you."

He looked at me. "What was it?"

"We think it's a container. Part of it's missing, but we found a blue powder inside, which we're analyzing."

"It was on my hands."

Selena looked at him. "What was on your hands?"

"Blue. I noticed it, just before I lost consciousness. Something blue was on my hands. But when I woke up, it was gone."

"Dr. Rashid had already washed you," I said. "Standard procedure in a morgue. It would have been rinsed away, along with any other trace."

Ru was silent for a moment. Then: "What does the container look like?"

We'd thought about showing him the photo. But if it really was a kind of ossified organ, something that belonged inside another demon's body, it seemed a bit obscene to produce a photo of viscera while we were having coffee. The consensus was that it would be easier on everyone to just describe it to him.

"It's this big." I measured about four inches with my hands. "It seems to be made of bone, but it's tensile. And we found blue powder inside with a high nitrocellulose content, which is a chemical that can be quite dangerous if handled improperly."

"Nitrocellulose," he murmured. "An Aikon."

"A what?"

His voice had changed. Quiet as it was, I could feel the anxiety creeping in as he spoke. "The Aikon is where we keep our life-text," he said. "It's an organ, below the heart. My grandsire's Aikon had an infection, and he nearly died. But they managed to replace it with a new one."

"Is it a recording of your life?" Selena asked.

"Not exactly. The word translates as 'kitchen.' It's our kitchen, where all of our memories are gathered. It's where we spend most of our time."

"How does it hold your memories?"

Again, he looked uncomfortable. It must have been like answering questions about some stranger's autopsied heart. "What you call 'powder' has viscosity during life. The memories swim in fluid. When we die, the medium dries up, like the rest of us."

"You remembered having blue on your fingers," Selena said. "Is there some way that you might have come in contact with this . . . Aikon?"

"I don't remember."

"Do you remember touching something? Carrying something, maybe?"

"You said it was buried. Do you think I buried it?"

Selena shook her head. "Not as yet. It was close to the surface, though, and we didn't find any implements for digging. We're still trying to figure out exactly how the debris got there."

"Why would I bury someone's Aikon? Would you bury a lung?"

"Possibly. Under extenuating circumstances."

"Where do the memories go?" I asked. "When we

die, our brains collapse, and everything that we were leaves us in a burst of electrical synapses. Do your memories just dry up and evaporate?"

"Ideally, there's someone with you when you die," Ru said. "They salvage the individual Aikon, and its serum can be added to the Uraikon. The family Aikon."

"So your relatives get to watch your memories?"

He laughed. "It's not a projection, like what you call TV. The serum is a liquid medium for thousands of intermingling memories. When you're with the Uraikon, you can see glimpses of past lives. But you can't pick and choose. I got to relive several embarrassing memories from a great-cousin."

"The organic technology might be something that we can duplicate," Selena said. "One of our technicians is working on passing alternating currents through the desiccated blue medium, in an attempt to unlock whatever may be recorded on it."

"Did you submit her overtime authorization?"

She gave me an odd look. "I did, thank you very much."

"You have to destroy it," Ru said.

We both looked at him.

"Destroy what?" Selena asked.

"The medium. It's the only way to release the memories. You can't duplicate the conditions found within the Aikon. But if you pass negative energy through the powder, you'll release what's left of the recording."

"How do you know that?"

"The Ferid learned how to do it." He stared at the

table. "They would kill us, then watch our lives from the beginning. Looking for secrets."

I parked across the street from the *daegred,* which seemed like any other apartment block in this area. The door had a small vampiric glyph, but it was in the top corner, obscured by wear, paint, and dust. You had to know precisely where to look. I rang the buzzer. A few seconds later, the door opened, and a large vampire appeared. She looked down at me.

"Yes? What do you need?"

"I'm here to see Patrick."

"What's your name?"

"Tess Corday."

"Oh. You can come in." She stepped aside. "He's upstairs."

"Thanks."

A few young vampires were hanging out in the main room, reading or just talking. There was only one computer, and they had to sign a log when they used it. Even immortals had to relinquish the PC when their ten minutes were up.

I went upstairs. Patrick and Modred were in the office. When they saw me, they both stopped talking.

"Agent Corday." Modred inclined his head. "How are you?"

"Okay. Mind if I talk to Patrick for a second?"

"Of course." He looked at the Magnate. "We'll continue our discussion when the timing is more agreeable."

He left.

"What are you two scheming?"

"Not scheming. More like urban planning."

"Care to elaborate?"

"I really can't."

I shrugged. "Understood. No fraternizing."

"We're not really fraternizing, Tess. I live in your house."

"It's your house, too."

"I know. I just mean—I trust you. But there are some things we can't talk about with nonvampires. Those are the rules."

"I get it. I didn't come to pump you for information. I really just wanted to see how things were going with you."

"Fine, I guess."

"How's life as Magnate? It must be stressful."

He frowned. "Tess, we could have talked about this at home. Why would you come all the way here just to shoot the breeze with me?"

I sat down. "I made a promise to Mia."

"What sort of promise?"

"To stop being so antivampire."

"You're not antivampire. You live with a vampire."

"I know. But lately, she's been curious about that part of her. The vampirism that we're suppressing with drugs. And I don't want her to open that door, but I also understand that I don't have a choice. I can't force her to take the medication. If she wants to transition, I won't be able to stop her."

"No. You won't."

"What would you do? If you were me."

"If I was Mia's mom?" He sighed. "Probably lock her up."

"I know, right? That's always my first impulse. But teenagers don't respond well to enforced confinement."

"If she does decide that vampire unlife is for her," Patrick said, "I can help her through the change. But that's all. She has to make the choice."

"I don't want her to change, though."

He smiled. "Yeah. Me, neither. I love her the way she is."

"Do you have any idea what she might do?"

Patrick shook his head. "You live with her. She's a tough fortune cookie to read. I've been watching her pretty closely, but for now, I think she's on the fence."

"Split evenly, or sort of listing to one side of the fence?"

"Is 'listing' a verb?"

"Yeah. It's a nautical term."

"Okay. Well, at this point, I think she's 'listing' toward not doing anything. She hasn't figured out who she wants to be yet."

"That's a relief."

"But it could change. She could change, without any warning." He met my gaze. "Look. I've spent a lot of time with her over the past few weeks. As far as I can tell, she's been taking her shots. I've never seen her miss a dose."

I looked at him. "It was scary for you, right? I mean, waking up in a strange place, not knowing how you got there. And you must have been hungry."

"I was fed intravenously."

"Oh. Well—it still must have been traumatic."

He nodded slowly. "I do remember my old life. Bits and pieces of it. They say the memories come back as you get older. Right now, I can only see flashes. I don't want Mia to have to know what that feels like. But she's also different, right? She has the potential to channel materia, and that could change everything. I have no idea what it would feel like for her to transition."

"Maybe she'll be a brave new vampire."

"Maybe she'll retain her memories. It's different for everyone. Some of us are turned more painfully than others."

I sighed. "I do trust her."

"But you also don't. Or you can't. I don't think you'd totally be a parent if you weren't somehow always worried about us."

"I'm not always worried. I'd just like to know what both of you are up to. It would be nice to have some kind of permanent audio stream."

"Is this a family, or a wiretap?"

I sighed. "The CORE may very well have bugged our phones a long time ago. So it could be a bit of both."

15

When I was about six or seven, I used to watch *Jem and the Holograms*, which featured a beautiful female protagonist with dual lives. By day, she ran the Starlight Orphanage, taking in misfit children and endangered runaways. But secretly, she was also a dynamic performer, and she could switch between these roles simply by tweaking a set of magic earrings. She had also, at some point, inherited a holographic computer named Synergy who lived in the basement of her mansion, but even at seven, I felt that this plot element was never adequately explained.

I had brief love affairs with other cartoons. On occasion, I would imagine what it might be like to step into the shoes of other dramatic female characters: Evil-Lyn from *Masters of the Universe*, Serena from *Sailor Moon*, and even that kid from *Wildfire* who rode the horse and had the magic amulet. But I really and sincerely wanted to be Jem. It wasn't that I had any interest in leading a band. I just wanted her power. The ability to step from one life into the next, seamlessly, day after day.

It also didn't hurt that she had an attractive blue-haired boyfriend. And I'll admit, I had more than a few fantasies about what I might do if I ever got a few minutes alone with Rio. But mostly, I was obsessed with the idea of a secret identity.

It didn't take long, however, to learn some critical lessons. Jem was independently wealthy. Serena was an alien princess. Evil-Lyn was part of an oppressive republic, and, as her name suggested, she was pretty evil. None of these women resembled me in any way. It didn't seem as if a blazing magical comet was going to visit my suburban neighborhood anytime soon. Unless I could get my hands on either a cosmic key or a moon prism, I was out of luck in terms of becoming a heroine.

But barely five years later, I woke up to find that something had changed. It didn't seem monumental. I hadn't grown horns or mastered the art of levitation. But I felt different, somehow. Later that day, when I was walking home from school, I came across a group of boys who were beating on a much smaller kid. I thought I could intervene, that maybe they'd listen to me. I had no idea why. Feminine mystique? At the very least, I figured they'd be afraid to hit me.

But I was wrong. One of them did hit me. At least he tried to. But before his fist connected with my body, I felt a rush of power, as if someone had plugged me into an unseen electrical current. I opened myself wide to something, and it swept through me, not frightening or angry, but strangely familiar.

That was the first time I channeled materia.

A few months later, my best friend, Eve, died in a fire. My powers weren't enough to save her. I wasn't strong or fast enough. It all seemed so cruelly unlike the cartoons I'd grown up watching. There was no magic earring to tweak. Eve burned to death, scared and alone, and no aliens or demons or talking cats arrived on the scene to rescue her. I saw her still, silent form in the hospital, blackened beyond recognition. That was when I learned my first lesson about real power.

It doesn't work for you. It doesn't listen to you. It just explodes, like a deadly solar flare, and everyone and everything that it touches is changed forever.

Tonight, I had to visit Mr. Corvid, the pureblood drug pusher who claimed to know my father. He also claimed to be old enough to have witnessed the dawn of the Celts, but demons were notorious braggarts. I was just hoping to return home in time to watch a few reruns of *American Dad* with Derrick. Miles was working late, which meant that I didn't have to spend the rest of the night watching them cuddle and make stupid eyes at each other.

I had to wait for Mia to go to sleep before I left. Otherwise, she'd ask too many questions about where I was going so close to midnight. Patrick was out late for the second night in a row, and as much as I wanted to lecture him, I didn't have the energy. I really had no idea what sort of effort was required to be a vampire Magnate. Maybe he also had late-night study sessions. Lucian had recently put it in perspective for me. *Just be thankful he hasn't eaten any of us yet.*

Meredith's athame was still in my purse. I had no idea what to do with it, but for some reason, I didn't want to set it down. I definitely felt a connection to it, but I still wasn't convinced that it belonged to me. In all the time that I'd known Meredith, I'd never seen it far from her grasp. It had always been an extension of her body, and now I felt like an interloper trying to hold it.

I sent Lucian a text as I was starting the car. *Be ready in 5.* Sometimes he took as long as I did in the bathroom.

It wasn't that I was afraid to meet with Corvid alone. I'd met with him before, and aside from the usual quea-siness of being in the same room with a centuries-old killer, I'd never felt that my life was in immediate dan-ger. I mostly just wanted the company. Not to mention the fact that having a necromancer standing behind you lent a certain emphasis to your arguments. Both Corvid and Lucian, despite their genealogical differ-ences, knew a lot about death, entropy, and annihila-tion. They may as well have been old college buddies.

My phone buzzed. It wasn't Lucian, but rather my mother, asking if Patrick and Mia had enjoyed the din-ner that she'd made.

Given Vancouver's recent ban on cell-phone use in cars without a hands-free headset device, I didn't want to get caught texting and driving. Plus, she should have been in bed. Weren't respectable mothers asleep by midnight, or at the very least reading a Rosemary Rogers book under the covers? They certainly weren't supposed to be having knife fights with their daughters.

By the time I got to Yaletown, Lucian was waiting outside. It was a mild night, even by West Coast standards, so he was wearing a black vinyl jacket over a chocolate brown shirt that matched his eyes. He grinned as I pulled up to the curb. He'd even shaved, and his face had a healthy glow to it. I couldn't remember what that felt like. If my face resembled anything these days, it was a mug shot.

He slipped into the passenger seat. "Good evening."

"Uh-huh." I started to pull away before he'd buckled his seat belt.

"Are you in a hurry?"

"Kind of. I don't want to spend the rest of my night entertaining a monster. I'd like to get in, get out, and be back home in time for cartoons."

"Ah. A stimulating night with Derrick, then?"

"You got it."

He was silent for a few seconds. Then he said: "You know, I like cartoons."

It took a lot of effort not to laugh. "I'm sorry, sweetheart. Are you jealous?"

"No. But it would be nice to be invited."

"I assumed that you might have more exciting things to do."

"But you're my favorite thing to do. And you're exciting."

"Not tonight. I'm putting on the bad jammies as soon as I get home. The ones with the baggy ass and the broken elastic."

"I like those ones."

"You're lying."

"Okay. They're not the best. But you love them, and the broken elastic does add a touch of class."

I chuckled. "That's me. Always a class act. You can stay the night if you want, but I can't promise anything exciting's going to happen. There's a good chance I'll fall asleep next to you while eating potato chips, though."

"Hot."

"I'm glad you think so."

"How's Derrick feeling?"

"Still kind of beat-up. He's improving, though, which also means that he's becoming annoying. He pretends that he can't do anything for himself, but when I'm not looking, he's making Bailey's milk shakes in the kitchen."

"Should he really be mixing alcohol with his pain medication?"

"He likes to live on the edge. Miles is a good nurse, though. He takes care of him without submitting to his bullshit."

"Yeah. They seem good together. How long's it been now? They've been together almost as long as we have, right?"

"That depends on how long you think we've been together."

He gave me an amused look. "How long do *you* think we've been together?"

"Well, if you count the time you showed up unannounced in my bedroom, it's been three years. But I did stab you, so it wasn't an ideal first date."

"I remember it being quite ideal, actually." He grinned. "I kissed you. Then you punched me in the face. Really hard."

"Yeah." I sighed. "Good times."

"I remember when I first saw you." He was still smiling. "You came to interview me at the club. You were scared, but you held your own. You looked me right in the eyes the whole time. I thought it was sexy."

"It was mostly adrenaline. I really was terrified."

"But you barely showed it."

"And you liked that."

"Yes. I did."

"Remember when I shot you?"

"Of course. I told you to."

I shook my head. "Occult relationships should come with a warning. *May cause sharp-force trauma*."

"That's what makes them fun." He put his hand on my knee. "Right?"

"I don't know about fun. But I'm not bored; I'll give you that."

We drove in silence like that for a while, his hand on my knee, my hand on the wheel. Eventually, my left hand found its way on top of his. It felt like closing a circuit. His touch was familiar, but it still made my insides hum. Even now, I was starting to think about things that had little to do with Mr. Corvid, or potato chips, or cartoons. Things you could only do after everyone else in the house had gone to sleep. Things that would possibly make you late for work in the morning.

"What was your favorite toy?" I asked as we turned onto Pacific.

"What? You mean, like—sexually?"

"No. Jesus. I mean when you were a little kid."

"Oh." He thought about it for a second. "Well, I did have a bear named Mr. Oso. My mom says that I took him everywhere, and I wouldn't let her wash him. I can't imagine how bad he must have smelled."

"I'll bet you were a cute kid."

"No. Lorenzo was the cute one. I had elephant ears."

Lucian almost never talked about his brother. I kept my eyes on the road, trying to appear as if I had no stake in the conversation.

In reality, I was dying to know more about him. Even after three years, I'd barely managed to assemble a skeleton of his life, and that was through piecing together random threads and mumbled anecdotes. I didn't know how old he was, where he'd been born, what his sign was. I didn't even know if he was a Canadian citizen.

"Lorenzo—was he born deaf? Or was it something that happened when he was young? I think Miles had rubella, or some kind of virus."

Lucian stared out the window. "Otosclerosis," he said. "It's a bone deformation. It's probably linked to rubella, though. He started to get terrible headaches when he was four or five. By the time he was seven, he had profound hearing loss."

"I'm sorry."

He shrugged. "It didn't keep us from communicating. I helped him learn sign language. He resisted it at first. He was angry and stubborn. But then I convinced him that we could have a secret language, just for us. It took our parents a lot longer to learn it, and they weren't nearly as fast."

Lucian chuckled. "Lorenzito and I would make fun of them, right to their faces, and they'd keep yelling at us with their hands, *Slower, slower*"—he made the sign for *slow*, putting one hand on top of the other and moving it slowly up his wrist, as if pulling up a shirtsleeve—"and we'd just laugh. They couldn't keep up with us."

"How did you learn ASL? Did you go to a special school?"

He made a face. "There weren't really a lot of schools like that around then, at least where we lived. We had a tutor. Her name was Pilar, but we called her *la vaca*. The cow. Because she was fat and mean."

"I'll bet she loved both of you."

"Yeah. We were little bastards. But in the end, she taught us pretty well." He shook his head. "Man. I haven't thought of *la vaca* in so long. She wore these hideous floral dresses. Each one was worse than the last. She wasn't deaf, but her sister was." He smiled. "Jalida. What a knockout. She was thirteen, and she used to come to our house to see Lorenzo. I caught them kissing in the backyard once. She taught him all the curse words in sign, and then he taught me."

We were almost at Corvid's building. I didn't want Lucian to stop talking, but I was worried that he'd notice if I suddenly took a detour. The light ahead of us turned yellow, and instead of running it, I slowed down like an obedient driver. We came to a stop at an empty intersection. The corporate superstructures and bank towers of the downtown core surrounded us, like planes of quartz, gleaming in the dark. The city was hibernating, but still very much alive.

"How long has it been?" I asked quietly.

Lucian looked at me, still leaning against the passenger-side window, one hand pressed against his temple. "Since when?"

"Since you saw *la vaca*, and Jalida, and Lorenzo?"

"Are you trying to ask me how old I am?"

"Yes. Is it such a difficult question?"

"Difficult? No." He looked away. "Just complicated."

"I'm a big girl, Lucian. And it's just a number. I can handle it."

He didn't say anything. He just breathed.

The light turned green.

Lucian gave me an expectant look.

"Street's empty," I said. "There's nobody listening. It's just you and me, and I'm not moving this car until you tell me."

"Tess."

I leaned back in the driver's seat. "I'm serious. It's been three years, and I've never pushed. But I think I deserve to know. It's not like I'm asking you to divulge all of your scary necromancer secrets. I just want to know your birthday."

He was silent for a while. The light turned yellow again, then red. The intersection remained empty. I could feel the steering wheel vibrating slightly under my hands. I sympathized with it. All that pent-up energy, and it was stuck here, in the dark, waiting. I often felt the same.

"June twenty-fourth," he said finally. "Nineteen twenty."

I didn't know what to say. I kept staring at the traffic light. Finally, a car appeared behind us. I pressed the accelerator, and we were moving again. I couldn't quite look at him. I wasn't sure why. It was only a number, right?

"I was born in Málaga," he continued. "Spain. I was sixteen years old when the civil war broke out. My parents moved us to Canada. We had an uncle who worked in Toronto, in a clothing store. I remember playing with Lorenzo in the back room, with all the piles of ugly shirts and slacks wrapped in plastic."

"I thought you said—" My hands tightened around the wheel. "I mean, once, you told me that all necromancers were stillborn babies. That they were taken to the hidden city right away. But you and Lorenzo grew up together."

He nodded. "Yes. I did say it was complicated, didn't I?"

"Come on. You're doing great so far. Don't stop now."

"But we've arrived."

He was right. Corvid's building was in view. I swore beneath my breath.

"We don't have to go in right away," I said.

He smiled. "Tess. You can't read the book of my life in one night. You have to be patient. It's not like we're on a deadline."

I sighed. "At least now I can buy you a proper birthday card."

"See? There you go." He kissed my cheek.

We locked the doors and crossed the parking lot. Corvid's building was one of the shining prefab towers that had gone up a few years ago, seemingly overnight. He owned the penthouse, and possibly several floors beneath it.

"Maybe I chose the wrong job," Lucian said. "I could be living here."

"You live in a Yaletown loft. You're doing fine."

"Sure. But I also pay a mortgage. I doubt he does."

"Purebloods must get a rate below prime," I said.

I was about to buzz his suite when someone exited the building. She was a normate, dressed in sweats and a jacket, possibly even going on a midnight snack run. I wondered if she knew that she was sharing her building with a monster. Probably not. You never really knew who your neighbors were.

She held the door open for us.

"Thanks," Lucian said.

She eyed him up and down. "My pleasure."

We stepped past her into the lobby. Lucian whistled softly.

"Yeah. I definitely chose the wrong profession. My apartment doesn't have marble pillars. Or a fountain."

"There's a sauna downstairs," I said. "He mentioned it once. God only knows what he does there."

"Maybe he just goes to relax."

"Purebloods relax by feeding on mortals. Or by hunting demons that are lower on the food chain. They don't need to go to the gym."

"Maybe he's just social that way."

"Trust me. He's got other things on his mind. Like how to keep the magical drug trade flowing across the city."

We stepped into the elevator. I pressed the button marked PH.

"How was it?" Lucian asked.

"How was what?"

"The Hex."

I stared at the LCD screen on the wall. The numbers leapt upward. I felt as if we might fly into the stratosphere at any moment.

"It was intense," I said. "I don't plan on doing it again."

"Never again?"

"Never."

"I've heard it makes your powers more accessible. That you can do things on Hex that you'd never be able to do normally."

"I wouldn't know."

"But you saw things, right? You dreamt. You saw your father."

I see my father practically every night. Whenever I

*close my eyes. That dream was no different from the
hundreds of others I've had since I was a child.*

"Yes," I said. "My mother, too. And the Iblis. It was
a party."

The elevator stopped. The doors opened, and I
stepped into the hallway. The air-conditioning made
me shiver.

"Sorry," Lucian said. "I've done other drugs, but
never Hex. I've often wondered what it would be like."

"Ask Corvid. He can hook you up, and the first
bump's always free."

"Look at you. Talking street."

"That's me. The essence of hard-core."

The hallway ended in a single door, since Corvid's
suite took up the entire top floor of the building. It
was ajar. That wasn't odd, since he usually left it open
when he was expecting visitors. What did he have to
be afraid of?

We stepped inside. Lucian surveyed the living
room, taking in the antiques and strange objets d'art
in glass cabinets.

"How old did you say he was again?"

"I'm not sure. He scares the shit out of me, though."

I walked down the hallway that led to Corvid's
study. Last time I was here, he'd told me about something that he was working on. Some kind of technology. I think he owned a few different companies
operating in Silicon Valley. He was always trying to
streamline the distribution and delivery of his prod-
ucts. In a perfect world, I imagined, he could deal
drugs that were purely made of energy. Little capsules

of light that went straight to your soul when you swallowed them.

I smelled something. It was a familiar smell, and not something that I'd ever associated with Corvid's hermetically sealed apartment. I paused.

"What is it?"

"I'm not sure. Something's wrong."

"Can you define 'wrong'?"

"Not yet. Just—" My eyes widened as I stepped into the office. "Don't move."

Corvid's head was sitting on top of his desk.

Even in death, his expression hadn't changed. He was still wearing the same black pearl earring. His long white hair was braided in tight dreads, and his mouth was bared, revealing a row of sharp teeth. Blood pooled around the base of his ruined neck. It was black, like Basuram's blood.

The rest of his body was lying a few meters away. Slowly, I approached his blood-spattered trunk and legs. One of his arms had been removed, but I didn't see it anywhere. Maybe the killer had absconded with it as a souvenir.

I stared at the headless body. Part of his spine was visible, gleaming as it protruded from the hole where his neck used to be. I was amazed to see that his bones were coated in a translucent material, almost like tempered glass. The overhead lights made the osseous material shimmer in prismatic patterns.

"His head was torn clean off," I said. "It wasn't a weapon. This was done by somebody's bare hands."

"What sort of thing could do that?" Lucian asked.

"I don't know. Until tonight, I'd say that Corvid himself was the only thing capable of doing something like this."

"He must have a lot of enemies."

"Of course. But not a lot of creatures would be bold enough to walk into his home and do this. He also has a lot of allies. Powerful allies who won't take something like this lightly."

"What do we do now?"

"I'm calling Selena. All you have to do is—" I stopped. I could feel something in the pit of my stomach. Something very wrong.

"What is it?"

I held a finger to my lips. I tried to quiet my thoughts, but they were all smashing into one another. My senses weren't telling me anything useful. I could feel Lucian's power next to me, and the residual power that still clung to Corvid's body, which was slowly disintegrating. But there was something else.

I looked more closely at the blood around his severed head. It was a passive blood pool, formed by gravity. The edges of the pool were only partially skeletonized. That meant that it was fresh. But I didn't know how fresh.

"Whatever did this could still be here," I whispered. "We need to leave, carefully and quietly. I can call Selena from the parking lot."

"Tess—" Lucian's eyes widened. "Are you feeling that?"

I swallowed. "I think so. Maybe it's just Corvid's ghost."

"No. It's different."

I took a step back into the hallway. "All right. Keep your defenses up. All we need to do is—"

Something flashed across my vision. A shadow. I reacted instinctively. Both blades were already in my hands. Meredith's athame was cold in my grasp, so cold that it almost burned. I held on tighter.

"Where did you get that?" Lucian asked.

"It was a gift. I'll explain later."

I heard something. A kind of shuffling. I took another step forward, and Lucian followed me. Great. Why was I always the one in front?

"If the killer was still here," Lucian murmured, "I feel like we'd already be dead. Anything that could do this to a pureblood would make short work of us."

"Maybe it's playing with us. Maybe it's a bastard."

I felt it again. A shadow presence. Not a demon, but something else. Where had I felt it before? It was driving me crazy.

Bang!

Something flung the closet door open.

I jumped back. Lucian yelled something, and I saw a nimbus of green energy swirl to life around his right hand. Then I heard another voice. *No, no, wait.*

What?

I blinked.

A man was standing in front of me. It looked as if he was about to collapse, and he was holding on to the edge of the closet for dear life. His eyes were wild, and he kept saying, *Wait, wait, wait.* He was staring at

Lucian's hand. The necroid materia made a crackling noise, like bacon in a pan.

The man finally looked at me. He was unshaven, and it looked as if he hadn't slept for days. He was trembling slightly. But I recognized him.

I lowered both of the blades. I gestured for Lucian to do the same, but the green light had already dimmed.

"Dr. Rashid?" I asked.

He stared at me. He looked at Lucian, and then at me again. He seemed on the verge of a nervous breakdown.

"What are you doing here, Dr. Rashid?"

"I—I live here. This is my building. I heard something. I called the police, but nobody came. So I went upstairs—and—" His eyes seemed to take me in for the very first time. They were all pupil. "You were there. Both of you—at the morgue. I remember. Who are you people? What's going on here? What is that—" He pointed in the direction of the office. "What is *that*? In there? It's not human. You're not human, either. I feel like I'm going crazy."

"You're not," I said. "You need to calm down. We can explain everything, but first, we have to get out of this building."

He blinked. "Are *you* the police?"

"Not exactly."

"Then what are you?"

Lucian put a hand on his shoulder. "Come with us," he said. "It's going to be a long night. But you're safe. For now."

"I don't feel safe."

"Yeah. Join the club."

I dialed Selena's number. "It's Tess. I'm at Corvid's. We need a forensic team and a veil, right away. We've got a code seven."

I hung up.

Rashid looked at me, still dazed. "What does that mean? Code seven?"

I sighed. "It means that you've got a lot of paperwork to fill out. And I'm not getting any sleep tonight."

16

Photographers were taking pictures of Corvid's head from every angle. I tried not to look at it, but I felt as if its eyes were following me. The rest of his body was scattered like a smashed marionette, but his head seemed oddly intact. Someone had dusted his earring for prints and then left a numbered evidence placard beneath it. The blood around it had been swabbed, hair samples taken, buccal texture scraped from the inside of the mouth, and now the head was just another piece of the scene.

I watched the forensic crew as they swept over Corvid's home, dusting, lifting, and taping off areas in grid patterns. They silently measured everything before placing it in a sealed and labeled envelope. In some cases, it was easiest to simply cut out and remove pieces of the wall and floor. In this way, the room was dissected bit by bit, while its surfaces were sprayed down with chemicals in the hopes of revealing spectral blood. We kept peeling back to reveal the flesh of the scene underneath, and the whole while, Corvid's sightless head watched us.

Nobody was mourning the pureblood's death. He'd be replaced by another aristocratic dealer, probably a younger one. But you also had to think that, over the span of a few millennia, you'd pick up a lot of interesting stories. You'd make friends, crash parties, do stupid things, have sex in strange places. Or was that just for the bottom-dwelling demons who aped human behavior? Maybe for a pureblood, it was all business. Maybe Corvid's whole life had been nothing but a nightmare of scheduling.

I guess a part of me wanted to see him as a teenager. Not that Corvid was his real name. It was just a moniker. It made me think about him as an ancient crow patrician, looking down on the activity of the smaller demons below.

Selena was talking to Dr. Rashid near the entrance to the study. Her voice was a shade softer than usual. He was in a minor state of shock, but his professional training had already kicked in. He calmly answered her questions about his medical research areas and proficiencies.

Tasha Lieu, our chief medical examiner, crossed the room to where we stood. She looked at Lucian. "Hello again."

He nodded and smiled. "Tasha. I haven't seen you since the Ordeño case."

"It's been too long."

"We really must stop meeting at crime scenes."

She gave him a long look. "You want lunch? I could do lunch."

"What kind of lunch?"

"Yogurt and apple slices. On a wild morning, I bring Grape-Nuts."

"I like the sound of that."

"Could you do this elsewhere?" I asked. "We have a head waiting for us. I'm not saying it's going anywhere, but I'd still like to get this over with."

Tasha took a step closer to the head. "Has it been moved?"

"No. There's a passive blood pool underneath."

"Was the blood still circulating when you found the head? Purebloods have been known to regulate their vital functions at the level of the spinal cord for up to several hours after death. Both the head and the trunk may have survived for quite some time following their disarticulation."

"That's really kind of horrifying," I replied. "But the blood pool had partially skeletonized when I arrived. I think he was dead."

"I won't be able to tell until I examine the borders of the wound. There may be hemorrhagic tissue."

"You go right ahead."

"We'll have to wait until he's on the table." She leaned in closer, squinting at the lacerated flesh of Corvid's neck. "It looks like a traffic accident. The head was separated at the level of the fifth and sixth cervical vertebrae, with ragged and contused margins.

I'm not sure what kind of weapon would do this. Tractor, maybe?"

"You can ask Dr. Rashid what he thinks. He's a pathologist."

Her eyes widened. "The code seven? I wasn't sure if that was just a rumor." She looked at Rashid. "Huh. Cute."

Lucian sighed. "I guess I should be devastated."

"What's his specialty?" Tasha asked.

"It's not analyzing demon heads; I can tell you that. He's scared shitless. But so far he's doing pretty well."

Before I could stop her, Tasha walked over to Selena. "Hi. Can we borrow Dr. Rashid for a moment?"

Selena shrugged. "That's up to him. Dr. Rashid—"

"You can call me Falih."

"Falih, I'm Tasha Lieu." She extended her hand. "I'm the chief medical examiner for—" She frowned at Selena. "What are we calling ourselves?"

"The organization."

"Fine. I'm the CME for the organization, and I could use your eyes. Would you mind taking a look at this head?"

"Of course. I'd love to."

The odd thing was, I believed him. Rashid and Lieu were both anatomists to the core, and it was clear that they enjoyed their jobs. I looked at Selena, but she just shrugged. At this point, we were so early into the "situation"—the intrusion of a normate—that everything was still very flexible. No rash decisions had been made, and Selena was still testing the waters. We needed to find out how much he knew, and how much he only thought he knew.

They examined the head together.

"It resembles railway interference," Tasha said. "Don't you think? The borders of the wound are avulsed. I suspect that the organs will be blanched from rapid blood loss. Both carotids transected along a jagged line."

"I had a decedent once," Rashid said. "Her head had blown through the windscreen of an automobile window. Snapped at the fifth cervical, and contusions all over the face. The head bounced off a tree and landed fifteen meters away."

"I had a decapitation by aluminum fence pole."

"Automobile accident?"

"No. It involved—" She frowned. "Well, let's just call them 'shearing forces,' for lack of a more descriptive term."

"Sharp-edged wound margins?"

"Yes. With tissue bridging. The epiglottis and hyoid were still intact, though."

Rashid looked again at Corvid's head. "Are you taking vitreous fluid? I mean—" He blinked. "I suppose I can ask, does he *have* vitreous fluid?"

Tasha smiled. "His species does. Usually. It's much harder to extract."

"How do you do it?"

"I think that falls under 'classified.' But trust me when I say that it's a giant electric needle, and quite fun to use."

"I believe it."

"What's your specialty, Falih?"

He blushed slightly. Only slightly, but I saw it. The effect was just a shade above adorable. Then he smiled and said: "Forensic pathology with an emphasis on osteological trauma. I graduated from the Dunn School of Pathology at Oxford."

"Did you work with Athanasou?"

"I did."

I half expected Tasha to offer up the spare room in her house to Rashid. She just nodded slightly, looking him up and down while still examining the head. I wasn't entirely sure which one of them she was more interested in.

"We were never introduced," Lucian said suddenly. "I'm Lucian Agrado. I work in a sort of consulting capacity."

Rashid shook his hand. "And what area do you consult in?"

"You could call it pathology."

Selena walked over to us. "Has anyone seen Sedgwick? I need him to keep an eye on the border situation."

"Which border is that?" Rashid asked.

"Not any of the ones you're thinking of." She looked at Tasha. "We're going to transport the head in a magnetic crucible. We'll move it extra slowly and try to preserve the more fragile tissue."

"I think the brain stem may be intact. Try not to touch it." Tasha walked away.

Selena turned to Rashid. "Dr.—"

"Really, Falih is fine."

"All right. Falih, we've got a bit of a situation here, and that's putting it lightly. We need to continue our interview at a more secure location."

"Secure, like an underground bunker?"

"No. An aboveground facility. Well, mostly aboveground."

"The best parts are underneath the basement," I volunteered.

"Who's going to be representing me when we get there?" Rashid asked. "Do you employ a public defender?"

"We employ an entire court of law."

"Then I'd like counsel present at my interview."

"We can get you someone."

"Good. Then I have no problem coming with you. I'd like to make one phone call first, if that's possible."

"It's not."

"That's a violation of my rights."

"True. But we've deactivated the transmission function on your cell. For now, you'll have to trust us and come along."

"Are you taking me across state lines? To some kind of facility?"

"No. Our building's downtown. West Pender."

"Really?"

"Yeah. It's nice. Air-conditioning, panic rooms, and a sweet little cafeteria. You won't suffer while you're there."

"I'm to take your word on that?"

"It would seem so."

They both stared at each other for a few seconds. Then Rashid nodded.

"All right. I don't trust you, but I don't have much of a choice, either. I do expect some form of counsel to be waiting for me, though."

"Don't worry. You won't be disappointed."

He shrugged. "Fine. Am I driving?"

"You're in no condition to drive. We'll transport you."

"I'm going with her, if that's the case." He pointed at me. "She can drive me."

"I call shotgun," Lucian said.

"No. Just her. No offense, Mr. Agrado."

I looked at Selena. "I don't care. We can swing by 7-Eleven if he wants, and he can ride in the front seat. Let's go."

"I'd rather be there," Lucian said.

"It's fine." I resisted the urge to touch him. "I don't mind. It's a short drive."

"I'll be tailgating you the whole way."

"If it makes you feel better."

"Flash your lights if anything happens."

"I will."

"There's a tracking device in your SUV," Selena said. "We'll be monitoring you the whole time."

"That's a real comfort. Where did they put the fiber-optic camera this time?"

"I don't know. It's the size of a dime, though."

"I wonder if Patrick noticed it."

"Who's Patrick?" Rashid asked.

I ignored him. "Do you have him on tape?"

Selena frowned. "Yes and no."

"What does that mean?"

"Well, sometimes he was moving too fast to be videotaped, so he's just a blur. And sometimes he seems less than fully material. More like a dense kind of mist. We've all seen it, and it's pretty creepy."

"I haven't seen it."

"Who's Patrick?" Rashid asked again.

"You probably don't want to," Selena said. "At any rate, we would have told you if he did anything too wild."

"Did you catch him with any girls?"

Selena nodded.

"Boys?"

She nodded again. "And combinations. Nothing R-rated, though."

I blinked. "You're right. I'd really rather not see it." I turned finally to Rashid. "Let's go. I'll try to answer your questions on the way to the lab."

"Are you going to answer them honestly?"

I looked at Selena. "I'm going to answer them to the best of my ability, in a way that won't compromise agreements that I made with this organization. Legally and spiritually binding agreements."

"I'm afraid to ask what that means."

"It's really best if you didn't."

"Text me when you get there," Lucian said.

"Thank you, Mr. Agrado. It's kind of you to be concerned."

I led Rashid out of Corvid's building and into the parking lot. He settled into the passenger seat, and I guided us out of the underground garage, merging onto Hornby Street. The night was repeating itself now. Maybe throwing that time bomb at Basuram hadn't been the smartest move after all. There could always be aftershocks. The last thing I wanted was to be stuck in a *Groundhog Day* situation involving a headless demon.

If I was going to repeat any moment in my life, again and again, it would be my first discovery of the salad bar at Bonanza. I could just lie underneath that soft-serve ice-cream dispenser and eat my weight in sundaes.

"Are you going to tell me what's going on?" Rashid asked.

"That depends on your definition of 'tell you.' I can give you limited pieces of information that might not make any sense."

"Limited is better than nothing."

"If it makes you feel any better, I think you're holding up very well."

"Thank you. I've been in surreal situations before. I'm not entirely sure that this is the craziest one. But it's in the top three."

"What was number one?"

"A case of advanced necrotizing fasciitis, in Iraq. An entire village. We had no idea what caused it, but the bones were so porous, it was as if the organic material had been sucked right out of them. What remained—it was like cinders."

"That's a terrible outbreak."

"I didn't think it was bacterial. But that was when I

was still a postgrad at Oxford, and nobody wanted to listen to me. I was just an annoying student yammering on."

"What did you think caused it? If it wasn't bacterial, I mean?"

He looked at me. "I wasn't entirely sure. But I'd never seen bacteria move that fast before. I wanted to write an article on it, in fact. But my supervisor convinced me not to. Five years later, and there's still no article. Something tells me that no record of the site was ever published."

"Oh, I'm sure it was published. Just not in a forensic journal that you can access through a common database."

"How large is this organization that you work for?"

"Large."

"Multinational?"

"Multidimensional."

"Right." He kept his eyes on me. "And you're not connected to the RCMP or to the Chief Coroner's Office?"

"We have access to their electronic archives. But socially, we don't attend the same parties. They're more or less unaware of our existence."

"More or less?"

"Well, there are certain liaisons. Certain political inroads. And of course there are also situations like this."

"You mean a code seven."

"Yes." I smiled. "That means 'Normate on Premises.'"

"Normate? Is that what I am?"

"Sometimes we say 'pedestrians.' I think that's mean, though."

"Is it like a Muggle?"

"Please. No Potter."

"Sorry."

"Let's just say that, in cases when a bystander manages to get involved with one of our investigations, we treat it seriously. Each intrusion is dealt with in the most efficient and humane manner possible."

"Humane. By my standards, or yours?"

"I can't answer that."

"Will you interrogate me?"

"Yes, but as Selena says, you'll have counsel present."

"I'm not sure I have any reason to trust one of your lawyers."

"No. You don't. But at this point, it's the best you're going to get."

"So—are there other organizations like you in the city? Are you in competition?"

"Not really. I mean, there are satellites. But we're the only fully equipped and funded occult forensics unit on the West Coast."

"How long have you been in operation for?"

"I don't even know. You'd have to ask our archivist, but I doubt you'll be visiting that level of the building anytime soon."

"Will you be holding me for the rest of the night?"

"Possibly longer. You'll be comfortable, though."

In actual fact, I had no idea where we were putting

Rashid. We couldn't keep him in the interrogation room forever, and he wasn't going anywhere near Basuram's neighborhood. I definitely saw the break room couch in his future.

"How often does this happen?" Rashid asked. "I mean, how often does someone like me stumble across one of your operations?"

"More often than you'd think. As I said, we judge every intrusion on a case-by-case basis. Some are more difficult to disentangle than others."

"Does my case qualify as difficult?"

"I'd go so far as to call it snarly."

"Should I be worried?"

"Not yet. But the night can always swing both ways."

"What exactly do you do for them? Are you a field agent?"

"I'm an occult special investigator. It's mostly field-work, but I do know my way around a lab."

"Should you be telling me this?"

"Possibly not. But you're going to figure it out in the next few hours, so I'm really just giving you a small head start."

"By 'occult,' do you mean Houdini? Or ritualistic killings?"

"Both. With a bit of *Exorcist* thrown in."

"So do you have an explanation for that headless body?"

I turned into the lab's parking lot. "What sort of explanation are you looking for? The kind that reassures you, or the kind that only further disturbs you?"

"I'd rather be disturbed than ignorant."

"You aren't the first person to claim that. Sometimes ignorance can be very useful. It can make your life a lot easier."

He shrugged. "I deal with ignorance every day. When I've got a body opened up and I'm looking at the organs, at the most intensely private part of someone—I try to determine cause of death, but just as often, it's like hunting for a shadow."

"Maybe, in those cases, it was simply better for you not to know what killed those people. Maybe the answer wouldn't have made any sense to you."

"Medical textbooks are full of things that don't make sense. But that creature back there—I've never seen anything like that."

"I'd be surprised if you had."

"His teeth were real. I mean, they certainly looked real."

"They're as real as his nine-inch fingernails."

"So—I mean—" Rashid looked at me. "That's not human. That body isn't animal and it isn't human. There's no way."

I was silent. I pulled into an empty space and turned the engine off.

"Should I run now? It seems like the opportune moment to run, if I was the kind of person who did that sort of thing."

I stared at him from across the driver's seat. "I guess you're right. If you're going to have a moment, it's now."

"I thought so."

We sat in silence for a while. Then he quietly undid his seat belt and got out of the car. He looked around.

"Isn't this the parking lot for the HSBC tower?"

"We share space."

"Are they aware of that?"

"Yes. They're not the only bank that we deal with."

"And the police. They must be in the dark?"

"We have people inside. They shield us. Not all the time, as you can see. But generally the system works."

"I guess that makes me the wrench."

"Be whatever tool you like. It doesn't matter to me."

He followed me as I walked across the parking lot. "I've lost my job, you know. Thanks to you and your organization. They're calling it flexible medical leave, but I'm never getting near an autopsy suite again. I know that."

"I'm sorry. We can try to grease some wheels, but there's no guarantee that you'll ever return to your position."

"So my career's over, just like that. Because I met you."

"I don't know about your career. But that particular job is over, most likely."

"I went to one of the finest pathology departments in the world to get that particular job, as you call it. I'm not going to stand idly by while the whole thing collapses in on itself."

"It may not. I mean, not a real collapse. Maybe it'll just be more like a lateral implosion, if that makes any sense."

"It doesn't."

"Yeah. Well." I yawned, holding the elevator door for him. "It's late. I don't have a lot to give you right now."

"I understand. And I appreciate your effort."

"Why did you make such a fuss about driving alone with me?"

He stepped into the elevator with me.

"I wanted to get to know you better."

The doors closed. I sighed.

17

"Dr. Rashid, can you state your birthplace?"

He took a sip of water. "Calgary."

"And were you raised in Alberta?"

"My parents came from Nablus. We went back and forth. I spent several years in the United Kingdom as well."

"Do you have Palestinian citizenship?"

"Yes. And Canadian."

"You have a Canadian passport?"

"Yes. I'm a dual national. Would you like to see the paperwork? It took four years to process. They looked at everything, including my father's transcripts from elementary school in Palestine."

"Were your grandparents from there as well?"

"My family has lived on the West Bank for over a hundred years. Is this an interview about my ancestry?

If it's to continue, I'd prefer to wait for my advocate. You did say she'd arrive twenty minutes ago."

Selena shrugged. "It's odd. She's not normally late."

There was a quiet knock. Selena stood and opened the door to the interrogation chamber. "Come in," she said. "Welcome."

A snow leopard walked slowly into the room.

"Whoa." Rashid stood up. He backed away until he was standing against the far wall of the room. "That's—you know—"

"Stop moving, Dr. Rashid," Selena said.

He stared at her. "Are you joking? What are you—"

The snow leopard was standing in the middle of the room, looking at him. She wore a braided golden collar with an engraved torque, just beneath her throat. Her eyes were so blue they looked burnished, like metal. They moved up and down Rashid's body, fixating on his neck.

"This is Latyrix," Selena said. "Don't move. She's your lawyer."

Perhaps the incredulity of Selena's comment was such that it actually got Rashid to pause for a moment. He stopped moving. Latyrix noticed this and took a slow step forward. Rashid was a statue now. He could barely move his fingers.

"She just needs to introduce herself. Among her species, introductions are extremely important. And sensitive. They can be life-defining."

Rashid was breathing quicker, but he didn't move. He kept his eyes on Latyrix. She had a beautiful silvered nose and black spotting on her head. Her pupils were very large, and her eyes were liquid, smooth in all their movements.

Her whiskers hesitated in the air between them. They were curled and stately, emerging like a kind of lacy textile from the sides of her face. The way each whisker curled up, it almost resembled the collar of a high cape, or a cravat.

Latyrix sniffed along Rashid's face. Her whiskers dragged against his skin, and he shivered, but didn't move. She sniffed down his neck.

"Thank you. I didn't mean to startle you."

Her voice came from the amulet, as if from a microphone. It sounded clear, but also slightly grainy. It wasn't her real voice, but rather the bare tone of her voice without any gestural information factored into it. I thought it sounded sometimes like a book on tape, but it was our most effective mode of communication with the animals who worked in the law court. I mean, really, they designed the law court. Most of the prosecutors weren't even mammalian, or barely so.

"Doctor," Selena was saying patiently, "Latyrix is your counsel. We're recording this session, and if necessary, she'll be your advocate in court."

"Is—" He tore himself away from Latyrix, who was still regarding him without any change in expression. "Is your court really run by animals?"

"Not entirely."

"Falih is scared and disoriented," Latyrix said. Her voice settled over the room, and we found ourselves going still. "That is the name you go by, correct? Rashid is your—what is the name for it"—she made a low growl in her throat, followed by a flick of her ears—"surname? Namelast?"

"Last name," Selena said.

"Yes." Latyrix looked at him for another long moment. Then she settled to her haunches, about a foot away from him. "This floor is cold. You need carpet."

"I agree, madam. But the floor is designed to be stain-resistant."

"Of course. You must get a lot of secreters in here." She looked at Rashid again. "I will call you Falih, if that is all right."

He nodded slowly. "Call me anything you want."

"I'm sorry that my appearance makes you nervous. It's a hard-coded biological response, and it will take you a few moments to work through it."

I was never quite sure if we were supposed to call animals "sir" and "madam" or not, but I did it out of deference. Mostly, I just copied Selena. But you could tell already how concerned the CORE was about Rashid being a code seven. I'd only seen Latyrix attending a deposition once or twice, but it was widely acknowledged that she was one of the best defense lawyers working for the CORE.

I knew little about the mechanics of occult litigation, save for the fact that panthers usually made the best prosecutors. Although I'd once seen a mink who was very persuasive in his closing arguments.

"Falih," the snow leopard continued, "it's important for you to know that you aren't being held here against your will. There's no evidence that can keep you here, and Officer Ward can't simply chain you to the table. You're free to go."

She moved her head slightly. "However. As your counsel, I would advise you against leaving. You're much safer here."

"Is someone going to rip my head off as well?"

"Quite possibly." Latyrix made a gesture that might have been a shrug. "Like it or not, you've blundered your way into a very serious situation. You've seen things that you shouldn't have. There's a mark of contagion on you now, and others will be able to sense it. Others will then be able track you."

He stared at her. "Who are these others?"

"The type of thing powerful enough to do what you saw in that office. The type of thing that makes even me nervous. Understand?"

He nodded. "I still don't fully believe that we're talking, though. I mean, I understand that I'm hearing your voice, or *a* voice; I don't know. I understand you. But I think I may also be hallucinating. Someone could have easily put something in this water. GHB, LSD, or a combination of the two."

"You aren't drugged and you aren't dreaming." Latyrix looked at him. "You're not supposed to be here, talking to us. But you are. We can't do anything about it. What we can do is figure out a solution that works for everyone."

"You really do kind of sound like a lawyer."

"That's because I am a lawyer. I have been my whole life."

"But—I mean—" He blinked. "You can forgive me for being skeptical, right? A talking leopard?"

"You think animals have no language?" She regarded him calmly, her eyes very still. "It's true, we have very little reason to talk to hominids like yourself. But for some of us, the situation demands it. As long as you manipulate the natural world, some of us have to live among you, to keep watch."

"Animals have always been involved in our justice system," Selena told him. "It may be hard for you to understand. But we're immensely grateful for the help and expertise that they offer us."

"Why are you telling me this?" Rashid shook his head. "Why not just shoot me full of drugs and leave me in my bed, at home? You made me forget once. I'm sure you could do it again."

"The procedure was imperfect," Selena replied. "It didn't take. You're risking brain damage if we attempt it again, and I can't allow that. So we have to do this properly, through the correct legal channels."

"Correct legal channels." Rashid closed his eyes. "I'm in an interrogation room, talking to a wild animal."

"Latyrix has no interest in harming you," Selena said, glancing at a folder in front of her. "We need to proceed. Falih, I've got all of your information here. Medical records, transcripts, DNA samples, relationship history—it's all in this file."

His eyes widened. "How did you get all of that so fast?"

"It actually took longer than usual, since you've

lived in so many places. But we have very good connections, and very fast computers."

"If you already know everything, then why are you asking me questions? Just read my life on paper."

"There are things that the file can't answer. Tests that we need to perform whose results aren't instantaneous. We'll need more time."

"Time for what? I don't understand what you're looking for."

"What Detective Ward means," I told him, "is that we're testing your blood to see if anything is out of the ordinary. You may have a preexisting condition. Something that would predispose you to—well—us. To who we are and what we are."

"You mean like a mutation?"

"You could call it that."

"You think I'm infected with something."

"We don't know anything yet," Selena said. "We just want to make sure that you're healthy and that your immune system is uncompromised."

"Do you think I was exposed to something? Back there, at the apartment?"

"It's possible."

"Great." He closed his eyes. "I've already lost my job, and now I might be sick. I can't imagine how this night is going to get better."

"Well, you are talking to a snow leopard," I reminded him. "And if that was the sort of thing you were able to tell your friends about, they'd probably think it was pretty awesome. But you can't tell them. You understand that, right?"

"I understand that you've basically kidnapped me and possibly drugged me. I don't feel ready to agree to anything just yet."

"You don't have to convince him," Latyrix said. "He's not going to tell anyone. They never tell anyone. Dr. Rashid would only be declaring himself insane if he shared the events of tonight with anyone else."

"I could say I was really drunk."

"But you don't drink."

"How do you know that?"

"Alcohol has a distinct odor. You don't drink, but you have smoked a cigarette recently. I don't believe you're anything but a casual smoker, though."

He swallowed. "That was close to a week ago."

"As I said. Recently." Latyrix looked at him. "Falih Rashid, let us be honest with each other. You don't understand any of this. Yesterday, you believed that you were a successful pathologist. Now you're talking to an animal, and you don't believe in talking animals. Nevertheless, here we are."

Rashid rubbed the back of his neck. He seemed to have lost some of his fear, but his body was still very stiff, and he couldn't take his eyes off the leopard.

"It's true," he said. "I'm not sure this is really happening. But I do know what I saw in that office. I can't forget that. I know what I felt, too. It was all over that body, everywhere, like an oil slick. Evil. I felt it. I know that I did."

"You're probably right," Latyrix replied. "Even someone like yourself, with no perceptible genetic anomalies or innate powers, can sense the presence of certain things from other worlds. Your body registers it as an electromagnetic disturbance. You feel it in your hair and your teeth, you smell it, just as I can smell it."

"Is that what it was? Evil?"

"It was certainly destructive. As your philosopher Blaise Pascal says, 'Evil is easy, and has infinite forms.' Maybe you sensed one of those forms. Whatever happened, you've been touched by it. Infected. And now whatever was after Corvid will also be after you."

"But I didn't do anything."

"No. You were at the wrong place at the wrong time." Latyrix looked at me suddenly. "And twice, if I'm not mistaken. Agent Corday, did you not encounter Dr. Rashid at the morgue originally, while you were retrieving the Ptah'li child?"

"That's right, madam."

The leopard almost seemed to wink at me. "I'm not that old. You can simply call me by my name."

"Sorry. You're right. We did meet that way."

"What's a Ptah'li?" Rashid asked. "Are you talking about the little boy?"

"Yes. His name is Ru."

"Is he here?"

"He's safe."

"Let me see him."

Selena shook her head. "I don't think that's possible."

"Look." Rashid exhaled. "That child was open on my table. I was cutting into his body, and he woke up. Screaming. Do you think that's ever happened to me before, in the history of my medical career? I can't stop thinking about it."

"Ru's fine," Selena said. "I promise you."

"I just need to see him for myself. Please. If he's here, it'll only take a second, right? Then you can get back to interrogating me."

Selena at Latyrix. "What do you think?"

"It couldn't hurt. We want them both to be comfortable, and they've cooperated so far. As long as we're all here, I don't see a problem in it."

Selena dialed a number on her cell. "Yes. Bring him to Conference Room C. I want a full guard detail accompanying him." She hung up. "Fine. He'll be here in five minutes. Then you can see that you haven't just been hallucinating all of this."

"Can—" Rashid looked at Latyrix again. "I mean, may I ask you a question?"

Her blue eyes held him. "If it is within reason."

"Please don't take this the wrong way. I mean no offense. But wouldn't you be more comfortable living in the wild?"

She flicked one of her ears. I interpreted it as a minor signal of annoyance. "Would *you* be more comfortable living in the wild?"

"I don't know. But we have very different instincts, you and I."

"It's true. I've undergone a good deal of conditioning to allow me to live among hominids. If I lived on a Siberian plain, I might be happier, more carefree. But I inherited the sacred duty of litigation. I chose this path, and I do not regret my choice. No matter how alienating it can be sometimes."

"I can relate to that. I think."

"A lot of us can," Selena said. "We've all inherited complex genetic legacies. You might even say some of us got shafted by our ancestral responsibilities. But we've all managed to build a life for ourselves."

"In this guarded complex," Rashid said. "No. Pardon me. In this secret guarded complex, which isn't supposed to exist."

"I didn't say it was perfect." Selena's cell rang. She put it to her ear. "I'm here. What?" Her eyes widened. "Oh, bloody—"

The lights flickered. Then an alarm sounded.

Rashid looked around him. "What is that? What's going on?"

Selena put down the phone.

"Ru's gone," she said. "And so is Basuram. Both cells are empty."

18

The lights went out.

The alarm was still going, and a few seconds later, the emergency lighting kicked in. It was basically the same as the floor lighting they always talk about in the safety demonstration on an airplane, just before take-off. Latyrix was the first to move. She stood up on her haunches, not growling, but making a very low sound in her throat, like the prelude to a growl. Selena walked over to the door and placed her hand on it.

"They're still here. Both demons. I'd say they're three floors beneath us and moving rapidly."

"Ru's fast," I said. "But I'm more worried about the path of destruction that Basuram's going to leave behind."

Selena crossed the room and hit the emergency PA button.

"Code Black," she said. "Evacuate all nonspecialized personnel. Combat-trained personnel are to cover floors one through fourteen. Use armor-piercing rounds for the Kentauros demon, and if you encounter the—"

The speaker went dead. Selena swore.

"They're in the subbasement." I looked at Selena. "Could they have gotten to Esther? The elevator won't even go there without a key card."

"The elevators aren't entirely demon-proof, unfortunately." Selena started dialing her cell. "Latyrix, if you'd be so kind, please escort Dr. Rashid and Agent Corday to a safe area. I have to organize a security pattern."

"Follow me," Latyrix said. "Agent Corday, are you armed?"

"Yes."

"Good."

Rashid approached me. "What are we doing? Are we supposed to blunder around this building in the dark, looking for two monsters?"

"Really, only one monster. But yes. That's the plan."

"I don't even have a weapon."

"You shouldn't need one."

"You think I've never heard that before?"

"Be quiet," Latyrix said. "And follow me." Then she walked through the open door and into the hallway. Nobody questioned her authority as leader of the hunt.

"Where are we going?" Rashid whispered.

"We need to cover each floor," I replied softly. "Ru is probably tracking us, and Basuram is tracking him."

"Basuram. Is that the creature from the morgue?"

"Yes."

"It looked like a centaur."

"It's a centaur with a whip, and it's angry."

"Where's security on this floor?" I asked Selena.

"They've been diverted elsewhere. We had a minimal presence on this floor already, due to Latyrix being here."

"Animal litigators can get stressed out by the presence of a lot of armed guards," I whispered to Rashid. "It puts them in a very defensive mood, and that's not good for depositions. So this floor was cleared of security prior to your lawyer's arrival."

"So we're alone?"

"Not entirely. There's an elaborate video system that runs throughout the building, and it's being monitored twenty-four/seven by a very dedicated technician. She can track our movements, and I think she's going to—"

I heard the chime of the elevator at the end of the hallway.

I looked at Selena. She drew her athame, holding it crosswise with her Sig Sauer in the way that a police officer would hold his gun and flashlight.

Latyrix stood in front of us, head lowered slightly. The leopard's mouth was partially open, and I could see her beautiful nest of teeth.

The elevator doors opened.

It was Ru. He saw us and immediately started screaming.

"Away from the wall! Get away! He's between the—"

I felt Basuram's presence glance off me, like a sting

to my shoulder. I grabbed Rashid and dragged him to the floor. He made an unintelligent sound as he fell, and I saw Latyrix weave to the left.

Basuram exploded through the wall. The demon emerged in a torrent of plaster and drywall, and it was as if a small hurricane had touched down in the hallway, right in front of us. There was a cloud of pulverized material, heavy with metal fragments. Basuram shook itself once, then looked at me.

"You were the last face I remember seeing before I lost consciousness," it said. "So I'm going to kill you first."

Latyrix growled. Basuram looked at her in surprise.

"What are you doing on their side? Has your famous court become so biased that you now associate exclusively with humans?"

"Who I socialize with is not your concern. The humans are under my care."

"That makes you my enemy."

"Yes. It does."

Latyrix leapt onto Basuram's back.

He started to yell something, but then she tore into his throat. Blood-spray blossomed as she hit the left carotid artery. Basuram screamed, trying to throw the leopard off. She only bit deeper. Finally, he smashed her into the facing wall. She untangled herself and leapt away, still growling. Basuram slammed into the leopard and both of them went through the glass of the interrogation room. I ducked, covering my face against the flying debris.

I looked behind me to make sure Rashid was okay.

He was dusting glass from his shoulders, quite efficiently, in fact. He looked thoroughly shell-shocked.

Latyrix was crawling through the shattered window of the room, her long body displacing the blinds. She growled and then leapt onto Basuram's back again. Before the demon could shake her off, she bit deep into the base of its neck. She ravaged the flesh, using her claws to drive the wound open farther. I thought she was going to keep digging until she latched onto the spine with her jaws.

Basuram howled. It tried to shake Latyrix once more, but she was single-minded and kept gnawing. Black blood was flowing, into her eyes and across her snout. The sound was disgusting.

Her beautiful coat's going to get all matted, I thought for a moment, stupidly.

Where was Ru? I looked around but couldn't see him anywhere. Then again, he might have been on the ceiling.

I wanted to call Derrick.

It was a ridiculous feeling, but I couldn't deny it. You need certain people present during FUBAR situations, and he was one of those people. I wanted him here even more than Lucian, because at least Derrick wasn't going to fuck me over at the end of the day. I loved Lucian, but I trusted Derrick.

Selena finally came running down the hall. She was yelling something into a headset, and all I caught was the word "incursion." Then she drew her athame and pointed it at Basuram. A cone of blue-white fire burst from the tip of the blade. The fire touched Basuram's body, and the demon put a hand to its face, snarling.

"What do you think you are?" Basuram screamed at Latyrix. "A higher being? One of the Bestia? You might as well be a corpse fly. You're just a clever bitch who's managed to outlive most of her kind."

Latyrix shrugged her sleek white shoulders as she rose. "I've been called worse by my ex-husband."

"The poor, cuckolded creature. I'll bet—"

"I'm giving you the chance to leave," she interrupted.

"As if anyone wants me to do that right now." Basuram smiled. "The thing you call Ru is pissing itself. You've got a wild animal and an old mage from a trashy family. This is getting operatic."

"Why are you even here?" Latyrix demanded. "Are you really so intent on delivering a child prisoner to your masters? I don't see the recompense."

"The child, as you call the Ptah'li, is a terrorist."

"He's done nothing, as far as I can tell from his file. You executed his family in front of him. He's merely trying to escape you."

"How impartial of you to say so. Is this how you perform in court?"

"No. I'm not ruled by emotion." Latyrix stared down Basuram. "I simply know you and demons like you. I know what your intensions usually are, and I know what you're willing to do to ensure the survival of your middle-class bloodline."

Basuram chuckled. "Is that supposed to hurt coming from a chained animal?"

"I wear a collar. That doesn't make me chained."

"It may as well be a slave collar. Do you think these humans care about anything but your performance as a commodity? They'll turn you into glue and bonemeal as soon as you outlive your function."

Latyrix advanced on him. "Then at least I'll see my death coming. I'll hear it in the cries of the slaughter-house."

"You'll hear it sooner than that—"

"Get back!"

It was Ru's voice. I turned to see him standing a few feet away. He was holding a familiar weapon. It was, in fact, the psychic sidearm that Derrick had used when we infiltrated the lair of the Iblis, two years ago. It had a sensor that interfaced telepathically with the user, making every shot perfect.

"I found this in a locked cabinet," Ru said. "The technology is primitive, but I'm not sure if even a Kentauros skull-plate can withstand twelve direct shots."

Basuram laughed. "You really think that's going to do something?"

Ru leveled the gun at Basuram's head. "I'm optimistic."

Basuram stepped forward. "You're pathetic. The Ferid are on their way. They'll do the same thing to you that they did to your—"

I felt a sudden coldness. The lights flickered.

Selena stared at something behind me. "What's—"

A dark cloud passed through the room. Something sparkled within its depths, and it moved almost voluptuously, trailing peals of black smoke. It swirled around Basuram's head, and the demon screamed. Blood poured from its eyes, nose, and mouth. It made a strangled noise and then collapsed.

The cloud was still for only a moment. Somewhere within, I thought I could see two gleaming points, like eyes. They were fixed not on Basuram's still form, but on me. I stared into the bright points. My own eyes widened.

"Arcadia?" I whispered.

The cloud trembled for a moment. Then it flew past us, vanishing through one of the air ducts in the ceiling.

"What the hell just happened?" Rashid asked.

Blood continued to pump slowly from Basuram's open mouth, as well as through what I presumed were its tear ducts. The demon appeared to be weeping in death, and as I watched, a black pool spread slowly around its head.

Ru set the gun gently down on the floor. "I suppose that's done," he said.

"It's you." Rashid stared at him.

Ru met his gaze. "Doctor. I'm sorry if I scared you."

He actually laughed. "You did."

"My body was hibernating. I came out of it just as you were—"

Rashid winced. "I'm sorry. I didn't mean to hurt you."

"I was not hurt," Ru said.

"I don't understand how this is all possible." Rashid stared at us. "How all of you are even remotely possible."

"Not understanding is the least of your problems

right now," I told him. "Let's just concentrate on getting you out of immediate danger."

"Can you really protect me?" he asked.

"We'll do our best. But a lot of wild and crazy things would like to see you dead, so don't expect miracles."

"We should get that printed on a business card," Selena observed.

I shrugged. "At least it would be honest."

19

My feet were dangling over the edge of the bed.

That was strange.

I rubbed my eyes. Light was filtering through a small window, getting in through the cracks that were visible in the cheap yellow roll-down blind. The pillow beneath my head was soft, but also seemed a tad small, like the bed itself. I groaned. I'd been having the strangest dream about berries and small demons that could spit green froth clear across the room. My stomach rumbled. I couldn't remember the last time I'd eaten. I felt emptied out and exhausted.

I started to sit up slowly. Then, as my surroundings actually registered, shape by familiar shape, I stopped. I wasn't in my room at home, although I was in a room that I'd seen many times before.

It was my childhood bedroom.

Everything was as I remembered it. The floor was old hardwood, rotting slightly at the edges. The window, I knew, would be a bitch to open, since layers of dried paint had long ago rendered it nearly immobile. There was a time when, after sliding it open inch by inch, I would have been able to crawl through and sit on the ledge with my feet hanging just above the ground. This provided convenient access to the backyard, where I staged most of my early duels with malcontents who'd invaded our garden.

I looked up. Sure enough, on top of my old redpainted bookshelf, there was a fish bowl. My unnamed goldfish swam inside, ignoring the colored stones that had settled at the base of the glass bowl. I'd never really warmed up to fish as a kid, partly because they smelled funny, but mostly owing to the fact that we always had cats. After holding more than one impromptu funeral service in the bathroom with my stepfather, I'd grown inured to the charms of anything without whiskers.

I pushed aside the Minnie Mouse quilt, which barely covered me anyway, and stood up. The sheets had that annihilated consistency of fabric that's been washed too many times, slightly pilled now, but soft as a dream. My pillow, rather than smelling of hair spray or shampoo, had no scent at all.

I had to move carefully, since the room was packed with things. My bookshelf leaned sideways beneath the weight of its *World Book* collection, filled with colored illustrations of insects, machines, and distant star clusters. A copy of *The Phantom Tollbooth* lay dog-eared on the top shelf. I remembered reading it when I'd been confined to bed after getting the mumps. I'd itched and hurt and wanted to scream and scratch every inch of my body, until I was nothing but a shaking bloody mess, but for a few hours that book kept me distracted.

Toys were piled in the corners of the room without any sense of organization. Snake Mountain stood against the wall, its hinged mechanism allowing it to open like a volume made of hard purple plastic. I had broken the microphone years ago, or maybe it had never worked to begin with, but you could still place action figures within the bowels of the castle. You just had to be the voice of Skeletor yourself, or God, or whatever thing you wanted to be in that moment.

The figures themselves languished in a plastic bucket. He-Man was endlessly replicated in varieties to suit any medieval occasion: battle action, riding action, chest-plate action with realistic damage, and one that was simply denuded and lying at the very bottom, facedown. I couldn't remember the precise scenarios I'd dreamt up for them all, but they usually involved deteriorating negotiations followed by disorganized combat. My mother never tried to buy me Barbie. She was wiser than that.

A few times, I think, Kevin suggested that I might want to play with more feminine toys, but I just stared at him, uncomprehending. He bought me a Rainbow Bright doll one Christmas, a Moondreamers doll the next, but they were immediately consigned to my closet. My Little Pony was okay in a pinch for cavalry scenes, but on the whole, I preferred actual knights.

There were a lot of questions I could have asked myself at this point.

Where was Ru?

Was this a dream? And, if so, how could it be so perfect?

Was I dead or dying or in some kind of perimortem state?

Maybe this really was the afterlife. I was barely eight years old when I'd lived in the bungalow on Young Street, in the town of Elder, with my mother and stepfather. From what I could remember, I'd been happy here. I guess settling here for eternity made about as much sense as settling anywhere else. At least there was a convenience store close by, the Honey Market, with an inexhaustible supply of Archie comics and Popsicles.

I stepped out of my bedroom and into the hallway.

The small bathroom was on my left, with its tricky toilet that always hissed. I peered inside. Sure enough, the counter was cluttered (although not in a messy way) with the tiny Spanish soaps and bath beads that my mother favored. I remembered being sick once and throwing up endlessly into that toilet, throwing up even water, even air, until everything in my stomach had left in a cold rush. Kevin sat with me on the couch. We watched the *Ewok* movie while my mom drove to the store to buy more ginger ale.

There was a mirror on the wall, which reflected the master bedroom. I'd seen them in bed together once, very late at night, when I was walking to the kitchen to get a glass of water. They were naked and seemed to be sliding around on the bed with each other, as if in a perfectly frictionless environment. They were both giggling.

My mother saw me in the mirror, even though it was dark and I stood very still. Later, she asked me what I'd seen. I said nothing, which was true at the time. I had seen nothing. It had registered as nothing, or rather, as a mystery that the mirror itself offered to me without any explanation.

The mirror reflected an empty bedroom now. The bed was in the center, its maroon quilt and matching sheets arranged neatly. An old poster of Robert Plant, from his days immediately after Led Zeppelin, was tacked to the left wall. On the right was a framed picture of a 1969 cherry red Mustang with black detailing. Most people thought it was Kevin's contribution to the room's decor, but both the poster and the framed print belonged to my mother. Her dream car and her dream man.

To the left was her dresser, and atop it her jewelry box. I could tell you its contents without even looking: oversized fluorescent hoop earrings, smaller silver hoops, cat brooches with emerald eyes, nothing gold on account of her allergy to the metal. She let me wear the clip-on earrings, but I had to wait until I was a teenager to borrow the real ones with their hooks that always pinched.

Under the bed, I knew, was a collection of lost metal and plastic backings, which the cat had secreted away for her own nocturnal amusements. This would have been before we had Misha, the amiable gray tabby who would stay in our lives for almost twenty years. In the old house on Young Street, we shared space with Tempest, a pampered Siamese cross who was my constant companion during archaeological expeditions in the living room. When I needed to exchange a sack full of sand for some guarded treasure, I would use Tempest instead, placing her carefully on the table and instructing her not to move. She would stay put for a while, examining her slim paws. Then she would eventually hop down and disappear into the kitchen, reasoning that her cooperation deserved a reward.

I heard a sound coming from nearby.

Slowly, I passed through the archway that led to the main room. It hadn't changed. The old black couch with no springs was pushed against the far wall. Beside it stood a table topped with yellow ceramic tiles, which my mother had rescued from one garage sale or another. A pack of her cigarettes, Matinée Slims, lay on the table, the plastic balled up and discarded next to them. My mother hadn't smoked in twenty-two years, but I could still smell her chosen cigarettes, still hear the sound of her unwrapping the gold foil that protected them.

An entertainment center dominated the far wall. Since it was still the late eighties, it consisted of twin tape decks and a JC Sound turntable, along with stacks of vinyl shelved neatly below. I could remember dancing with her, my feet on top of hers, my arms clasped tightly around her waist. We danced to Blondie's "One Way or Another," and "Cupid," and "Twistin' the Night Away." Every time she dipped me, I would laugh and laugh, like a little maniac. So she'd dip me again, until it seemed as if I was about to touch the floor, as if I'd surely fall, but I never did. She always held on to me, and she was stronger than she looked.

I heard the noise again. A kind of shuffling. After the incident with the pager, I was wary, but also annoyed with myself for suspecting everything. I peered around the edge of the couch, thinking it might be the familiar noise of the baseboard heater finally kicking in, tapping and burbling to itself.

A cat looked up at me.

She sat on the floor calmly. Her eyes were electric blue, and she had a long, thin tail that crooked into a question mark as she regarded me.

"Tempest?"

She leapt onto the arm of the couch, purring. She butted her head against my hand, and I rubbed her. For a while, that was all I could do. Just stand there, breathing, while she purred, our reciprocal noises already familiar to each other.

I hadn't seen her since I was eight. She'd been hit by a car one day while I was at school. My mother told me that she ran away, but I knew better. I never dreamt that I'd be able to touch her again. But she was here, and very real. She opened her delicate pink mouth and yawned.

Then she leapt off the couch. She looked at me for a few seconds, as if gauging my intelligence. I returned her gaze.

"Are we playing?" I asked her. "Is this a game?"

Tempest looked disappointed. I wondered if I'd

completely misjudged the situation. Then she turned and padded slowly into the kitchen.

I followed her. She jumped onto the old Formica table, which was pushed against the window overlooking our backyard. The window was open, and a glass mobile stirred within its frame. The hummingbirds jangled against one another, even though I couldn't feel a wind coming from outside. I couldn't smell anything, either.

I didn't have to open any of the cupboards to see how they were arranged. I remembered the placement of every spoon. I remembered when I was even younger, and I'd transformed the kitchen into an apothecary, brewing potions solely for my mother's delectation. She would comment on how wonderful each one looked, especially if I'd added food coloring. Then, when my back was turned, she would dump it down the sink. She always scrubbed the stainless steel afterward, to eradicate any trace of colored liquid that might suggest her betrayal.

Tempest looked at me once more. Then she walked down the short flight of steps that led to the laundry room. It was less of a room, really, and more of a clumsy add-on, probably from the 1970s, with unfinished concrete floors covered in a thick layer of ropey gray paint. I used to pretend that it was *pahoihoi* lava, a particular kind that I'd read about in one of my *World Book* volumes. I'd also read about pillow lava, the result of pyroclastic eruptions, which I'd assumed was an actual pillow for fire-sprites and other incendiary elementals. Back when I still tacitly believed in such things, but had never come across one. That didn't happen until puberty.

The cat gave me another look. Then she walked over to the back door and sat down in front of it.

"You want me to go outside, eh? You're quite the tour guide."

She said nothing.

"All right. We might as well check out the yard while we're here. Who knows if I'll ever have the chance to visit this dimension again?"

Of course, I didn't know whether or not it was a parallel dimension, or some splinter of an afterlife, or a fever dream, or the last eclectic firing of my neurons as my brain slowly died from lack of oxygen. It could have been all or none of these things. It could have been a trap set by Basuram, Arcadia, or anyone.

My pockets were empty, and I had no purse. I didn't even have an athame. I had no idea if materia worked in this twilight place, and I wasn't quite ready to try it out yet. Aside from my lackluster training in jujitsu, I was pretty much humped if a demon came calling. Or worse.

I opened the door and walked into our backyard. There was a small square of concrete, on which sat a picnic table with rusty iron bolts just barely holding the pieces together. A child's delight. Beyond the concrete was a slightly larger square of yard, bordered by a low, mostly ornamental fence separating our house from the others on this quiet block. I walked along the perimeter of our garden, which had always mostly been stinkweed and rhubarb. Still, I can remember holding my plastic sword among the purple rhubarb, staring up at the roof of the house and wondering: What sort of levitation spell might get me up there? And what benevolent sorceress might I procure it from?

Back then, I thought a lot about magic. And I hadn't even begun to radiate power yet. It wasn't until I hit twelve that I really started leaking materia all over the place, like a radiator with its cap off, just oozing its contents slowly onto your driveway.

I looked down. Tempest was at my feet, looking up at me. Her paws seemed slightly offended by the prickly grass.

"Let's keep walking," I said. "See if there's anyone else in my coma dream. Maybe we'll run into my second-grade teacher, Miss McGrath, and I can tell her what I really thought about her ceramic penguin collection."

There was a hedge that ran the length of Young Street, and I touched it as we walked. It felt as I remembered, although it had seemed larger, far more uncanny, when I was a child. I had imagined that it hid orcs and spies, as well as those unsettling mice from the Mrs. Brisby movie.

The Honey Market was at the corner of the street and just past Central Elementary, which I could hear from my house. It was weird. Seeing my old house was disturbing, but seeing the old market seemed almost worse. It was one of the first real *other places* I remember as a kid. You've got your room (semiprivate), the yard (public), and then maybe you've got the park (surveilled). The corner store was the first place I remember actually being myself, and where I first began to really be aware of myself as a consciousness separate from others. I could read Archie and Silver Surfer comics for hours, and if I spent too long, they'd get a call from my mother: *Sorry; is she reading all your magazines again?*

"Let's go."

Tempest walked in before me, as if to lessen the blow. I was grateful.

The store, like the street outside, was empty. Maybe the city was empty. If this experience was just my own private neural collapse, then I hoped my subconscious would at least have the decency to let me run into another person. Not that the cat wasn't fine company, but she wasn't wearing a golden collar and didn't seem to have Latyrix's gift of speech. Unless she suddenly developed a very interesting hobby, I knew I was going to be feeling every moment of this eternity.

I walked in. The floor was mismatched linoleum, mostly red and black, but with one inexplicable blue patch where the freezers stood. There was no one behind the counter, although I could see from its light that the cash register was turned on.

The magazine rack was stocked with copies of *Thor*, *X-Factor*, and *Elektra*. In a battle between Thor and any other superhero, save for the Silver Surfer, I felt that Thor was always going to win. He had a hammer, named Mjolnir, and it could pretty much break Odin's jaw. What were the New Warriors going to do against something like that? You think Speedball's going to use his fun kinetic energy to bounce all around Thor, in the hopes of confusing him? This is an Asgardian. Not even Speedball is bouncing back from an open skull fracture.

Tess.

I looked sharply at Tempest. "Did you just say something?"

She didn't answer. The voice hadn't seemed to be coming from her to begin with. I peered around the corner of the shelves, but all I could see were endless rows of Pop-Tarts and Hamburger Helper.

Tess.

It was coming from the direction of the magazine rack. I stared at the comics, the sci-fi magazines, and the neat, colored block of Archie digests.

"Maybe one of these things is a weapon," I said to the cat. "It could look like anything. It could be a plug, or a calculator. Is it wrong that I kind of hope it's an ice-cream sandwich?"

Tess.

I blinked. Was the voice actually coming from the ice-cream freezer?

It was right next to the comics. I peered in at all the sleeping Revello bars, the lime Creamsicles, and the coveted Drumstick cones. I couldn't hear the voice anymore. I placed my hand on the sliding door. It was slightly warm.

"Maybe this is how I'm going out. A conversation with ice cream."

I slid open the door. The cold air touched my fingertips, and I could smell something sharply metallic inside.

Tess.

Was I really going to put my head inside a freezer?

I didn't feel quite ready to be the fatal girl in the movie, at least not yet. I kept both my hands planted firmly on the freezer door, but I leaned in slightly.

"Hello?" I asked finally.

Jesus. It's about time. I've been yelling your name for twenty minutes.

I blinked. "Derrick?"

Hi.

"Do you want me to try to broadcast my thoughts to you, instead of just talking out loud?"

Have I ever once asked you to do that?

"No."

Are you a trained telepath?

"Well, obviously not. But, I mean, I've done focus exercises—"

Don't try to think-talk with me. It'll just get messy. I know it's weird, but you just have to keep talking to yourself.

"I can always just talk to the cat."

There's a cat with you?

"Yeah. My parents' old cat, Tempest. She's the only living thing I've run into here. Elder is completely empty."

You're in Elder? And there's a cat with you? That's so weird.

"I know, right?" I looked once more at the freezer. "Is your psychic presence anchored to the ice-cream freezer, or can I close this?"

It's not anchored to anything, but this is the spot

where I seem to get the most reception. Can you describe what you're seeing to me?

"I'm in my old favorite corner store. The one on Young."

Do you feel like you're dreaming?

I sighed. "I feel like you don't have a fucking clue where I am, or why I'm here. How is describing the place for you going to help me?"

Okay. You've got a point.

"Awesome. So, nobody knows anything. And I have no body."

You must have one somewhere. Otherwise, your psyche wouldn't have survived. I've heard of full severance before, but it's rare.

"Because rare things never happen to us. Okay, I love you, but I can't stand here for the next two hours talking to an ice-cream freezer. I'm going to keep walking."

All right. I'll try to follow you.

I walked slowly past the soda fridges and the shelves full of baked goods.

"Can you still hear me?"

Yeah. There's some interference, though.

"Maybe it's all the lima beans." I shook my head. "You know, I really loved this place. It had the best chocolate cherry blossoms you could buy anywhere."

They were made by Nestlé. You could buy them in fun packs from Safeway.

"But these ones just tasted better."

I approached the back of the store. There was a door marked PRIVATE, a door I'd never opened as a child, but always been curious about. I stood in front of it for a while. I couldn't decide what to do.

"Still there?"

No reply. I took a step backward.

"Derrick?"

He was gone. We'd lost the connection.

I looked down at Tempest. "Guess it's just us, then. You ready?"

She was sedate. Her lack of concern gave me a twinge of confidence.

I pushed open the door. I heard a sound as I left the store behind. Maybe it was Derrick saying something, but I couldn't hear. I was already too far away. I felt a coldness on my shoulders.

I turned and saw a glimpse of something, like a cloud with eyes. Then it flowed over me, blanking out everything, even my name.

20

I woke up on the couch of the break room. Maybe I was just going to keep repeating this morning until I got it right. Except that it wasn't morning. It was ten thirty-five at night. I sat up, rubbing my eyes. Half of my face felt like a sandbag. At least someone had been nice enough to throw a blanket over me. I gave myself a moment, waiting for the planes of my head to equalize. No drool this time. Bonus.

I reached for my purse. There was a Post-it note affixed to it:

> *Fresh coffee was made for you at: ~~4:00~~ ~~6:00~~ 9:30*
> *Inquire at Ru's.*

I smiled at the thought of Derrick coming into the break room every few hours and leaning over me to cross out each pot of coffee that had elapsed. I stretched and threw on my sweater, which I'd slept on. It was reassuringly warm.

I walked in a slight fugue down the hallway. The security guard nodded at me when I got to the lab's suite, which had unofficially become Ru's place in our minds. Like that movie where Tom Hanks can't leave the airport. Or not.

There was music playing. Ru must have figured out how to use the television as a stereo, because it was playing *The Marriage of Figaro*. Mia and Patrick were on the couch, both reading. Derrick stood behind them, talking on the phone. Miles and Ru were playing with Baron. He was tugging on a blue toy that looked like either Thing One or Thing Two from *The Cat in the Hat*.

"Has Selena seen the dog?" I asked.

Everyone turned to look at me.

"That's right. I fell asleep. It was a stressful day."

Derrick hung up. "Baron has clearance."

"He needed to be walked," Miles said. "And now we've gotten him all riled up with Thing One."

"It is amazing that he has been domesticated," Ru said. "I have seen lupines from other worlds, but never this particular mutation. They are very friendly."

"Is there a current iteration of coffee?" I asked.

Derrick handed me a to-go cup. "This was brewed across the street. But we've kept it warm for you. Patrick made a tea cozy."

He looked up from his book. "It was for sewing class. We have to do some knitting, too, and that was the only thing I could make."

"Well, it worked like a hot-damn," Mia said. "I'd say market them, but I'm afraid the East Vancouver textiles posse would probably break your legs."

I took the cup. "Where's Falih?"

"Oh." That got Mia's attention. "Are we on firsties now with the forensic pathologist? I think Selena's talking to him."

I looked at Derrick. "How much have you been telling her?"

"I think you forget what a really good listener she is." He walked over to where I was standing. "Did you sleep okay?"

"So-so. I had a dream where you were inside an ice-cream freezer."

"That's a little weird, even for you."

"I know."

"Not much has changed since you passed out. Dr. Rashid is still filling out paperwork. Miles came over around seven, and I told him to bring Patrick and Mia with him, since I figured you'd want them here."

"This hotel room is pretty much the safest part of the building. So I'd say your instincts were on target, as always. Don't let Latyrix see the dog, though."

"She went home. She said she was tired and needed to wash."

"Her fur was a mess."

"Her species would not submit well to domestication," Ru said. "I doubt I would be able to rub her."

"No. I wouldn't try it." I yawned. "Has Cindée already done the electrical resistivity tests on the powder?"

"She's been doing tests for the last four hours. I think she's almost done."

"I can't listen to any more opera." Mia got up. "I'm plugging my BlackBerry into the television. Anyone have any objections?"

"Nothing by Bright Eyes," Derrick said.

"Oh, you love Conor Oberst." Mia switched off the opera. "And he's done nothing to deserve your ire."

Bette Midler came on. "Otto Titsling." Ru listened with great interest, not even bothering to ask about any difficult vocabulary.

When the Editors came on, I turned back to Derrick. "Okay. Number one, thank you for this coffee. Number two, I visited the *daegred*, and I think we should give them our old computer."

"You mean my old computer."

"Maybe I should have been more specific. I mean the computer that you haven't used for three months."

"Right. Well, that seems like a good idea."

"That's cool of you," Patrick said. "I was going to buy another one, but I'm still, like"—he blinked—"nine hundred dollars short."

"Don't they give you a Magnate credit card?"

"No way. There's a line of credit for refurbishing the space and buying supplies, but Modred's really possessive of it."

"Huh. I thought you'd have like a Diners Club card or something."

"What's Diners Club?"

"Something from the eighties. Never mind."

"Anyhow, thanks for the computer, Derrick."

"Not a problem. I should at least update some of the software before I give it to you, though. How dire is the lack of Internet situation?"

"Most of us can just use our phones," Patrick said. "But some of the older vampires don't agree with hand-held technology. So they can get a bit cranky while they're waiting twelve hours for nightfall."

"I'll get on it, then."

"What are you reading?" I asked Patrick.

"*Beowulf*. Modred says it's required reading."

"Sometimes I like how Modred thinks."

"I'm reading the GRE handbook," Mia said. "Not that anyone cares."

"That's a test for graduate school."

"It's only four years away. Three if I get accelerated."

"Is that like brownnosing?" Patrick asked. "Because I'm sure you'll be able to chat up all your professors after reading their articles."

"Hey. Don't snap at me just because you got a C-plus in sociology."

I looked at Patrick. "Really?"

"We had to read all this stuff by Max Weber! I swear to you, Tess, the guy does not know how to write."

"Are you going to redo the assignment?"

"The prof won't let me."

"He's scared to ask the department head," Mia clarified.

"I am not."

"Oh, my God, you clench up whenever I even mention the idea of you visiting her office. You need to grow a pair, my friend."

"Nobody's pair is in dispute right now," I said. "Patrick, you should go talk to the department head. It's part of their job. And if she's inflexible, tell her your parents are absolutely barking mad, and as a result of that, you've had to suffer adversity."

"I don't think she'll believe it. She studies social demographics."

"Well, you could always tell her you're a vampire."

"I don't think she'd believe me."

"Show her your fangs," Mia said. "Better yet, show her Puppy."

"Shut up."

"Is Puppy a person?" Miles asked.

Mia broke into laughter.

My pager buzzed. I looked down and saw it was a message from Cindée.

"I have to go," I said.

Ru stood up. "Does it have something to do with the Aikon?"

"It does."

"I would like to see."

"What's an Aikon?" Mia asked. "Like the camera?"

"That's a Nikon," Derrick said.

I shrugged. "You have a right to see whatever we've found. It may upset you, though. You need to be prepared for that."

"I am," Ru said.

"All right. Come on."

"Text me when you're done," Derrick called after us. "I'm trying to organize a take-out order, and I'll need input later."

"Agreed."

Ru and I made our way to the trace lab. I heard Cindée talking to someone. As we stepped through the doorway, Lucian came into view.

"I don't know about wavelength," he was saying, "but there is a way to channel something broad-spectrum. It might be enough."

"Enough what?" I asked.

Cindée saw Ru, and her expression shifted slightly. "Don't you have better things to do than watch science unfolding, kiddo?"

"I want to see what you've found," he replied evenly.

She nodded. "Well. We can try. But so far, I haven't had any luck with the different materia frequencies. I called Lucian Agrado as a last resort."

"That's me," he said. "I'm like the opposite of Mulder."

"Oh, please." I grinned at him. "You're so Scully."

"You wish." He turned to Cindée. "Okay. I'm going to channel a weak stream of necroid materia. I don't have complete control over it, but I can regulate the intensity and try to keep it from debriding too much of the vessel's surface."

"You're doing house calls now?"

He shrugged. "I'm on retainer." Then he looked at Ru. "I don't know very much about this case or you. But I hope this works for you. I hope you're able to recover some of your lost memories."

"Thank you," Ru said.

Lucian stepped closer to the reconstructed Aikon. He held out his hand, and I felt necroid materia begin to gather itself in a concentrated point inches away from his outstretched fingertips. Green flickers attended the power, and I smelled something almost barometric, like the slow condensation of a storm.

The Aikon glowed. It was dim at first, but the light grew. It cast broken green shadows on the wall. Now the smell changed to burning powder. I could see that Lucian's energy was slowly dissolving the bonds that held the Aikon together. The materia shimmered as it was consumed.

In the green shadows, I could just make out blurry things. What might have been a floor. Someone's hand. An open window. A hallway.

Then a young demon's face appeared. He looked like Ru but was slightly larger, his horns more noticeable. He smiled. Ru made a low noise.

"Do you recognize him?" I asked.

He nodded slowly. "It's El," he said. "My brother."

I cleared my throat. We stood in the serology lab. Linus had his back to us and was looking through a microscope. Ru hadn't left my side for the last two hours. He'd made it clear that he didn't want to be touched. He didn't even particularly want us to acknowledge his presence. He followed me like a moth. He made no sound, but would settle in the background, seemingly comfortable.

"He's not a computer," Selena had said. "Time is of the essence, but we can't keep pushing him. We just forced him to watch his dead brother's memories, projected on the wall like some fucking scene out of Proust."

"I don't know that reference," I admitted.

"Ask Derrick."

"Ah. Gotcha."

Linus sat down, holding a file. He looked at it and frowned. "I don't know why I'm holding this. For a moment, I thought I kind of looked like Greg from *CSI*."

"That's sad, Linus."

He blinked. "Yeah. I guess. All right, this is what's going on with Mr. Corvid. Which isn't his name, by the way."

"He never told me his real name."

"Actually, the body is intersexed. Tasha said the genitalia were tucked into the pelvis, like an avian's reproductive system."

"Huh. Is that common?"

"You'd have to ask her. I don't think she's seen very many purebloods in situ. When they interact with our world, they don't tend to leave traces behind."

"The Ferid are not pure," Ru said. Linus and I stared at him. These were his first words in more than two hours. "Or, they are not predominantly pureblood. The Senators are, and of course, the Invictus."

"What's the Invictus?" I asked.

"The Invictus controls the Senate. The Invictus is what you might have called a Caesar in your world's antique period."

"And that's who Basuram thinks you tried to assassinate?"

He laughed. "That would be suicide. Basuram was

given a cover story to engage the potential trust of the locals. But the Kentauros was sent after me because my memories are important. The Ferid cared nothing for El's memories, but they're eager to devour mine, because only I remember how the three of us got here." He suddenly looked at Linus. "I apologize, Doctor. Please go on about the demon's remains."

Linus smiled slightly. Who didn't like hearing themselves referred to as Doctor? He couldn't prescribe medication, like Dr. Hinzelmann, or prosect a body, like Dr. Rashid, but he could run a refractive index test on bits of bone and broken glass from another world. Plus, there was now the "military training" mystique that Selena had mentioned to me, in a rare moment of naked gossip for her.

Not that I found soldiers particularly sexy. Although I did once sleep with a member of the Israeli Defense Forces who had alopecia, which meant that his chest was hairy, but his head and legs were smooth. I kept being really sassy, pretending I knew something about the Middle East because I'd read *Drinking the Sea at Gaza*. In the morning, we ate fried chicken at a place across the street.

Focus. God.

I blinked, returning my attention to Linus.

"We took vitreous fluid from the demon," he said, "whose name appears to be Blq. At least, that was the repeating rune we found in his RNA."

"Blq," I murmured. "Like that goblin in the Tom Cruise movie."

"Blq is what we unofficially call a Bercilak-demon.

That is, like the giant Bercilak in *Sir Gawain and the Green Knight*—"

"Blq can survive decapitation."

"Not indefinitely, though. The erythropoietin levels in the brain were quite high. The serum EPO is 119, and that elevation can indicate severe tissue damage with a prolonged perimortem phase before actual death."

"That sounds about right," I said, "given that Blq was still alive after being disarticulated and disabused of his head."

"I'm going to examine the vitreous fluid closer," Linus said. "The proteins may tell a story. Although, to be honest, it's pretty much like staring at a glass of water."

"All right. Do keep me posted on that. And thanks for all your hard work, Linus. You really are an integral member of the forensic team."

He opened the file. "I'm going to pretend you never said that."

"Thanks. That's probably for the best."

We began walking down the hall to Trace.

"I know where it is," Ru said. "At least, I think I do."

"You know where what is?"

"The apartment. From the memories."

I stopped in the middle of the hallway. "Ru. We don't have to rush this. You've just remembered that you have a brother."

"I had a brother. He died in that place. With the shiny yellow floors and the brown walls. And the big bowl."

"What big bowl?"

"It was made of a smooth material, like marble. He said that he filled it with water, but I was skeptical."

"A claw-foot tub."

"It did have feet, yes."

"That could be half the apartments downtown," I said. "Although—you mostly find claw-foot tubs in older buildings."

"The street outside was strange."

"Strange how?"

"Made of little stones."

"Cobblestones. That's Gastown."

"Tess. I need to find whatever is left of him."

"And you know he's your brother?"

"As surely as you would know one of your own family."

"Basuram said you were alone."

"The Kentauros lies. The Kentauroi are soldiers. They are paid to fight the wars of the Ferid. But Basuram almost told me about El, just before dying. My brother's name was on the tip of the demon's tongue."

I exhaled. "All right. Come with me."

I took Ru into the audiovisual lab, which was empty. I sat down and logged into the computer. Ru frowned.

"Why are you searching for real estate?"

"I'm doing a Boolean search for apartments that may have some of the characteristics we saw. This search engine links to Craigslist and KiJiJi, as well as to private listings. Let's see. Claw-foot tub. You said there was a window."

"I did?"

"When Derrick was reading your mind."

"Oh. I do not remember everything I said."

"He's really sorry about that, by the way."

"I have already accepted his apology, which was unnecessary."

"Was there anything special about the window?"

"It was hard to open. It—what is the word—became jam?"

"Jammed. Did you push it up? Was it heavy?"

"Yes. The glass was thick."

"What about around the frame of the window?"

"There was a design. Sculpted."

"Crown molding." I added that. "Did you look out the window?"

"Once. I saw a big metal building." His eyes widened. "I'm remembering more now. There was an arch. And a flying vessel, moving along a stone aqueduct."

"The cinema in Chinatown. That's on Pender. We're definitely in the vicinity of Gastown." I kept thinking. That was a bit of a shabby area, although the city was aggressively gentrifying the neighborhood. It was close, in fact, to an apartment building I'd visited more than three years ago, belonging to a vampire named Sebastian.

I clicked the search button. Eleven results appeared.

I opened each listing. They all had images, but they weren't great images by any stretch of the imagination. When I clicked on 29 ABBOTT STREET, I felt Ru suck in his breath slightly behind me. I looked at the pictures. The apartment had faux paneling, original hardwood, and walls with at least fifty years of paint coating them. The kitchen was floored in tacky yellow linoleum.

"This place was put on the market two days ago." I stood up. "I have to go declare it an active crime scene."

"I am going with you."

"I don't think that's a good idea, Ru."

"That place is all I remember about my brother. I need to see it."

I looked around. "Damn. Where's Selena?" I dialed her extension. It went straight to voice mail.

"This is Tess," I said. "I've got an address. I'm taking the Denali, and if something attacks me, I won't think twice about using it as a tank."

"What's a Denali?" Ru asked.

I was already dialing Lucian. "It's like a chariot."

"Hello?"

"It's me. I need you to meet me at Twenty-nine Abbot Street in Gastown. And I need you to drive like you aren't ninety years old."

"Can you give me any more information?"

"No. But I'll buy you a drink later tonight."

"That's fair." He hung up.

We took the elevator down to the underground parking. I made sure that Ru was strapped in tightly on the passenger side, then carefully guided us aboveground. It was dusk. Why was it always dusk?

"This part of the city is interesting," Ru said. "Like a sunken ship."

"It does feel that way sometimes."

"There are a lot of people living outside."

"Not everyone can afford a place to live in a city this big."

"What is strange," he replied, "is that you think this place is big."

I parked across the street from the walk-up building. "How hot was it in the apartment building?" I asked. "Were you sweating?"

"I do not perspire."

"Fine. Did you feel hot?"

"Yes. It was dry, and the air was full of dust. I also smelled something very pungent. An odor that was like polymer melting."

"Roof tar. Let's start with the top floor."

I walked up to the entrance and rang the manager's suite. Nobody answered. I pressed a few random buttons. There was a buzz, and the door opened.

"People are dumb," I said.

We climbed the stairs. I was breathing more heavily by the time we got to the top, which brought me to the conclusion that I needed to step up my cardio.

"You lead the way," I told Ru.

I followed him slowly down the hallway. He stopped at 304.

"This might be it," he said.

The door was locked. I took the athame out of my purse and touched it to the dead bolt. I channeled a spike of earth materia, letting it agitate the metal, until I heard a satisfying click. The door opened.

The apartment was empty and had been recently cleaned. The tang of bleach was still in the air. The hallway seemed familiar, but only in flashes. Ru walked slowly around the living room. The moment his foot touched the linoleum floor, I saw a shudder go through him.

"What is it?"

He looked down. "El died here."

"You're certain."

"Yes. I can feel him."

I grabbed a spray bottle of luminol from my reagent travel kit. I took pictures of the floor from several angles, including a ruler for scale. Then I sprayed the tiles, which were cracked, their edges beginning to curl upward. When every inch of the floor had been treated, I stood up.

"This might be upsetting," I told Ru.

"You keep saying that," he said. "But I am past being upset. Now I just want to know what happened to my brother. I want to know what he was doing here in the first place, and what made me come after him. I wish I could remember."

"Just"—I swallowed—"be prepared."

I pointed the athame at the window. Strands of earth materia stirred the dust on both sides of the glass, encouraging it, making it fecund. Gradually, the window darkened as earth, grit, and heavy smog thickened on it, until the kitchen was almost completely dark. I turned around, passing the athame over the linoleum floor. Blue light struck the yellow, and dazzling patterns emerged. Markings like frost that glittered blue, forming arcs and glowing satellites.

"Ru," I said slowly. "These are signs of arterial blood loss. Someone's body exsanguinated on this floor."

"He couldn't get up." Ru's voice was soft. "But I put my head in his lap. And he touched my hair. He said, *You're my partner in crime*. He said, *I love you, even though you are an ill-bred puppy*. And then he showed me."

"Showed you what?"

"How to recover the Aikon. How to save the memories." Ru extended his hand, fingers hovering in the air. "There was a hole in his chest. I reached inside. He said, *Lower*. I reached lower, until I found it. Then I pulled it out."

I felt all the color leave my face. "He was alive when you took the Aikon?"

"Every body is different. He needed to tell me. So I took it, and I carried it into the bathroom. I saw myself in the mirror. That must have been when I noticed the blue all over my fingers."

I walked into the bathroom. There was a tiled floor and a claw-foot tub, just as Ru had remembered. The vanity was a full-length mirror, like the kind my mother still has in her closet. As soon as I got near it, I felt strange.

"This is not supposed to be here," I said.

The edges of the mirror were gilded, but the more I tried to look at them, the less defined they grew. I felt a pain in my head.

"Go downstairs," I told Ru. "Take my phone. Dial one for the lab."

"I have no wish to leave you."

"Something's not right here. Go downstairs."

The mirror was getting darker. I could no longer see myself in it. I felt the floorboards beginning to vibrate.

"Tess—" Ru pointed to the glass.

It was steaming.

"Get out of here!" I shouted.

"No! I want to stay with you!"

I pointed the athame at his feet. I closed my eyes, channeling a braid of earth and air materia. The power formed itself into a curtain of light, hazy, like smoked green glass. Ru stared at me in disbelief. He yelled something, but the barrier absorbed the sound of his voice. It was for his own good. If it protected him.

I turned to regard the mirror. Now it was a pane of blackness, hanging like a mineral scar in the air. I took a step forward, raising my blade.

The steam condensed. It turned red, until it looked like a spout of whirling embers. Somewhere in the shifting flames, I saw two steady points, which were fixed on me. The cloud drifted forward. I stood my ground.

"Arcadia," I said.

My phone started to buzz. I knew it was Lucian, but there was no time for anything but this moment. I turned. Ru was gone. He must have run downstairs. I silently thanked whatever power might be listening.

"Tessa Isobel Corday."

I turned at the sound of my full name. Arcadia was about a foot away from me now, hovering at eye level. Her form was like a vermilion nebula compressed into a trembling water spout. She had no discernible mouth, but her eyes were unmistakable.

"Arcadia," I repeated. "What do you want?"

"The question is, really, what don't I want, Tess."

She hung in the air before me. She was kind of a dark miracle, floating, and she didn't actually have a face, which made it difficult to judge her expressions. But her eyes grew brighter when she was emphatic.

"You look like the water spout from *Loom*," I said. "The one you have to unweave using your distaff."

"I am a Vapor. My touch will atomize you."

"Right. Kind of like what happened to Blq."

She drew into herself. "That was not supposed to be. The Bercilak was unyielding and refused to see reason."

"I don't understand your connection to Mr. Corvid."

"*Mr. Corvid.* Is that what the demon went by?" The debris of energy that swirled within her rippled, contracting slightly.

I kept looking for something like a heart, since I had no face to fix my eyes on, but there was only a kind of glowing ribbon that moved within the cloud. I wondered if she had a wandering soul.

"Blq was a Mound-Dweller. An old one. Blq had a contract with the Senate, but failed to honor a clause."

"Which clause?"

"The promise of his psychic essence to be held in receivership by the Senate."

"Well. To be fair, I wouldn't want to fulfill that end of the agreement."

"The Invictus lent the Mound-Dweller a favor. The gift increased the demon's business, but it came with a price. Blq's time was up."

"So Blq's execution had nothing to do with Ru."

"Wrong. It has absolutely everything to do with

him." Arcadia flowed over to the mirror, which was still dark, still humming. "The Senate authorized an incursion into your world. The goal was to retrieve Blq's essence. But when the rift was opened, the two Ptah'li escaped."

"Were they really involved in a coup?"

"They are subjects of interest."

"To whom?"

"The Senate."

"And what is your relationship to this Senate?"

Arcadia flowed closer. I could feel her electromagnetic field raising the hair on my arms. The heat of her eyes was strong on my face. *This is what it feels like to have an intimate conversation with a spinning barbecue.*

"I am a Senator's daughter. As are you."

Those three words knocked the wind out of me. I took a step back.

"We're sisters?"

"Half sisters."

"Half sisters." I spread my arms. "You're a homicidal water spout. What the hell does that make me?"

"The Ferid are part of you. But the rest of you is human."

"Right. The fucking *Ferid* are part of me because your father attacked my mother. I never asked for this."

"He did not attack her. She is not telling you the truth."

"I'm supposed to trust you over my own mother."

"Has she not deceived you before?"

"I feel like you guys have still deceived me a lot

more. Your father's the reason I've had nightmares since I can remember."

"No. I am the cause of your nightmares."

"What?"

Arcadia's form contracted. She moved almost fractally, her vague insides glowing as they shifted. Suddenly, a young girl was standing in front of me. She was dark-skinned and had green eyes.

"I remember you," I whispered. "You were in my dream about *las meninas*. You were the *menina* I didn't recognize."

"I gave you all those dreams."

"Why?"

"So you would hate him as I do."

"Well, you could have saved yourself the trouble, because I already hated him without having to endure creepy nightmares about him."

"You hated him because you thought he forced himself upon your mother. I believe you will discover that he did not, or at least not in the way you surmise."

"You just admitted that you've been mentally tormenting me since I was a little girl. Why should I believe anything you say?"

"Because I have also helped you."

"The dreams weren't all premonitory."

"But they made you think about things differently. They allowed you to harness your own creativity as an investigator."

"What am I supposed to say? Thanks for the nightmares?" I gestured to the apartment around me. "His brother died here. Did you kill him?"

"I meant to wound him. But he moved suddenly. He moved to protect his brother, and my presence grazed him."

"Well, your presence gave him a penetrating chest wound. He bled to death on that ugly floor. And for what? What was his life worth to you?"

"Next to nothing."

I swallowed. "I think I'd like to officially become estranged from your side of the family. That's effective immediately."

"El saw something he should not have. The Senate needs his memories back."

"That's tough. His memories are gone."

"Not completely. Some of them were transferred to Ru when he carried El's remembering organ to the beach. El must have told him to destroy it, and the water is close by. Possibly, he tried to drown the organ, or smother it. But finally, he thought of burning it. As you've seen, it's highly combustible. The blast would have knocked him out, scattering the fragments of the vessel."

"But why did the two of them go through the rift in the first place?"

"Because they were in the wrong place at the wrong time. When it was realized that they had breached your world, the Kentauros was sent to extract them."

"And then you were sent. To extract the Kentauros."

"I never left. I remained here after settling Blq's debt."

"Watching me?"

"Pitying you. Wondering if I should put you out of your misery."

"Do it, then, you fucking cow. Atomize me."

"Why do you seek disambiguation?"

"Because I'm tired of talking to Mound-Dwellers and Vapors and purebloods. I'm tired of talking."

"If you wish to die," Arcadia said, "by all means, approach."

I took a small step forward. The cloud did not move. I could feel thrills of electricity moving along my body now. I inched forward again. Her heat was burning my face now, but it felt good, somehow. Like steaming water from the bath that was too hot, but only just.

That was when I remembered the bathtub. It was made of solid porcelain. If I gave it a massive charge, I might be able to disrupt her electromagnetic field. I might even be able to leech power from it.

I didn't draw my athame. I just stood there.

Arcadia's form seemed to exhale slightly. I felt stings go down my body. My cheeks and my neck burned, and I could feel blood welling up in the cuts.

"Ru is under my protection," I said.

"A lot of people seem to share that honor." She drifted back slightly. The cuts throbbed. I bit my lip. "One vampire. A half vampire. An addled telepath."

"Derrick's not addled."

"He thought he touched Basuram's mind, but he was wrong. It was my mind the psychic touched, as he was blindly fumbling about."

"What did you do to him?"

"I accelerated his potential."

"He's not going to become a zombie-king for the Ferid."

"He will become whatever we wish him to become."

I sighed. "Give me one thing, at least."

"What do you wish?"

"Tell me the bastard's name."

"Is that your only question, Tess? It's unoriginal."

"Arcadia. Please." I felt a strange pressure leave me. "Whether we like it or not, we're family. And you owe me."

She was silent for a moment. Then her eyes became two points of light, so brilliant I could barely look at them.

"You have always known it," she said.

Then Arcadia flowed back into the mirror. Its edges gradually softened, until it became a regular vanity again.

I was shaking violently. The curtain of materia I'd thrown up had dissolved a long time ago. As I slowly made my way out of the bathroom, I saw Lucian.

"Hey." He put his hand on my face. "What did this to you?"

"A falling-out."

He put his arm around me. "Let me help you."

"I won't say no."

Ru and Selena walked through the door. Ru immediately crossed the room and stood next to me.

"Now you've seen them," he said. "Now you understand."

"No. I absolutely don't understand. I do know one thing, though." I reached out and grabbed his hand. "We're going to become better friends."

"Will we? That's exciting."

"Yeah. I kind of thought so."

Selena gave me a tired look. "This is the part where I give you the speech about not following protocol, borrowing the Denali, endangering a subject in an active investigation, et cetera. But I think I'm going to save it this time. You look beat-up."

"I am beat-up." I took out my gun and laid it on the sofa. "I'm tired of telling everyone how tired I am. But mostly, I'm unhappy. And life's too short for that."

"I don't understand."

I laid my CORE badge on top of the gun.

"I quit."

I walked out with Lucian and Ru. Derrick met me at the foot of the stairs. I looked into his bright face and was once again astonished by what an amazing person he was, and how much I loved him.

"What just happened?"

I kissed his cheek. "I just completely screwed us over."

About the Author

Jes Battis was born in Vancouver, British Columbia. He teaches and writes in Regina, Saskatchewan. Visit his website at www.authorjesbattis.com.

M828T0111

From the #1 *New York Times*
Bestselling Author
PATRICIA BRIGGS

RIVER MARKED

~~~

Car mechanic Mercy Thompson has always known there
is something unique about her, and it's not just the way she
can make a VW engine sit up and beg. Mercy is a different
breed of shapeshifter, a characteristic she inherited from
her long-gone father. She's never known any others of her
kind. Until now.

An evil is stirring in the depths of the Columbia River—
one that her father's people may know something about.
And to have any hope of surviving, Mercy and her mate,
the Alpha werewolf Adam, will need their help . . .

Now available from Ace Books

M773T0311

Explore the outer reaches
of imagination—don't miss these authors
of dark fantasy and urban noir who take you
to the edge and beyond . . .

Patricia Briggs	Anne Bishop
Simon R. Green	Marjorie M. Liu
Jim Butcher	Jeanne C. Stein
Kat Richardson	Christopher Golden
Karen Chance	Ilona Andrews
Rachel Caine	Anton Strout

penguin.com/scififantasy